THE PLACEHOLDER

www.mascotbooks.com

The Placeholder

For more information, please contact:
Mascot Books, an imprint of Amplify Publishing Group
620 Herndon Parkway, Suite 320
Herndon, VA 20170
info@mascotbooks.com

Library of Congress Control Number: 2022901637

CPSIA Code: PRV0522A

ISBN-13: 978-1-63755-219-3

Printed in the United States

ALSO BY LYNDA WOLTERS

VOICES OF CANCER

VOICES OF LGBTQ+

THE *Placeholder*

LYNDA WOLTERS

MASCOT®
BOOKS

CHAPTER

1

The last thing I expected to be as a seasoned attorney in her forties was a defendant in a lawsuit, but here I am.

I have only sat in a witness box one other time, which was during a mock trial in my last year of law school. I was a 3L at the University of Idaho (Go, Vandals!) and in love with Hank Robinson. He was a rich kid from mining country who, little did I know, was engaged to a gold heiress named Beatrix, with an "x." I roll my eyes every time I remember the x. Hank was our trial team captain and my boyfriend. We won first place in the competition, but I lost Hank to the girl with the x. Today, in similar fashion, I am losing my husband, Clint, to the floater from my firm's typing pool. I'm such a good picker.

Both relationships were fraught with infidelity, both men having a wandering penis. If I am honest, there have been plenty of times when I visualized pulling a Lorena Bobbitt and severing those single-minded members from their owners and flinging them out the window. Had I ever acted on those thoughts, this case would be far more salacious. Fortunately for everyone involved, I have a modicum of self-control and a severe aversion to blood. Today's suit is not about something heinous I did, it is about something I didn't do—or rather couldn't: bear children. Apparently, a deal-breaker for my husband.

My mind drifts back to Hank and how similar my life still is years later with Clint. Hank was my first love, obsession, heart-break, first everything. He appeared one day as if jumping from a page of a bodice-ripping novel, dressed in a smart blazer and crisp, white button-down, his dark hair held in place with just enough pomade not to look greasy. I hadn't initially grasped why there was a group of other young men in the wings, dressed as sharply, cupping their hands over their mouths and snickering. I thought they were laughing at my coke-bottle glasses or the way I stammered when I introduced myself, so taken aback that someone like Hank would talk to me; neither turned out to be the case. I was Hank's prey, his experiment, his plaything, and those other young men knew this—I was a game.

Clint was a widower when I met him a decade after the Hank fiasco. He had two darling little girls, Elise and Hailey, and the three of them were lonely, desperate, and looking for love. We made an instant match, made perfect with a bit of tweaking on my behalf. After all, I rationalized, I did make more money. I bought a new house to accommodate children, complete with a large backyard and redwood playset, in the most desirable school district. I purchased a soccer-mom-style SUV with built-in DVD players and garaged my convertible. I even dyed my hair. Clint liked blondes.

"For the love of Peter, Paul, and Mary," Carolyn yelled when she caught me researching plastic surgeons a few years into my marriage, "what now?" (Carolyn is an attorney in the same firm as me. She is both friend and boss, which at times, can make our relationship awkward.)

"I'm thinking about a boob job," I had said, not looking up from the monitor.

"Because Clint wants you to have bigger tits," she stated. This was not a question.

"No, well, yes, but I think he's right." I cupped my smallish breasts to examine their size.

"Clint is a douche. Get over him. You'll find someone better."

"That douche," I yelled back, "is my husband." And then, in a whisper, "And he has my babies."

"I know, we need to get the adoption papers drawn up; I just haven't gotten to it. I'm sorry." She sounded genuinely apologetic.

"No rush." I smiled, still looking at the different sizes of breasts on the screen. I settled for a 34C, which admittedly did seem a bit large on my five-foot-three-inch frame, but I knew Clint liked a large "rack," as he would say.

A year after my boob job, I ran crying home to my mother. "I must not be showing him enough love," I said. "I've tried everything—sexy negligees, role play, Kama Sutra . . ." I stopped myself short of admitting to cosmetic surgery.

"Wouldn't matter," Momma said, unflustered by my disclosures about my sex life, "No amount of creativity or changing will ever make you good enough."

"But why?" I wailed, balled up in snot and tears, "Because I can't have children?"

She shakes her head, takes a long pull on a cigarette, and stared somewhere far away. "The same thing went wrong with you and Hank, Serenade Jean. It's not your inability to have children," she blows out the smoke, "you aren't Clint's beloved. You are not his one true love."

Momma is right. My desire to be someone's chosen consumes me. Every. Single. Time. It doesn't matter who I am with, that person becomes my world, and that becomes the new me. But never for Hank or Clint had their worlds been all things Serenade.

And now here I sit, about to be a broke divorcée. Against my attorney's advice (who uncomfortably is Carolyn), I am giving up the house, part of my retirement, and my cherished 1960 Stingray all in the hopes of sweetening the pot for what *I* want: visitation rights.

"Sera," Carolyn says, leaning in from her chair next to mine. Her tone is authoritative and no-nonsense. "You need to come to terms with the fact that the judge may not be feeling . . ." Taking in a deliberate breath, she mulls her next word, ". . . generous."

"I'm not budging," I whisper through clenched teeth. "He can set a precedent." I squint at Carolyn, and she stares back: two attorneys locking horns in a battle for dominance. Carolyn blinks; I grin.

"And the house?" Carolyn slides a document in my direction. "He wants the house."

I glance down at the deed. "I know. I don't care."

"You must pay him part of your retirement as well," she reminds me.

I snap, in no mood to suffer her pragmatic attorney-speak. "Carolyn, we've been over this."

She taps her pen on the table and closes her eyes. "And the car?"

"I want visitation," I say, "everything else is replaceable."

"But—"

I hold up my hand, "It's non-negotiable."

"You know this may end badly."

I shrug off the comment and focus on the room as if I hadn't been inside it a hundred times. I cannot lose. I will not lose. I am going to lose.

"All rise." George, the bailiff, announces Judge Shockley's entrance. "Court is now in session. The Honorable Ned Shockley is presiding. You may be seated."

I slump into my chair, weary from the months of fighting.

"Sit up," Carolyn hisses with a sharp elbow to my ribs.

"I've read the pleadings on file," Judge Shockley says, his bulbous nose flaring outward. His deep vibrato voice fills the courtroom, pushing out what little air is left. "I've considered the declarations, the memoranda, and today, it falls to me to help you two sort the last of your affairs."

I snort at his choice of words. He gives Clint a long, hard stare and then shifts his gaze to me, holding his attention on me equally long.

"What say you, Mr. Walters?" Judge Shockley says, addressing Clint's attorney.

"Thank you, Your Honor," Stan Walters begins. "As you have read, the parties are at an impasse regarding a settlement. Negotiations have broken down, and mediation has failed. My client apologizes for this inconvenience to the court."

Inconvenience? My blood boils. I tense, and my face turns red. *This inconvenience is my life, asshole*, I yell silently at Stan.

Carolyn rests her hand on my arm, sensing I am ready to leap. She rises an inch from her chair, "Your Honor?"

With a wave of his hand, Judge Shockley seats Carolyn and speaks to Stan. "Mr. Walters, let's not start the day slinging mud."

His long exhale sounds to my ears as, *Let the shitshow begin.*

Stan dips his head, saying, "My apologies, Your Honor. If it pleases the Court, we would like to call Serenade Kincaid to the stand."

And here we go.

"Ms. Kincaid," Clint's lawyer starts, "may I call you Serenade?"

"Sera."

"Sera," he corrects himself and smiles a toothy grin my way. "Isn't it true you shoplifted in college?"

I gasp. Until last week's trial prep with Carolyn, I had only ever told one person this story.

"Objection!" Carolyn flies off her seat. "Relevance."

Stan holds up his hand, halting Carolyn, and continues, "Do you think this type of behavior is a good example for children?"

Carolyn reaches behind her, feeling for the chair, and sits, our eyes glued in horror.

"I, I—well, it was a long time ago, and I wasn't charged. I was surviving on Top Raman and server tips, drowning in student loans, so I took the cardigan. My boyfriend told me he would love to see me in the sweater." The words have fallen from my mouth before I could stop them. "I brought it back to the store," I whisper, then clamp my lips tight. My eyes burn with tears, and I wish for lasers to shoot from them and into Clint's heart. He smirks from across the courtroom.

You bastard.

CHAPTER

2

"**M**s. Kincaid, while your argument is compelling and your story pulls at my heartstrings, I find no law to support your request for court-ordered visitation of your stepchildren," Judge Shockley rules from the bench.

I stifle a gasp, covering my mouth with my hands, as tears spill onto my cheeks.

The magistrate turns his attention to Clint, and I whisper a prayer. "Please, please make him find it in his heart to let me see my babies. I'm *begging* you."

"It would be my hope," the judge continues, "both as a father myself and an advocate of the family court, that you consider a continued relationship between the two little girls and their stepmother." He waves a large hand at the court reporter, "Off the record, please." The reporter stops typing.

"It is apparent you have already made plans regarding the direction you wish to take your family." He nods toward Angelica, the seven-months pregnant former typist at my firm sitting behind Clint in the gallery. Disapproval washes over Shockley's face. "But a child cannot have enough love and affection. Your girls have suffered a lifetime of grief and pain with the loss of their mother. I would encourage you to reconsider forcing them to lose a second mother."

I turn to Carolyn. Has she caught that too, that little bone of hope the judge just threw? But Carolyn refuses to look at me, fixing her eyes straight ahead, her face stoic.

"Did you hear that?" I whisper, frantic for reassurance. "He called me their mother." I am tense with excitement. "He is all but telling Clint to give me visitation."

Carolyn draws in a slow breath, and closes her eyes, still not looking at me.

Regardless of how tiny the hope, I heard the judge say it, and I want—*need*—my friend to celebrate with me. Carolyn, who has been through so much with me, my marriage and failed attempts at conception, now sits beside me as a frenemy. At this moment, I hate her. *Has she done her best for me? Did she fight hard enough? Is this retaliation for something I did at work?* My mind whirls, desperate for answers, looking for a reason I shouldn't be allowed to see my stepdaughters. I shift my gaze to Judge Shockley and then Angelica, resting my icy glare on Clint.

The gavel falls and the courtroom empties.

Long minutes pass. I sit alone, weeping, curled into myself and rocking back and forth. The bailiff and Carolyn make their way to the back wall and give me privacy while I cry and mourn. Making occasional squeaking noises, I do my best to dam the anguish building inside me. At some point, the two escort me from the courtroom. They guide me by my elbows through the windowless bowels of the building generally reserved for transporting shackled criminals away from the scrutiny of the public eye. I lumber, dazed, and defeated, weighed down by grief as I make my way through the empty hallway, void of its usual murderers, child molesters, and gangland malcontents. George and Carolyn lead me to the locked exterior door bearing the words, *prisoners only.* The weight of my sentence bears down on me: a life without children.

Carolyn's car and driver are waiting outside for us. George scoops me into his arms and loads me inside like a rag doll.

"I've got your work covered for the next few weeks," Carolyn says on the drive back to my place. I sit mute, staring out the window.

The driver takes us to my new residence—the tired, old motel that needs a facelift. It has been my home since I vacated the marital house leaving it to the children, which means I left my home to Clint, Angelica, and their unborn child.

Carolyn settles me onto the stained couch that sits between the tiny living room and kitchenette. She recoils from the mystery smell wafting up from its sour cushions, soiled from years of God-knows-what. She wraps a blanket around me, scrunching her nose as she leans in, doing her best to keep at arm's length distance from the smelly couch. Then she goes to the kitchenette, returning with a glass of water.

"Take this," she commands, giving me a pill. "Drink." She shoves the glass into my hand.

I place the pill on the back of my tongue and swallow.

"Now sleep. I'll be here when you wake up."

I nod, my eyelids heavy from the events of the past several months.

———

I wake to the sound of chirping birds and Carolyn throwing open the hefty, dust-laden curtains.

"Time to get up." She is wearing fresh clothes. "I brought you a few things."

"I don't want anything," I whine, my eyes clamped tight against the sunlight.

Dropping an armload of books with a thud, she says, "You have homework."

Then she hands me a to-go cup filled with a suspicious-looking green froth. I raise an eyebrow.

"It's kale, carrot, wheatgrass, and some other crap that the guy at Tree City Juice said would be good for you." She shrugs as if that made it alright for me to drink this unknown concoction. "I told him I wanted a hangover cure," she says with a wink.

"What was that pill?" I am still hauling myself out of my drug-induced stupor.

A Cheshire grin spreads across her face.

"Now, up," she says, deflecting my question and gently slapping my cheeks. "You have work to do, and so do I."

I squint, unsure what she means.

"You don't see it, do you?" she stands with her arms folded across her chest. "You are a fierce attorney, the best in court—a little dynamo. But you are also wrapped up so tightly trying to prove yourself to everyone and find that special certain-someone that you lose yourself to other people. Sera, you are so desperate to find love, you fall for anyone who pays you attention."

She is making my head hurt. I knead my forehead, wishing she would stop, but she doesn't.

"Girl, you need to work on becoming more self-reliant."

I glance up through still heavy-lidded eyes but cannot argue. The trial and the pill have knocked all the wind out of my sails. I sip the juice, making a face akin to eating strained vegetables and lamb—a baby food option I tried while going through my immersion phase of willing a pregnancy. I had rationalized that conception was all about mindset, so everything in my life became all things baby, including what I ate.

"I also brought a carafe of coffee and a Grand Slam from Denny's—a tried-and-true hangover cure." Carolyn runs her hands down her perfectly pressed skirt, whisking away any imaginary wrinkles. "I'll come back with lunch. Eat. Sleep. Read." She chuckles, apparently finding herself humorous, and points to the book on top of the stack, Elizabeth Gilbert's *Eat, Pray, Love.*

"You want me to read a memoir about spaghetti and meditation?" I scoff. "I've tried this self-help mumbo jumbo before; it's bullshit."

She looks at me, a mixture of exasperation and irritation crossing her face. "Just read it. You might learn something."

"Such as?"

"Such as you can't do life by yourself."

I think about her words after the door closes behind her. I do morph for every man, I can't and don't ask for help, and I am a pro at being bullheaded (and have the history to prove it). I honed my craft at the tender age of six when I punched Sammy Red Feather Roberts in the face. I broke his nose. I was a small girl from a small town, born with the wrong-colored skin, now living where pigment and lineage meant everything, and I had just punched the Chief's son. While I could justify my actions after being bullied, I was still in big trouble and would get my first taste of the legal system. I blame that incident for me wanting to become a lawyer.

"You're petite," Momma said when I came home with a note stating I needed to appear in front of the tribal court. "I don't know why you can't get that through your head and stop fighting."

"But, Momma, he called me teeny *sooyaapoo*," I cried.

"Serenade Jean Kincaid," she stood, her eyes boring through me, "you are non-Indian."

Even at six years old, I knew I was not just a petite non-Indian living on the reservation. I was the pasty white, near ghost-like, thirty-two-pound type of petite non-Indian. I had frizzy dishwater blonde hair and nowhere close to the right shade of brown eyes. They were hazel. Even now, I loathe the color.

"How can my eyes be the color of a lady's name?" I once cried to my mom, referring to Hazel Eggers, the old lady who lived a quarter mile down the road.

"There, there," Daddy had soothed, "Hazel is a beautiful name and a perfect color for eyes."

"The color is like pea soup," Momma said.

I remember wailing at her hurtful words, but she continued: "I'm not sure what the good Lord was thinking, but if ever there was a mistake . . ." Mom pointed at my face, wagging her cigarette-stained finger inches from my nose, ". . . it's those eyes." She cackled the raspy laugh of a longtime smoker.

"God doesn't make mistakes," Daddy whispered into the crown of my head.

"She knows I'm kiddin'," Momma said defensively, and then counseled me: "Someday you can get yourself some colored contacts." And I did, in the perfect shade of deep brown. But that was several years and many insults later.

As promised, Carolyn stayed by my side day and night, only leaving me alone and unchecked for brief periods before, like any good fairy godmother, reappearing with sustenance and more reading material. She also brought a wooden chair from home and sanitized it daily; she could not bring herself to sit on the couch.

"Afraid of a little dirt?" I smirk.

"Nope, afraid of cooties." She glances toward the couch.

My days blur with buckets of coffee and mountains of self-help, how-to, and get-over-him books that now cover the bright orange carpet and the table that serves as both a place to eat and pile books.

"Learn anything today?" Carolyn asks a few days into our new routine.

"Why, yes," I say, sarcasm oozing, "to brave the wilderness, I must first understand my love language so I can be untamed on a Sunday."

Carolyn looks confused.

I laugh and explain, "I used the Brené Brown, Gary Chapman, Glennon Doyle, and Oprah book titles." I line up the books on the table. She is not chuckling.

"Not funny?"

"This is serious, Sera." Carolyn again sounds irritated. "You have no clue who you are, why you do what you do, and where you're going." She towers over me as I sit in my unbathed state, adding to the couch's stink. "You think everything is a goddamn joke. You're a fucking mess."

She turns on a heel and slams the door.

Alone, stinging from Carolyn's words, I amble to the bathroom to survey my condition. My eyes are swollen, red, and crusty. The smudge of three-day-old mascara darkens the skin beneath my lower lashes. My hair, no surprise, is matting together with the beginnings of dreadlocks. I lift my arm, still in the blouse I wore to court, sniff, and wince.

"Good God, you *are* a fucking mess," I tell my reflection.

I climb into the shower for the first time in days.

Carolyn did not show up this afternoon or evening: suicide watch must be over.

That isn't funny, my inner voice scolds, knowing I had stood on the brink.

"Okay, so what do we have here?" I stand over the growing pile of books, my hair and clothes now clean.

"Sorry, Ms. Gilbert, but I didn't like the movie; not sure I can stomach the book." I set aside *Eat, Pray, Love.*

There are fresh additions to my growing self-help Tower of Pisa, including Maya Angelou and Gandhi, and an intriguing one from Steve Harvey, *Act Like a Lady, Think Like a Man.* "Good on you, Steve," I say to his picture on the back flap, as if we are old friends.

The last day's enticer is *The Badass Life: 30 Amazing Days to a Lifetime of Great Habits—Body, Mind, and Spirit,* written by a woman named Christmas Abbott.

"Love your name, girlfriend." Her picture is as expected; she is gorgeous. "You are badass."

I place the book on my head, balance it, and close my eyes. "Learning through osmosis," I say with a giggle.

"Glad you think this is funny."

Carolyn's voice startles me, and the book falls with a thud, just missing my toes. "Jesus, you could knock." I gulp, catching my breath.

"I wanted to check on you, but it looks like you are doing fine. Still sloughing off personal responsibility and growth, I see." She sniffs and smiles. "At least you've showered."

"What do you want, Carolyn?" I ask, unamused.

"To tell you we are going to Steve's Bar. I thought you could use a distraction"—she pauses— "from all your studying." She wears a deep scowl, her gaze landing on the cover of one closed book to the next. "We leave tomorrow."

I do not argue. Steve's Bar is fantastic, as is its proprietor.

CHAPTER

3

The beaches in Puerto Vallarta, Mexico, are not the city's draw; they are thin, pebbly, and unwalkable without sandals. Only the city's fanciest resorts have the luxuriously soft white sand most people expect at tropical destinations. Unbeknownst to most tourists, however, that postcard-perfect sand is hauled in by dump trucks under the veil of night.

I love Puerto Vallarta's old town with its narrow, cobblestone roads that snake past shops selling trinkets to foolish Westerners. The barrage of smells (exhaust, fried fish, and salt air) and sounds (honking horns and shop owners calling out, "Miss, very beautiful, you buy? Only one dollar for you today") intrigues me and, strangely, comforts me. I feel at home when I am in PV.

My law-school buddy, Steve, brought me here for a spring break during our 3L year. Hank had insisted he needed to go home, to attend some mysterious event, alone—his engagement party, I would later learn. Steve, witnessing my meltdown upon Hank's departure, encouraged me to come with him to the "most special place . . . Puerto Vallarta."

"What makes it so special?" I asked Steve on the flight to Mexico.

"The people," he said, matter-of-factly. "They are brash and openly rude, harassing the Westerners to drop American dollars for their inauthentic wares."

"Inauthentic?"

"Most are made in China." Steve chuckled, shaking his head.

"And this makes the people 'special'?" I asked, not seeing anything special about deceitful behavior.

"No, Sera," Steve scoffed, as if I were the one talking nonsense. "They are special because they bust their asses to stay out of the cartel's stranglehold. They have figured out that we gringos want two things from our visit to Mexico: drugs and souvenirs. And we want a deal on both."

Steve paused, reflective. "They take their hard-earned money and gladly distribute it to their families and friends. And most nights they have fiestas, celebrating everything from births to deaths, from a sunset to it being a Tuesday." Steve closed his eyes. "Unlike us Americans, the people of PV don't need a reason to party. Every day that they can avoid gangs and warlords is worthy of a party." Steve sighs, the look on his face envious. "Being alive is a good enough reason for them to celebrate."

I admired that, and I liked Puerto Vallarta before I arrived.

After my week with Steve, I too made PV my go-to destination whenever I needed a quick dose of sunshine or a break from my life in Boise, Idaho, or just a reminder that not all things revolve around money.

In the years I had known Carolyn, she had joined me several times at my favorite haunt. However, after our first trip together, when we stayed in what I could afford—a cockroach-infested, non-air-conditioned room—she now insists we only stay at New

Amber, a posh resort in Jalisco, fifteen minutes out of town, complete with tourist sand. She pays.

Steve, who was not kidding about his fondness for the city, moved to Puerto Vallarta permanently a few years after law school, realizing he wasn't cut out for the grind. He and his long-time girlfriend, Marin, purchased an old building a few streets off the beaten path. Together, they happily run a US-style sports bar with big-screen TVs streaming real-time sports, and serving up finger steaks and fries, aptly named Steve's Bar Americana.

I'm busy throwing the last-minute, mostly unnecessary items into my carry-on—hairclip, umpteenth lip gloss, condoms—when Carolyn barges in using the spare key she never gave back after the custody hearing. Maybe she still worries about me being alone.

"Could you at least knock?" I call out from the bedroom, startled.

Unfazed, she throws her bag and jacket on the chair. "Got a bottle opener?"

"It's ten o'clock," I remind her, pointing to the kitchenette. "I thought we were heading to the airport?"

She waves a dismissive hand, rummages through the only drawer for an opener and pops the cork from the chilled bottle of Chablis she has brought with her. "Not for another hour. Thought we might get a jump-start on our vacay."

"Vacay? How old are you?"

She giggles, and we clink our glasses.

"To Mexico," I say.

"To margaritas."

"To men," I add with a wink.

I hail a cab and do the talking, always surprised by how poor Carolyn's Spanish is, given her fluency in so many other languages, including pig Latin.

"¿Adonde?" The cab driver catches my eye in his rearview.

"Steve's Bar, por favor."

"Si."

CHAPTER

4

Two months have passed since the divorce proceedings. My tan is fading, the lessons learned from the few self-help books I actually read are a distant memory, and now I am drowning in debt, self-pity, and work.

Despite my workload, Carolyn storms into my office and drops an armload of files on the desk and slams down her mug. Coffee sloshes over the side onto her folders and my research.

"What the hell?" I glare, looking at the wet, brown-stained papers.

She sets her jaw. "We need to talk."

"I can meet this afternoon."

"The dogs nipping at your butt?" she asks, referring to my clients.

I shake my head. "More like I'm up to my ass in alligators." I point to the brief in the Sampson case lying on my desk.

"This can't wait." She grabs a tissue from the box sitting on the desk's corner and dabs at the papers. "I've always been straight-forward with you, Sera, but last weekend when we went out for drinks—"

Here we go. She will not give up on this.

"—and then you take off, and I'm sitting there waiting, looking like an idiot."

I work my pen, clicking it repeatedly. A habit of mine that drives her crazy.

She knows sex has become my vice, my way to escape the loneliness. I do not see a problem with a good bottle of red, some companionship, and a few orgasms.

Over my glasses, I see her mouth moving, enunciating each word in a way that exaggerates her full, red-painted lips.

"And what's with you and having sex in bathrooms? Why there?" She pauses, waiting for a response.

"Are you slut-shaming me?"

Tension fills the room. When Carolyn speaks again, her tone is measured, her pitch low. "I've been in your shoes," I hear her say. "You may not think I do, but I understand."

I glare at her. There is no way Little Miss Silverspoon understands what I am going through.

"Just because we're friends," she starts again.

Oh, so now she's playing the friend card. Okay, that catches my attention. *But is she rambling about my sexual habits or my work performance?*

"Sera," Carolyn slaps her palm on the desk, and I jump, "Are you even listening?" A droplet of spit hits the paper in front of me.

"Pretty hard not to, boss lady," I feel heat rising in my cheeks.

"You do an outstanding job at the firm, but you're floundering in the other areas of your life."

"Look," I say, doing my best to regain my composure, "about the other night, I was lonely, he was available—"

"Jesus, Sera. Not everything has to do with sex." Carolyn's voice booms through my office. Marta, my assistant, reaches around the corner and shuts my office door, carefully staying out of Carolyn's view.

"It's your finances that are concerning me. I don't care who you have meaningless friction with, just keep it together here."

My eyes widen. I didn't see that coming.

"You know what I'm talking about." She waves her hand, fluttering her fingers. "Meaningless friction—dipping the wick? Copulating? Bumping uglies?"

"Just wow." I shake my head in wonderment, Carolyn never ceases to amaze me. I see the wheels turning and she adds an insult to the injury: "Do you even know his name?"

I roll my eyes, unsure if the answer really matters.

"You've gotta get a grip, girl." Carolyn's voice is still louder than I wish. "You're sexually finding yourself after the divorce, understandable, but hellfire and brimstone." Her words fade, and there is a pause in the tirade. She then says, "You're a partner in the firm now."

I nod; she has a point. But if I am honest, I cannot seem to fill the void left by my little girls and, I begrudgingly admit, Clint.

"You have a responsibility to at least show some level of decorum."

I continue nodding; she isn't wrong.

Carolyn plops down on the chair across from me.

Oh God, she's staying.

She shakes her head and, lowering her voice, says, "Look, the entire office knows."

"About the bathroom sex?" I'm suddenly horrified.

She raises an eyebrow. "About your money issues."

"Oh." I am now both embarrassed and interested in what she has to say.

"I've even heard the talk. God knows these women cluck, flapping around like hens in a coop, but come on." Her voice rises again in volume as she says, "You need to get your shit together, Sera."

"I'm busy here. I've got no time." I gesture to my desk piled high with papers and folders.

"Don't hide behind your career. You're in a funk. I get it. But what's it been, a year since he left you?"

Her words hit home.

"It's only been two months since the divorce was finalized," I say, seething.

"Semantics," she counters. "You're still living in that rundown motel drinking boxed wine out of red Solo cups." She peers over the rim of her mug. "Reused, red Solo cups."

I shrug. I grew up on red Solo cups; I do not see the problem.

And then she jabs, "Don't let this affect your work."

"Damn, I got it."

"I care for you." Carolyn's tone is soft for the first time since barging into my office. She gathers her stained files and stands to leave. "And I'm sorry you lost the girls. You were an exceptional mother to them, and you deserve visitation. If only we'd filed for adoption before the divorce . . ." Her voice trails off, and I hear her regret—the room fills with the *if only.*

"I don't blame you, Carolyn," I offer, and I mean it. "Judges don't give visitation to stepparents. But I had to try."

"Yes, but you gave Clint everything, Sera. You didn't have to do that," Carolyn says, now in consolation mode.

"I felt he deserved it."

"Jesus, Sera, you're infertile, not a criminal." Her words are kind, but they still cut as if I am a criminal.

Carolyn and I look at each other. There is an understanding between us, having both experienced the loss of a child.

"I had my assistant, the new one, what's her name? Some sort of spice."

I scoff; Carolyn runs through help like most people change clothes. "Sage," I remind her.

"Right. I had her . . . *Sage*," she corrects herself, "book you a flight and a room at the Marriott for a Dave Ramsey seminar. It's this Saturday and Sunday in Salt Lake City. You leave tonight at five."

"What the hell? You can't plan my life." I hang my head; I'm running out of fight. "I have things to do. I need to write this brief . . . and I have plans." I throw in an outright lie, but she sees through it.

"You never have plans. And the Sampson brief isn't due till next Thursday. I looked at the scheduling order." She is out the door when I hear her say, "You're going."

———

Staring out the window of the cab, I see my stone-faced reflection looking back. I can't unhear Carolyn's words. My cheeks flush, remembering the tongue-lashing, both about my sex life and my finances that has brought me to downtown Salt Lake. The driver yammers on about the cityscape. "And over here," he says, "is the Mormon Temple." He points to a massive building that, regardless of my mood, I admit is remarkable. I count six spires reaching to the sky, and a tall figure sitting atop the building's capstone, which the driver informs me is the Angel Moroni. I know this angel from the Book of Revelation; he is the one who is to welcome in the Second Coming of Christ. My feelings about organized religion aside, the compound is breathtaking.

"They don't want to be called Mormon anymore or LDS," my driver continues. "They prefer 'The Church of Jesus Christ of Latter-day Saints.'"

"Hmm," I mumble, disinterested. I gave up my churchiness as a faithful Catholic about the time I let Thomas Jefferson (yes, really) shove his hand up my dress at senior prom. (Poor kid, saddled with such a moniker.) Any belief I had left went totally by the wayside somewhere between going batshit crazy over Hank and losing my stepdaughters to Clint.

I can no longer swallow the strict set of "thou shalt nots" and "thou musts." I've lived that life. I did my job and prayed daily for God to grant me children, but the omnipotent failed in his side of the bargain, leaving my womb empty and then insulting me further by taking away my stepdaughters.

"We're here, Miss," the driver says, stopping outside the Marriott. I grab my laptop and roll bag from the seat next to me and pass some cash to Mister Chatty Cathy.

"I hope you find your happiness," he shouts as I slam the door.

"Jerk," I whisper between clenched teeth. How dare he think he knows anything about me?

"Good day, ma'am. How may I help you?" the hotel clerk asks without looking up at me.

"Reservation for Serenade Kincaid."

"Yes, ma'am. Here for the seminar, I see." I focus on the click-clacking of the keyboard.

"You're on the twelfth floor, room 1247." He gives me a well-re-hearsed ho-hum spiel: "There are complimentary appetizers in the lounge and a continental breakfast at six. The workshops are in various conference rooms on the second floor. Is there anything else I can assist you with?" His too-polished smile screams, *I hate my job.*

"No, thank you."

I slog my bag to my room, irritated I'm here and that Carolyn has the power to send me. *Damn, Serenade,* I think, *you are just flat-out grouchy these days.*

———

There is a lot about Carolyn that's enviable. She is tall, wealthy, and, since the death of her husband, she's been in a monogamous relationship with a cowboy who would lasso the moon for her if she'd let him. Me, on the other hand, I'm living hand-to-mouth and lily-padding—Carolyn's term.

"You are the frog, honey," she corrected me after I complained about kissing a lot of them, "jumping from lily pad to lily pad, hoping to find Prince Charming."

Carolyn is exasperating and, in most ways, the antithesis of me. We're both forty-something, have each lost children and a husband, and are an only child of parents who were also only children. But that's where the similarities stop. I am the daughter of a third-generation wheat farmer and a crazy mother from the sticks. Carolyn is the heiress to the Wetzstein-Yates fortune—the two men who started our firm. Carolyn was, is, and ever will be spoiled to the nth degree, and I will always be the financial disas-ter, teeny *sooyaapoo* from the rez. Yet we gel.

CHAPTER

5

The gathering of fiscally unsound individuals who schmooze one another, hand out business cards, and put a best foot forward is almost more than I can handle. I can't get past the false vibe presented. If any of us had our lives together, we wouldn't be here.

"Hi. Dean Anderson," the man in front of me says hastily, thrusting his hand out. Dean has mischievous, pale eyes and unruly, sand-blond hair that hangs in unkempt bangs over his forehead. In what I guess is an attempt to stop his hair falling into his eyes, or is a nervous habit, he regularly tilts his head and shakes the hair away, resulting in a flashback look of Justin Bieber circa 2007. Nevertheless, he is semi-handsome, cheerful, and comes off simple and lacking pretense. His mixture of boyish good looks and innocent charm is refreshing and intriguing.

"I'm Sera." I smile, placing my hand on his. Electricity runs through me as I shake his cold, clammy hand.

"You ever been to one of these?" he asks, releasing my hand and wiping his palm down his pant leg. He glances up at the mop that has fallen back onto his face. He is conscious of both his sweat and unruly mane.

"No, you?" I look at him but continue to thumb through the conference brochure. He seems more attractive as the minutes pass and the wine takes hold.

"Yeah, my company sends me to these." He blows wisps of hair off his forehead. "They call it 'continuing education,' which is ridiculous since I don't have a degree and, therefore, don't know what it's continuing," he babbles. Chuckling, he says, "Do you need continuing education?"

I grin, "Yes."

"What do you do?"

"I'm an attorney." My words come out guarded; I am always ready to defend my chosen career.

"Oh, wow. That's great. Are you an Ivy Leaguer?" he pumps at the ceiling with open palms.

"No. The University of Idaho."

"Sweet. Go, Vandals." He adds, "That's impressive."

"Thanks, I eked out the JD." Sensing he was unfamiliar with the term, I add, "Juris doctor?" Nothing. "Law degree."

"Ah," he nods, comprehension filling his eyes.

I look back to the brochure and mark the session entitled *Personal Wealth and Investing, How to Overcome Debt.* Dean sidles up to me, oblivious that he's invading my space.

"Hey, I'm attending that session too." He taps the pamphlet, nearly knocking it from my hand. "I heard it's at capacity. I'll get there early and save you a spot, and you'll be in like flint," he says, gesturing like a player sliding into home plate.

"Flynn," I correct.

"What?"

"The saying . . . it's in like 'Flynn,' not 'flint.'" I roll my eyes.

"Oh, right," he snorts, and I watch the reference fly over his head.

"Well, what do you say? Save you a seat?"

A warning goes off in my head. The few books I have read explain that I will continue to pick the same type of destructive relationship unless I consciously choose someone completely different from previous partners. My inner voice runs through a quick checklist. *Is he like the others? Will he suck you in, and will you change? Is he the leaving kind?*

This man-child with the pop-star hair feels different, at least at first blush. He seems harmless.

"Thank you. Please save me a seat."

I excuse myself, make a beeline for the food cart, grab a few appetizers, and head up to my room, patting myself on the back for not jumping into anything physical with this stranger on our first meeting.

In the capacity of a friend, I call Carolyn to update her on the event, "You would *not* believe how many people are here."

"I *can* believe it. I've been to a Dave Ramsey seminar."

"No, kidding." And there's the answer as to why she was so adamant I attend.

"Yes, years ago. I was dating this law school jerk. Okay, it was my contracts professor," she admits without provocation. "But he was still a jerk."

I cringe. *Carolyn dated her professor.*

"He insisted that 'anyone who spends time with me must be fiscally responsible.'" She groans, and I giggle at her impression of a dry New England accent.

"He gave me the worst grade I ever received in law school."

"Ouch."

"Yeah, I dumped his ass. But I attended the Ramsey seminar, and I learned a lot from it."

"Duly noted, counselor." I yawn. "I'll call you tomorrow." I slip between the sheets and drift.

———

"Okay, you were right," I say to Carolyn that Monday at the office, "I enjoyed the seminar."

"Oh, my good God, who is *he*? What's happening?" she throws herself into the chair across my desk.

"No one. And nothing. Why do you think that?"

"It's never nothing with you, Sera, and you've got that shifty look."

"I'm pretty sure I didn't end up in a bathroom with a stranger, if that's what you're implying." I grin and enjoy watching Carolyn's eyes grow as big as saucers.

CHAPTER

6

join Dean's bowling league two weeks after we met. I am horrible at the game. I carry a handicap of ninety-two, which makes me shudder when I learn it is the equivalent of a low D in grade terms. Dean likes to joke with the guys on the team about how my handicap helps us beat the other teams. His words hurt. But I play along, shutting out the tap on my shoulder, reminding me this new guy may not be all that different from the other losers I have picked. I am enjoying not being alone, so I ignore my inner voice.

At my desk, I swipe away from Facebook and onto the page displaying the ten-pound glittery pink bowling ball I just purchased and smile.

"Plans for the weekend?"

"Could you knock?" I ask, looking up to see Carolyn. "And yes, I'm going bowling with Dean. Look at what I just bought." I proudly shove my phone in her direction.

"Here we go," she mumbles, humoring me as she looks at the screen.

"What does that mean?" I prickle at her tone, grab my phone, and scroll back to social media.

"Are you telling me you're a fan of smoky bowling alleys and sweaty old men in polyester shirts?"

"You don't have any idea what you're saying. Smoking is banned in bowling alleys." I cock my head and continue swiping.

She chuckles, "Checking out your dating apps?"

"No, smarty, I'm checking out Facebook. Dean still hasn't accepted my friend request; it's kinda weird."

I look up, and Carolyn has closed her eyes and is shaking her head.

———————

"Hey, Sera, I need to ask you something," Dean says on our way to my motel from the bowling alley. My stomach churns: I am not ready for this.

"Dean, you know I'm only like seven minutes out of my disastrous marriage. Can't we keep doing what we're doing? Without labels?"

Dean looks at me, perplexed. "I know how you feel about that, Sera. That's not what I need to ask." He grows silent. "I'm embarrassed to say this, but I'm a tad short. I was wondering if you could spot me two hundred dollars. I get paid in a couple of days."

I am relieved that Dean only wants money, not a commitment to be his girlfriend or meet his parents, just a small payday loan.

So much for the Ramsey seminar. I give him two crisp bills.

———————

Two days later, I am over at Dean's for dinner. He has again cooked his famous spaghetti for the third time in as many weeks.

"Thank you," I sigh, finishing my meal, which wasn't half-bad.

Dean grins and whisks me out of my chair, throwing me over his shoulder.

"Dean. Put me down," I squeal. "What are you doing?" I protest, playing the game. I know he is taking me to his bed.

He flings me down, unzips my jeans, and yanks them and my panties off in one quick tug. He fumbles for a moment with the buttons on my blouse. Exasperated, he grabs a fist full of material in each hand and rips it open, the buttons spraying onto the bed.

"What the hell?" I yell as I sit up.

"I'll buy you a new one."

With my money, I suppose.

He pushes me back on the bed, pinning my arms above my head, the moisture of his palms sticky on my wrists. "No talking."

His mouth finds mine, and my breath catches. He makes his way skillfully down my neck. I am surprised how confident his performance is, given his usual childish behaviors. He pauses at each breast, paying attention before traveling downward. I close my eyes and melt into the pleasure.

It is dark when I open my eyes. The house is quiet, and the bed empty; I've dozed after our lovemaking. I turn on the bedside lamp and blush when the light illuminates ten crisp twenty-dollar bills fanned out on the nightstand. A rush runs through my body, titillating me and warming my face.

"Shut the front door," Carolyn emphasizes each word after I tell her the story over our morning coffee and case review. "That is the sexiest thing."

"Right?" I twirl around in my chair and squeal.

"But no more lending money," she wags her finger.

"I know, I know. But he paid me right back, with interest." I wink, still riding the taboo wave of being paid for sex.

"Did he ever accept you on Facebook?"

"Why are you digging for something?" I am annoyed by her suspicion.

"Just be careful. You hardly know the guy. And what would your books say?" she asks on her way out of my office.

"They'd tell me not to let my friend spoil a fun time," I call after her and then hear myself dispute the fact. *No, Serenade, those books, if you'd read them, will surely tell you what you already know. Carolyn's right—you need to be careful.*

———

I text Dean.

"Hey babe. Taking a rain check tonight. Have deposition in the morning and need sleep."

I debate for a moment and then add a heart emoji. I gather my files, make my way to the motel, get ready for bed, and lay the phone on the pillow, expecting it to vibrate. Instead, I wake to the alarm and a blank screen, still no text.

———

"I'm ready," the court reporter announces. She sits in her chair, ramrod straight, her fingers poised over the keys of her steno machine and looks up at me over the top of her glasses in anticipation.

"Thank you." I take a breath and focus on the moment, pushing Dean out of my mind.

An hour of questioning the less-than-truthful deponent has crawled by when my phone vibrates with a text notification. I have intentionally not silenced it.

"I'm so sorry," I lie about the disruption. "Let's take a ten-minute break."

I open the message. "Ms. Kincaid, please call the office ~ Marta."

"Hey, Marta," I say when she answers. "What is it?"

"It's your doctor. They said it was important and to please call."

"Thanks. I'll take care of it when we finish."

———

"Thank you for calling, Ms. Kincaid," the voice on the other end of the line says. "We need you to come in and get a diagnostic ultrasound."

"What's the problem?" I ask, my stomach lurching.

"The radiologist noticed something suspicious on your mammogram."

I lean against the wall for support. In a well-rehearsed tone, the voice pauses and finishes with, "We have you scheduled for tomorrow morning. No need to worry."

I slide down to the floor. My thoughts, disjointed, fracture into hundreds of directions and race at warp speed. *No need to worry. What the hell? Do I have cancer? Am I dying?* Worry seems an excellent place to start. I push number three on my speed dial and go straight to Dean's voicemail. I wait a minute and try again.

"Damn it." I don't leave a message.

"Where the hell are you, Dean?" I yell at the dark screen. "Why aren't you answering?"

I pace back and forth, from window to door, waiting for a call from Dean. I move the sheer aside at the window, lift a slat in the blind, and stare out onto the empty street below, searching for the familiar old maroon Ford Taurus.

"Maybe he's coming up the stairs," I try to reassure myself.

I cross the room, and on tip-toes peer through the peephole . . . nothing. Dean isn't texting back, answering my calls, driving up, and he is *not* lurking in the hallway.

"Where are you?"

I reach for my phone again, ready to push speed dial number two, Carolyn, and then stop myself. Her mother died of breast cancer. That wound runs deep, is still raw, and off-limits. I will tell her later, and only if necessary. I know better than to touch the number one on the speed dial queue. For different reasons, both Dad and Mom are forever unavailable.

Exhausted and filled with irrational thoughts about tomorrow's ultrasound and Dean's whereabouts, I scream into the phone when his name lights up my screen. "Where the hell have you been?"

"I told you I was at a seminar today." I hear the slightest stammer.

"Right," I say, sure he's not telling me the entire story. "Well, you didn't send me a goodnight text, and you haven't answered my calls all day. What's up with that?"

"I'm sorry. I was busy and couldn't talk. What's going on, Sera? I'm coming over."

"No. I don't want you here now," I say. Something isn't right. He never told me about a seminar; I forget very little. He is lying to me, and I am in no mood for that.

"It's late, and I'm tired. I have an early appointment. I was just pissed when I didn't hear from you."

God, I could use a cigarette. I'm not a bona fide smoker but do indulge in an occasional puff when I drink too much or my nerves are upended, like now.

Ashamed of my suspicious behavior and fearful of losing him, I lower my voice and say, "I'm sorry." I wipe my nose on the back of my hand, transferring the contents onto my pajamas, childlike.

"Sera, you never ramble. What is it?"

"Nothing. I'll talk to you tomorrow." I end the call.

Thoughts of the next day's test keep me awake.

Am I going to lose my breasts? I wonder if Clint will let me see the girls before I die. Clint. *Oh, God, who will take care of me if I'm sick?* I thought it would be Clint when we got married, but now that's a no-go. I run through my mental Rolodex of candidates and come up short. Mom is incapable. The firm keeps Carolyn too occupied. Maybe Dean? I roll my eyes at the thought.

I grab my laptop and open Facebook. I spend a few minutes checking recent posts and confirming a friend request from a girl in my high school class. I wonder as I look at her profile how she could have five children when I couldn't seem to have one. My list of friends is short, and I can't care less about my work acquaintances. It takes no time scrolling through the updates for my mind to go back to the nagging question: why won't Dean friend me on social media?

What are you hiding, Dean Anderson?

My fingers hover over the keyboard as I ponder my next move and then type Dean's name into the Facebook login screen. That bit is easy. Now for the password . . .

"People are predictable," Clint had told me. "Their passwords are often something personal, like a birth date or an anniversary, mother's maiden name, pet's name, or the street of their childhood home."

Everything else aside, Clint is an excellent private investigator.

"Alright, Dean," I say to my laptop, "Let's try your garage code, 2120."

"Invalid password," replies Facebook.

Think, Serenade. You're smarter than this.

Tap, tap, tap. My finger touches the keys, hoping to conjure a password as if this were a Ouija board.

Maybe it's Millie, his dog's name, and his birth date. Millie0701, I type.

"Invalid password" flashes again, goading me to try one last time before locking me out.

Come on, Serenade, you've got this.

I wait a minute, clear my head, and try a different route. Dean often talks about his desire to restore a car, an Oldsmobile, which he refers to as the Olds, with a four-barrel carburetor, four-speed manual transmission, and dual exhausts known as a "four-four-two." I type Olds442, hold my breath, and through squinted eyes, push "enter."

My heart races with excitement. The screen shows Dean's profile picture, a cute photo of him and Millie, taken when both were much less gray. I can see he has reacted to several posts from friends, a picture of someone's dinner, a meme of an angler catching a roll of toilet paper, captioned "brown trout fishing." I then notice he has an unopened message in Messenger. I click it open and read:

"I miss you too," a woman named Pam writes. My shoulders sink, and I scroll back through the text.

"I miss you." The line above appears, Dean's image in the circle next to it. I roll the cursor up further and read from the beginning of the day's message thread.

"I'm hard," was Dean's first clandestine message.

"LOL," her intelligent response.

"I want you," he wrote.

Smiley face emoji from Pam.

"I want to taste you."

But why? I choke down the sob that threatens to burst from my mouth.

I can't take my eyes off the train wreck, can't stop reading their parlay, can't keep the hot tears from streaming down my face or vomit rising in my throat. I continue to scroll, torturing myself until I've read every graphic and sordid entry, including how Dean wanted to have Pam again as he had earlier in the day.

I am hyperventilating. Once again, I am consumed with a man who isn't consumed with me, and this consumption now has me hacking and cyberstalking, and who-knows-what other criminal activity in due course.

I click on Pam's name.

Her profile opens to a lovely picture of a blonde in a crisp white blouse and blue jeans. Her hair cascades over her shoulders, her blue eyes match her jeans. Next to her sits a handsome man in similar attire, a white shirt, and jeans. There is no doubt he is Mister Pam.

Three adorable young children complete the frame. All are barefoot, posed in perfect Rockwellian-style, caught mid-laugh, capturing the family's idyllic essence. Pam is a gorgeous married mother.

I taste bile, slam the laptop closed, flick on the lamp beside me, and reach for my phone.

"How dare you." I spit my words like venom when Dean answers. "I needed you, and you were out screwing a married woman. Stay the hell away from me."

I end the call with a tap on the screen and long for the good old days when you could slam down a phone receiver or yank the base from the wall and fling the entire contraption across the room.

Thirty minutes later, there is constant pounding on my door. I glance at my nightstand where I keep my loaded 9mm and shout, "Don't you dare come in here, Dean."

Before leaving for my ultrasound, I check Dean's Facebook page, wiped clean as a whistle.

CHAPTER
7

Breathe, *Serenade,* I tell myself over and over, *this will be okay.* I am wearing a hospital gown, open in the front, and have settled onto the examination table. The magazine I brought from the waiting room lies limp between my hands. Beneath me, crinkling every time I move, is the paper sheet covering the vinyl on which I am sitting. My heartbeat feels a thousand times faster than it should, and it occurs to me that I may die of a heart attack before the start of the ultrasound.

This cannot be happening. I have so many things I want to do, so many places to see. If I get out of this okay, I will live more, see more, and do more. I smile, despite my fear, at the way I am bargaining with the unknown.

How much longer?

"Patience," I whisper.

Maybe I need to pray, I think.

You need to pray even when not in times of desperation. The voice of my fifth-grade Catechism teacher, Sister Mary Katherine, rings through my head.

I used to pray, Sister. Say my Rosary, the whole shebang. But my prayers went unanswered. I always wanted a family, but Clint took the girls away. And now this. A sob escapes my throat.

A quick rap at the door saves me from my fit. I jolt back to the present. The paper crinkles beneath me, and the magazine falls to the floor with a splat.

"Sorry." I fumble getting off the table to rescue the reading material.

"Don't be nervous, hon," the lady says, leaning down to retrieve the magazine instead. "I'll be doing your ultrasound." She smiles, showing me her yellow-stained teeth and cigarette wrinkles.

I nod. My mouth too dry to speak.

"This won't hurt a bit. I've warmed up the gel and will put a dab on the end of the wand. I'll use it to look around at the tissue, click a few pictures, and then the doctor will look at it while you wait, okay?" The sweet lady with gray hair clipped back in neat pins smiled again; this time, I see experience and patience in the folds of skin on her face. "You'll have your results before you leave today," she says, patting my hand.

Will I live long enough to get wrinkles? I lie back on the noisy paper, and a tear rolls out of my eye and into my ear.

"Whatever the outcome, we are here for you." The technician holds my gaze, releasing it only when I nod.

She touches the skin of my breast with the warm, gooey wand. I lay motionless, not breathing, and stare up at a poster tacked on the ceiling. It's a picture of two stick people, one is holding the straight, center "body" line of the other. The caption reads, "I've got your back." It's supposed to be funny, but I don't laugh.

The technician finishes and leaves the room to confer with the doctor. I am alone again with my thoughts. *Does a quick result mean a good outcome? Or was it the other way around?* I feel pressure in my chest. *Yep, I'm having a heart attack. Maybe it's anxiety.* I take a stab at self-diagnosis. *Of course, it's anxiety. Jesus, I'm going crazy. Please, someone, save me from me.*

Another quick rap at the door again causes me to jump. An academic-looking woman with glasses perched on the end of her nose steps in and introduces herself as the radiologist.

"I've looked at your scan, Ms. Kincaid, and see nothing abnormal. Your breasts are fibrous, which can often appear as lumps or worse. In your case, what they saw on your mammogram looks to be fibrous tissue. You'll be fine." She reassures me with a nod and turns on her heel.

As the doctor leaves, the tech comes in, "Okay, you're all done."

Choked-up, I mouth, "Thank you." The corners of her lip curl. I release the breath I don't know I am holding.

"I'll leave you to get dressed, take all the time you need." With that, she slips out of the room.

I sit alone, weeping, overwhelmed by immense feelings of relief and loss. My boobs will stay with me; Dean will not.

CHAPTER

8

"What are you working on, Sera?" Carolyn asks, throwing herself on the chair in her usual spot.

Dressed in haute couture, Carolyn slumps low, her head resting on the chairback, her legs sprawled over an arm. She acts like an adolescent wrapped in a fierce attorney's body; she is the literal definition of a hot mess.

"Nothing much. Just making a list," I say.

She sits up, intrigued, and grabs for the pad. "A list of what?"

"Nosey." I move the paper out of her reach. "It's a list of things I want to do."

"Oh, a fuck-it list?" She amuses herself.

I roll my eyes as she drums her manicured red nails, trying to draw me in.

"I suppose." I shoot an annoyed look over my glasses, my childishness now equaling hers.

With lightning speed, she snatches the paper and begins reading it aloud: "Belly dancing, horse riding, river rafting, backpacking." She flings it back on the desk. "This list is more like a boring exercise regimen. Where's sex on top of the Eiffel Tower and orgies in the courthouse?" She laughs. "That seems more your style."

"A girl has one tryst in a bathroom, and she's marked for life," I joke.

I could see her wheels turning. "Is there something you're not telling me?" She raises a brow.

Carolyn is empathic, or I'm guilt ridden, a byproduct of my churchgoing days on the prairie; either way, she sees through me. I can never keep secrets from her.

"Okay, I had a breast ultrasound, but it was nothing."

"What? When? Why didn't you say something?"

"I just got back a little while ago, and I didn't want to, well," I stammer, struggling to find a word that isn't annoying or hurtful, so I choose, "burden you."

"Burden? You didn't want to burden me?" She exaggerates the words and blinks fast. "Telling me you had an ultrasound isn't burdensome. You dying without telling me, now that's a burden." Then to lighten the mood, she adds, "I'd get stuck with all your work."

"Thanks for being so understanding." I chuckle.

"Is everything okay?" I hear a slight crack in her voice.

"Yes. I promise."

The flash of fear on her face takes me back to when I first worked under Carolyn as her lackey associate. I was doing grunt work, research, and witness interviews, when Carolyn's mother received her stage four metastatic breast cancer diagnosis. They gave her a grim two-month prognosis.

When Carolyn received the call, she came into my office, eyes red, purse in hand. And in a wavering voice said, "You have the helm."

It was trial by fire.

Carolyn left for the next three months without so much as a caseload explanation or rundown. She sat by her mother's side for days on end, taking part in her version of a living Shiva, refusing to work, and only occasionally taking time to bathe or change her clothes. She wouldn't allow the television or radio to play in her mother's room, insisting she read to her so that her voice was the only thing her mother heard. Carolyn refused to sit on anything other than a metal stool reserved for the doctor. "If she's uncomfortable, I can't be comfortable." She stayed with her mother until she passed.

Carolyn clears her throat, bringing us both back to our current conversation. "Now, what's with the list?"

"I've lost myself, that's all." The look on Carolyn's face prompts me to revise my statement, "Okay, maybe I've never known myself."

She grins.

"I went from Hank to marrying Clint to some guy in a bathroom to hooking up with Dean. Years have gone by, and I've done nothing but chameleoning. So, I made a list."

"Chameleoning?" Carolyn shakes her head. "Did you just say that?" She slaps her leg and snorts.

"I did. It's stupid but true. I turn into a chameleon with whatever guy I'm dating." I pause, giving her a chance to gather herself. "What do you think of the word, not bad, huh?"

"No. It's horrible. It's fitting but horrible." Carolyn wipes a tear. "If you want to mark off rafting, I know a guide. I think you'd like him."

"That'd be great."

"You sure you're okay, friend?" Carolyn stops at the door, and her eyes lock with mine.

"I'm sure," I smile.

I think back to the first time she called me that. It had been following her mother's death, after I'd covered her work for months, sat quietly with her as she wept, and asked if there was anything I could do for her. She responded with a simple, "You're doing it. Just being available is what I need. Thank you, friend." And our worlds intertwined.

My phone vibrates, and I glance down to see that Carolyn has texted me her guide friend's contact information. It reads, "Captain Tim, pirate."

———————

"Ms. Kincaid," Marta's voice chimes over the intercom, "I have a Captain Tim on the line for you. He says you'll know who he is." Marta's worked for me for the better part of three years and refuses to call me Sera or Serenade. "It's not proper in the workplace," she claims.

I pick up the phone. "Hi, Tim? I'm Sera Kincaid, a friend of Carolyn Scott. She gave me your number and said you—"

"Yep."

It annoys me he spoke over me, but I listen as I want to raft.

"She said I should call you," he continues. "What can I do ya for?"

Oh my, he sounds like a winner.

"Carolyn mentioned you might go on a trip in a couple of weeks. I would like to join if there's space."

"You ever been on the river?"

"Yes, I have. It's been a while, well, a long while, but I have," I stammer, hoping I haven't just talked myself out of a seat.

There is a lengthy pause, and I assume the captain is weighing his options. "It's a four-dayer. You up to that?"

"I've done nothing like that before, but I suppose I could do it."

Another interminable pause as I hold my breath.

"What the hell. We need another body to round out the group. I'll shoot you the deets."

Shoot me the what?

As if reading my mind, he says, "Got an email? I'll send you the information."

Ah, the deets.

A four-dayer, I learn through the captain's email, starts deep in the backcountry, putting the rafts into the river and coming out four days later. No civilization, no communication except a satellite phone with spotty reception for emergencies—just twelve rafters and the river. We will carry all our supplies with us, raft several hours a day, "take-out" at pre-designated spots, make camp, cook, sleep, rinse, and repeat. It will cost me two hundred dollars and will require me to help prepare meals the day before the trip.

As I read the email, Carolyn taps on my door and lets herself in. "Well?"

"Are you kidding me?" I shake my head in disbelief. "Do you have my office bugged?"

"Better," she winks. "I have spies all over town. So?"

Click, click, click, I work my pen. "Yes, I'm going."

Carolyn lets out a yip. "You're going to love it, and you'll like Tim, I assure you."

———————

"Sera. Sera, we're here." I wake up in the backseat of a pickup at the edge of the Snake River in Hells Canyon, the Oregon side. Tim is leaning in, one eye looking at me, the other looking over my shoulder, saying, "We're at the launch." Three hours flew by while I slept.

As my vision comes into focus, I can't help but stare at Tim and his cockeyed gaze. I hadn't noticed it in the dark when we loaded up at four-thirty this morning, but I see it now; he has an eye thing. Now I get the "pirate" reference on Carolyn's contact.

I wipe the drool off the side of my mouth, still staring. "Sorry, I didn't sleep well last night."

He taps below one eye and whispers, "It's fake," and then turns his attention back to unloading the truck. He wears a loose tank top that exposes his man-boobs and faded red shorts that are two inches short of the day's style. A ball cap pulled low protects his eyes from the sun's glare but does nothing to hide his mullet. He looks hokey but has a certain *je ne sais quoi* about him. He has a powerful personality, and I like the way he commands attention. It doesn't hurt that he has a legendary reputation on the river.

I rub the sleep from my eyes and roll out of the truck. I trip over a bag on the ground and fall against a stack of oars leaning on the pickup. They create an enormous commotion as they topple.

"Yard sale," someone calls out, and everyone laughs.

"What's yard sale?" I ask Tim as I begin picking up the paddles and restacking them against the truck.

"You are," he chuckles. "When a skier crashes on a run and all their gear flies off, everyone says they look like a yard sale all over the mountainside."

Great, already I'm the butt of the jokes. I brush it off. Who cares about them?

"Ah," I say, hoping my wounded feelings don't show. "Hey, Tim, I . . ." I falter and start again, "I'm sorry about earlier, I didn't mean to—"

"Please," Tim holds up a hand, "Don't apologize. I lost it years ago; caught a blade to the eye playing ice hockey." His thoughts drift. "My pappy said, 'Don't you go on the ice today, son. You got chores.' But I was just a kid, so I thought I'd play a quick pickup game before I went home to do my work. Best damned lesson I ever learned." He smiles.

"I'm sorry for your loss," I blurt out, instantly regretting it.

A dozen of us stand on the loading ramp after the rafts are in the river and the equipment is secure. Someone calls out, "Last time to use a civilized shitter, take advantage." Regardless of my distaste of the reference, I need to pee and so make a beeline for the outhouse.

The group is a mix of young, not-so young, educated, and not-so much. There's an engineer, two college students, a kid from Canada fresh out of high school in his gap year, two skydiving instructors and their female roommate, Tim, me, and a guy called Cutter. Two others drive up late, just as we are ready to shove off; I don't catch their names.

"Okay, everyone, gather around so we can get some housekeeping out of the way." The pirate addresses the crowd. "My name's Captain Tim, and I'm in charge. I only have a few rules. First, whatever shit you pack in, you pack out. And I mean *whatever*, including the human type. We've got a groover strapped to Cutter's cat."

I bite my top lip, unsure what a groover is and missing the feline reference. Tim, seeing my confusion, announces, "Cat is short for catamaran." He points to a boat in the water, "That pontoon-looking craft that seats two is a cat." The group of seasoned river-goers whoop at my expense.

Leaning close, he says, "A groover is where you, well, you know . . ."

To my surprise, he wrinkles his nose the way Carolyn does.

"Okay, in all fairness, this is Sera, otherwise known as Yard Sale." The crowd laughs again at my earlier incident. "She's new to the river, so let's be kind to her, teach her the ropes, and keep an eye out for her."

I lift my hand and let out a sheepish, "Hey."

"How's it hanging, Yard Sale?" one guy asks. I fight the urge to roll my eyes.

"Back to the shit," Tim calls for attention. "No crapping anywhere except in the groover. And, I have to say this; toilet paper is a necessity, ladies, not a luxury." Tim glances in my direction and then to the only other woman. I see a slight pink tinge cover his face. "You need to pee elsewhere; the groover is only for, well, you know."

My stomach clenches, knowing I will never be able to use that thing. *I'll be holding it for four days.*

"Second," Tim's voice rises, "we wear PFDs through the rapids, no exception. Yard Sale—"

I snap to attention.

"That's short for a personal flotation device."

I nod.

"Third, I'll be the lead cat. I want the kayaks to follow me, the rafts next, and Cutter on his cat, bringing up the rear. Kayaks, if we have swimmers, you'll be able to reach them first. Have 'em hang on until me or Cutter can get to you." The group nods and mumbles their understanding.

"Last, remember, what happens on the river stays on the river."
A round of shouts and laughter befalls the group. "And yes, ladies,
you can earn these." Tim lifts a handful of beads he has around his
neck. Catcalls and whistles erupt. I catch the Mardi gras reference;
flash your boobs, earn a strand of beads.

I cover my chest with folded arms. *There will be no flashing of
these ta-tas.*

The other woman howls like an excited dog.

"Now, let's talk about the river. Hells Canyon's one helluva
river to navigate. She's runnin' high and fast, and some of her
rapids are closed."

Tim leans in again to me and explains that the National Forest
Service deems when a rapid is too dangerous to traverse.

"Thanks." I smile, looking only at what I believe is his real eye.

Tim returns his attention to the group. "The first rapid is the
Green Room, and it's a no-go zone. It's closed. You won't make it
through in a raft, period. The rumble in the distance is the Green
Room." The roar was unmistakable.

"I need to repeat this, do not pass through the Green Room," Tim
emphasizes every word. The eleven of us nod our understanding.

"Okay, kayakers, get in, rafters next. Cutter, you all set?"

"Ready, Captain," says Cutter.

"Then, let's roll."

There are hoots and hollers as we load the gear.

"Sera, I want you with me, at least for now. You cool with that?"

Relieved to be with the rafting expert, I look up gratefully but
self-consciously, unsure which eye to meet. "You'll get used to
it," he says and walks off towards his catamaran, leaving me
red-faced.

I settle into the front of the vessel, and less than a minute later, Tim is yelling. I can only hear snippets over the roar of the river and the thudding of my heart in my ears. "Dig your feet . . . grab . . . rope and hang . . . if . . . don't panic." His face is red, his mouth forming words. I understand enough to jam my legs under the front frame and wrap my hands rodeo-style around the bronc rein.

"Here we go!"

Mouth wide open, I let out a scream from the depth of my soul. Lunging forward, we plummet over the outside edge of the rapid. I hang on, white-knuckled to the rope. My stomach drops several feet as the catamaran tips point straight downward. The plunge lifts me off my seat, and I am standing, my legs locked under the frame as I keep a death grip on the nylon braid between my hands. The curve of the kick catches the water and shoots us upright, slamming me back into my seat and the boat into the tranquil water on the other side of the Green Room.

"And that, Yard Sale, is just the fringe of a rapid. You are in for a real ride next time."

I nod, drenched in water and weak from the rush.

Tim turns our vessel to watch and wait for the others. My heart pounds and my breath is quick with excitement. The kayakers follow, screaming with the same satisfaction and glee when they plunge over the periphery of the rapid. The supply raft with its occupants is next, and they negotiate expertly around the Green Room.

The raft carrying the two skydivers, their female roommate, and the two people I don't know follows and, as if not just hearing the stern warning minutes prior, head straight for the middle of the rapid.

"We got swimmers!"

CHAPTER

9

Tim calls for a rescue before the raft enters the rapid. Three of the swimmers pop to the surface as soon as the call goes out.

"I got one," yells a kayaker.

"I got two," calls the other.

"Tim, there, I see him," I say, excited and relieved to see the third man's head just above the waterline. "I got three," I yell.

The woman who became number four in our headcount somehow is still in the raft, standing, arms extended to the sky, like a gymnast who just stuck a perfect landing. She hollers at the top of her lungs, "Woo-hoo!"

The fifth person is unaccounted for; it is one of the men late to the dock.

"Where's five? Where the hell is five?" Tim curses, scanning the water. "Anyone got eyes on number five?" Tim strains, pulling mightily on the oars against the powerful current.

I sit helplessly in the cat's bow without so much as a paddle. Tim calls out again, desperate, "Anyone got eyes on number five?"

The silence is deafening above the roar of the rapid. We have only been on the water for a matter of minutes. I feel nauseous and wish I were back at home.

"Cap," calls out a kayaker, "I got eyes." He points to a body bobbing downriver on his back, not moving.

Cutter reaches the lifeless man first and, using his sheer size and adrenaline, pulls the limp body into his vessel.

"He's hurt but will be alright," Cutter yells.

A collective sigh ripples through, and we all cheer. Cutter, a physician's assistant, I learn, continues to perform a quick assessment.

"Looks like he has a concussion and has swallowed gallons. Possible broken ankle. He'll make it, no question. We just need to get him outta here."

"We'll give you enough food and water to make it to the next take-out. It's about twenty miles," Tim calls, taking charge. "It'll take you the better part of the day. You okay with that?" Direct orders and decisions replace his carefree manner and goofy beads.

Cutter gives an affirming salute, and Tim continues.

"You got your cell? Use it at the take-out; there's coverage there. We'll keep the sat phone in case there's another, uh, incident." Tim looks around at the somber faces, then back to Cutter. "You good?"

"I'm good."

"Anyone wants to bail and go with Cutter, now's the time." Tim looks around, pausing at each one of us, waiting for our answer. No one says a word. I suddenly feel a kinship to each person here.

The man with the broken ankle moans in obvious pain, and two rafters quickly strap the groover onto our cat and help push Cutter away from the bank.

I now understand Tim's celebrity status.

The mood for the rest of the day is subdued, and we ride the rapids and float in near silence. The heat reaches a sweltering 117 degrees, and my skin is a bright shade of pink. My lips crack under the relentless rays of the sun. I slide down the float tube, shivering as my sunburned body touches the coolness of the water, and reflect on the day's events, my bucket list, and my mortality.

"What do you say, Yard Sale?" Tim calls down from his perch on the back of the catamaran. "Wanna take a kayak and do a solo down the next rapid? Only one more before camp tonight."

"Mmm, I'm not sure." I make my way back into my seat in the bow.

"I think it would be a good idea." He whistles between his teeth and waves over a kayaker. "You saw an awful thing today. You don't get back in the saddle, you may never come back to the river." He pauses, waiting for my answer. "Come on, Sera, it's exhilarating. I'll be right behind you."

I stare at him, glancing from eye to eye. He points to his right eye, and I focus on it.

"Okay."

"She's in," he calls out. Everyone, it seems, knew of his plan.

Tucked tight inside the kayak, Tim adjusts the straps on my PFD and my helmet, then gives me a refresher on paddling: "Straight down, pull back, feather, and plunge deep in front. Got it?"

"Got it."

"Paddle through the rapid, just keep digging, keep it straight, and no matter what happens, don't let go of that paddle. Yard Sale, you hear me?"

"I hear you. Hang onto the paddle." My heart is pounding.

"Okay, Sera, now go get 'er," He shoves my boat away from the cat.

I start tentatively, timid in my strokes, self-conscious that the others are judging the depth to which I plunge the paddle or the way the craft drifts off course and floats sideways until I recenter its nose. But when I look over my shoulder, no one is paying attention. They are all doing their own thing, chatting, splashing each other, swimming, or just taking in the scenery. It becomes apparent I care more about their judgment of me than they do.

I hear a locomotive in the distance. Tim has slipped his craft next to mine, and as if reading my thoughts, calls over the noise. "That's not a train, Yard Sale, that's the rapid."

I nod, check my straps on my helmet and jacket, take a deep breath, and dig in my paddle. "Stroke," I hear Tim call out, "stroke, stroke, straighten it up. That's the way, keep paddling."

The water is swift, whitecaps form, coming closer as I paddle on the right side of the kayak and then the left, alternating with precision to keep the craft aligned to enter the rapid head-on. My belly rolls as the boat falls into the center of the wave, down, then up; water crashes onto my face, dousing my body as I pull hard on the oar, right side, left side. My arms burn and I scream, caught up in the thrill of running the river. I gulp water, sputter, and keep paddling. Through it all, I hear Tim's voice, "Stroke, stroke."

The rapid ends as quickly as it started, and I am on the other side of it, the river calm and flat with birds floating on its surface. I did it! I've conquered a rapid in Hells Canyon, in a kayak—by myself. I hold my paddle in both hands and thrust it over my head, letting out a canyon echoing, "Woo-hoo!"

"Nicely done, Yard Sale," another kayaker slaps his paddle with mine—the river equivalent of a high five.

"Way to go, girl," the woman calls out, lifting her top in celebration. On a whim, I mirror her. Tim throws us each a set of beads.

At the bank, we moor our rigs, make supper, and choose our sleeping spots. Tim calls out, "Gather 'round. Everyone grab something to drink and hold it high."

I hold my wine cooler in the air, watch the other rafters pour out a small, symbolic amount for our fallen rafter, a libation. I follow suit.

"Cheers," Tim calls.

"Cheers," we answer.

I sit with the others around the campfire, listen to their rafting stories, drink an initiation shot of Fireball, and chase it with a beer. The day's heat and lack of hydration hits me hard, and I am drunk in short order. Glad to call it a night, I find my way to the spot I've carved out as mine and lie on top of my sleeping bag, fanning myself and slapping at the insects feasting on my sweat.

A twig snaps nearby, and I grab my flashlight, shining it around, trying not to think about mountain lions. "Who's there?"

"Hey, it's me, Yard Sale," I recognize Tim's voice through its gruff whisper.

"What are you doing? You scared the hell out of me."

"Just wanted to make sure you were okay."

I am glad he came. I'm reeling from the highs and lows of the day and am afraid sleep will elude me if I try.

"Why'd you insist I solo that rapid?"

"Two-fold, I suppose. First, you needed to after what happened. But second, Carolyn told me you need some encouragement to find your way." He shrugs, "I don't know anything other than the river."

Carolyn . . .

For an instant, I'm angry with her. But the voice in my head reminds me that her conversation with this stranger came from a place of love and rafting that rapid was a highlight in my life.

"That scared me today; what happened at the Green Room."

"Me too."

"Really?"

"Yes. I've never lost a rafter. Today was the closest." Tim pauses and brushes hair from my cheek sending a warm current through me. "I'm glad you're here, Sera." His voice low.

"Me too." I surprise myself and slap at a bug.

"Mind if I climb in?" he points to my sleeping bag, "I'm getting eaten alive."

"Me too."

Tim snuggles into my bag, smaller than a twin-size bed, and we lie with the tips of our noses touching, breathing in each other's exhales. I feel his fingers graze the length of my arm, up and down, then draw rhythmic circles on the inside of my wrist until a small sound of pleasure escapes my lips. On cue then and with deft precision, Tim lifts me and scoots me under him and rolls on top of me, our bodies sticky with sweat and bug spray. He nuzzles into my neck, eliciting more low moans. Buzzed with drink and high on life, I close my eyes and ease into him.

I reach to unzip his shorts, but he grabs my wrist and holds it. "Let me take care of you first." His voice is husky as he whispers, and it thrills me knowing the others are lying just feet away. He kicks out of the bag and works my panties down to my ankles, his breath hot on my inner thighs.

He plays and teases.

"Please . . ."

"Shh."

"I'm trying to shush," I giggle.

Tim sits up, unbuckles his pants, and poises himself over me as he moves his hips up and down until his breath comes fast. It is hot on my burned skin.

Something's not right. Where is he? I am suddenly sober.

He continues his gyrating, rhythmic motion, grunting with pleasure as my mind whirls with the possibilities as to why I can't feel him inside me.

Did he miss? Jesus, how embarrassing. Oh, my God . . . I'm too big. I feel my face flush as I panic, and Tim continues to groan, dripping sweat on my face.

He must be inside I rationalize and then freak out again, *but why can't I feel him?*

The missing penis has wiped away all previous signs of passion or buzz. I lie limp, waiting for Tim to finish thrusting, pumping, and grunting until his breath comes in ragged bursts, and he buries his face in my hair, stifling something between a moan and a scream.

I remain still as he exhales and collapses his full weight on my chest. Shimmying out from under him, I pull my panties up and my t-shirt down and creep by the moonlight to the river.

I wade out to my knees in the tepid water and sit down to rinse myself and splash my face, slapping my cheeks, trying to knock some sense into myself. Tiptoeing back to the sleeping bag, I climb in between the zippers, and leave Tim passed out on top of the bag, naked. A shiver runs through me as the temperature plummets.

In the morning, the sun beats down on my face. I lay drenched between the layers of my sleeping bag, the heat already on a quick rise through the canyon. My cohort still lies splayed out next to me. I peek over the bag, my gaze following the hairline down the contour of his belly where I stop, frozen, staring at the unkempt, thick mound. Nestled, cozy on top of its hairy bed, lies his flaccid, pinky-sized penis.

I gasp and slap both hands over my mouth—*a micropenis.*

CHAPTER

10

s. Kincaid?" Marta's voice chimes over the intercom. "I have Captain Tim on the line again." She pauses. "He asked to speak with Yard Sale."

"Marta," I bark, "I'm not taking his calls. Tell him I died." My voice booms over the speaker. "Tell him whatever you want. I don't care. But I'm not taking his calls."

Carolyn rounds the corner to my office, and I hiss, "Do not come in here."

"Why not? What's wrong?"

"You said I'd like him." I stand, arms akimbo.

"And did you like him?"

"Yes, very much, but Jesus, Carolyn, you could have warned me."

"About what?" She asks batting her eyes.

"Don't tell me you didn't know about his . . . impediment. And I'm not talking about his eyesight."

"You slept with him?"

"Maybe. Well, yes."

"Jesus."

"What's wrong with that? You said I would like him."

"Yes, as in he's a good guy and a fabulous river guide. I didn't mean sleep with him, Sera. You know, you don't have to sleep with every man you meet."

"Well, I did, and you don't have to be such a bitch about it."

Her eyes narrow. "And you don't have to be such a trollop."

"Trollop?"

"Yes, trollop. God knows I don't want to be accused of slut-shaming again."

I grab my stapler and threaten to throw it. Carolyn backs out, hands up in surrender, smirking.

"Marta," I say after Carolyn leaves and I've simmered down, "I'm going to the M for a chai. Can I bring you something?"

"Thank you, no," she replies politely. There is disapproval in her tone.

The Flying M, a coffeehouse with an eclectic, nostalgic vibe, sits in the corner of a historic, renovated building at the end of restaurant row. A rainbow sticker on the door and Vance, the daytime barista, are the primary reasons I frequent the place. I feel love whenever I enter the M, and Vance's carefree zeal for life makes me happy. Over the past many years, he and I have become friends and gossip like schoolgirls.

"Hi, Vance," I say when it's my turn to order.

"Heyya, yourself." He breaks into a full smile. "Come, give me some shugga." He patters around the island and holds me close. "It's been a dog's age since I've seen you," he says, scampering back to his side of the counter. "What have you been doing? Or should I say, who?"

I roll my eyes. "You and Carolyn, real comedians. The usual, please." I'm not in the mood for more insults.

"Small, skinny chai, half-shot of vanilla, hot," he calls over his shoulder, ignoring his coworker's complaint about why he isn't making the drink himself.

"What's going on? Let's sit." He removes his apron, drops it on the counter and proclaims to no one in particular, "I'm taking a break."

We sit at my favorite back corner table, next to a window. It has terrific light to work by and makes it easy to people-watch. I spend a good deal of time here, thinking it a safer option than a bar, and liking it much better than my seedy old motel room.

"Tell Vance all about it," he says.

"I'm just in a rut, ever since the divorce."

"Small, skinny chai, half-shot of vanilla, hot," interrupts a sweet young person with a smile.

I sip the foam from the top of the drink, making a slurping noise. "You know I hate being alone."

Vance flicks his wrist at me. "We all hate being alone," he says and then leans in, "I have a new beau."

"What?" I choke. "Who? When? Why didn't I know?"

He laughs, "Hold on now; I don't tell you everything."

"You don't?" I feign disappointment and shock, lifting the back of my hand to my forehead.

"Okay, so there's this guy down at the new One Nineteen building—you know, the boujee condos on Tenth and Grove?" Vance looks at me as if I know all the goings-on in the Boise real estate market. My blank stare informs him otherwise.

"Oh, come on," he leans back and chuckles. "Sera, you gotta check it out, those are right up your alley, and you need to get out of that nasty, pay-by-the-hour motel."

"It's not pay-by-the-hour. And how do you know?"

Of course, Carolyn.

He looks sheepish, and then waves it off and starts again: "Okay, so down at the One Nineteen, there is this fine young thing who handles the door—"

"Wait, this place has a doorman?" I interrupt.

"Yes, ma'am."

"That *is* boujee," I say, taking another sip. "Continue, please."

"Anyway, I met him at the Balcony the other night. It was ladies' night, and I said to the bouncer, 'Honey, I'm wearing my best heels,' and I lift a Jimmy Choo so he could get a good look. He let me in for free!" Vance throws his head back, reliving the moment.

"And when I walked in, it was like God himself parted the sea of people." Vance fans himself as if he's suddenly faint, "And there he was. Stefan."

"Moses parted the sea," I correct.

Vance rolls his eyes, continuing, "Well, Stefan looks like a god, and he parted the people at the club, and we've been inseparable ever since."

I smile at him and take another sip before asking, "May I ask you something, well, quite personal?"

"Ooh, this could be fun."

"Seriously. I had an experience . . ." I pause, wrestling with how to say the next words, ". . . involving a penis."

"Yas, Kween!" Vance draws out the phrase, clapping his hands; he's proud. I've heard him use this term before when referring to what he believes is a *BA female*. Given the context, however, I'm not feeling so badass.

I drop my shoulders, draw a breath, and try again. "It was more of a problem than an experience. Like a spatial thing."

"Ohh, do tell."

"Good God, Vance, you are like a teenager." We both laugh. "It wasn't a *good* spatial thing." I hold up my pinky and waggle it.

Vance gasps, "Oh, dear Lord. You had a micropenis encounter." He slaps his hands over his mouth and looks side to side as if he just recited aloud the code to arm a nuclear weapon. "You poor thing." Vance said and then added, "That poor man."

"So, it's a thing?"

"Indeed." Vance was still shaking his head.

I release a sigh of relief. "Oh, thank God. I mean, not thank God that he has a small penis but that I, well, I thought it was my issue."

"What? Oh, girl. You thought your vajayjay was . . ." Vance makes a large circle with his arms.

I grimace and look away.

The sound that Vance makes roars through the room, halting all other talk and hubbub. He laughs until he cries. "Honey, I've gotta go back to work, but come back soon. I can't wait to hear more stories." He leans in and air-kisses my cheeks.

I take the long way back to work; the response to the discovery requests I've got sitting on my desk can wait another day. I walk the several blocks to Tenth and turn south, peering into the shops as I pass; it seems eons since I simply meandered through the city I call home. There is a new bagel shop where Andy's Deli had been for decades. I smile at the sight of Mixed Greens, my favorite trinket shop across the street; it has been a while since I've browsed its aisles. I pass the Wear Boise clothing store with a t-shirt in the window that reads, "Boy-See." I chuckle, making a mental note to take one to Steve the next time I go to Puerto Val-larta. He, like most outsiders, refers to our beautiful little capital city as "Boy-Z"; it drives us native Idahoans mad.

I find myself at the corner of Grove Street and Tenth, where there is a building under construction, staring up at a large vinyl sign with bold lettering waving in the breeze: "One Nineteen. Experience Downtown Boise like never before. Open for tours."

I wander inside.

CHAPTER

11

"**M**s. Kincaid?" Marta's pleasant voice comes over the speaker. "I have Melanie Charles on the line."

"Great, thanks." I lift my head from my desk, my mind filled with nothing work related. Melanie is a peripheral friend, soft-hearted and kind, but not someone I see or speak with often. On the "peel the onion" scale, which I've learned about in one of my self-help books I'm still not telling Carolyn I've dabbled in, Mel is somewhere in the second or third layer as a friend. Today, however, she is a welcomed distraction.

I fumble for the speaker button. "Hey Mel, what's up?"

"Hi, nothing. Are you okay? It sounds like you're in a tunnel."

"All good, thanks, and you?"

I may as well be in a tunnel, with no light at the end.

"I'm great, thanks. Hey, Carolyn called me."

"Oh, for God's sake." I pop my head up, grab the phone, take it off the speaker, and clear a stubborn frog in my throat.

"You sick?" Mel asks.

Sick of Carolyn, maybe. I clear my throat again, "I'm fine. Just allergies."

Always the mother, Mel says offhandedly, "Take an allergy pill. The over-the-counter ones are just as good as the prescription nowadays." Then, without skipping a beat, "You know she means well."

"She might mean well, but she's a buttinski," I shout toward the door. Marta, the dutiful, rises from behind her desk and shuts my door.

"Regardless, she has your best interest at heart."

"If that's how you define a busybody."

Mel ignores my snarkiness. "Now listen, she said you and that guy broke up a few months ago."

"What guy?" I ask.

"I don't know, and it doesn't matter. Martin and I talked about it after putting the kids to bed last night, and we have decided we have a friend who may be what you need. He'd make a terrible boyfriend, mind you, but I'm sure you two would get along great in other ways."

"In what way would I need him if he'd make a terrible boyfriend?" I ask, my curiosity piqued. "And now Martin is in on my love life?"

There's a muffled voice in the background, I assume is Martin's. "We think you two would be, you know, compatible," Mel sounds embarrassed. "Truth be told," she whispers, "I would screw him if I weren't with Martin."

Martin makes an outraged noise.

"Mel!" I scoff sarcastically at the bold statement. So out of character for the normally prudish mother of two. There was a scuffle in the background and a playful squeal from Mel.

"What?" she laughs. "I'm just saying. He's hot. He's an ex-Marine." I'm not sure if she says this for my benefit or Martin's.

"*Former* Marine." I correct her, having learned the proper term from a client. "I'm told that once a Marine, always a Marine. Oorah." I pump a fist in a poor imitation of my client.

"Whatever. I'm sure you'd like him. Keep in mind, though; he's terrible boyfriend material."

"What does that mean? You've said it twice."

"It means he's fresh out of a marriage and wants nothing to do with another relationship. He told Martin he's only looking for company and fun. Kinda like you, right?" She sounds pleased, as if she's involved in espionage or juicy playground gossip.

"I appreciate your concern for my, um," I pause, and clear my throat again, "wellbeing, Mel, but a friend with benefits? Is that something done in one's forties?"

"Come on, Sera, everyone knows about your proclivity for sex." Mel giggles. "And he could be a placeholder until the right person comes along." She then whispers, "Maybe help take the edge off some of the loneliness?"

There is a moment of silence as I ponder this arrangement. I could hear a pin drop on the other end, envisioning Mel and Martin fighting for ear space near the receiver. Fact is, I've never contemplated being with a man purely for satisfying my physical needs. Instead, I try to find one I can mold into all the boxes: romance, companionship, sex. This fantasy person would laugh with me at our inside jokes and enjoy shoe shopping. They would follow the daily goings-on of the royal members of the House of Windsor (including the rebels who moved to America); sit beside me through B movies, sharing popcorn and theater candy; wipe my tears at a funeral; and mutually enjoy the physical pleasures of sex.

A shiver runs down the length of my body; perhaps this is where I've been going wrong. What if there isn't just one person for me? What if I am an anomaly, a rogue human who doesn't fit the conventional monogamous standard pounded into her since she was a child? Does this make me abnormal? A freak? Immoral? Am I damned to hell?

"Sera?" Mel says.

"Still here."

My track record of searching for Mr. Conventional speaks for itself; I confuse the need for physical touch with sex, and I blur sex into love. I break the silence with Mel at last. "So, how would I go about meeting this hot former Marine who's interested in screwing but not committing?"

There's a collective sigh from the other end of the line, and Mel releases a giddy, teenaged squeal of delight. I hear hands clap and imagine Mel and Martin just high fived.

"I'll set it up," she says. "I'll get you two in touch, and whatever happens from there, you're on your own. Deal?"

"Deal," I say to my pimp, and then add with sincerity, "and, Mel, thank you, both of you."

"You're welcome," Martin says. "What are friends for?"

I put the phone down and my mind races. The thought of having someone in my life to fulfill my physical needs somehow feels right, liberating, freeing. If I was to take sex and orgasms out of the equation for my end-all, be-all, would it uncomplicate my life? I had been reading those self-help books like a child after bedtime—under a blanket with a flashlight—not wanting to admit to Carolyn she's right. They tell me I need to figure out my "love language" and stop the personal madness of conforming to societal norms. The authors preach to give up worrying about what others think of me. And they tell me it's okay to give up the guilt of religious chains.

———————

I receive my introduction to the potential boy toy via email.

"Sera, meet Zac. Zac, meet Sera. You two are now on your own. Good luck. Love you both, Mel (and Martin)," complete with a wink emoji.

Through emails, I learn Zac is in fact, recently divorced, is in his thirties, has a decent job doing something computery, and rides a Harley. I divulge I am an attorney with no children . . . and I am a few years older than him, though I don't give him the exact number of years' difference.

In my last email, I ask for a picture and then wait.

Carolyn strolls in unannounced and flops on the chair in front of my desk. "Hey, what's on the agenda today?"

"Waiting for a picture from some guy."

Her judgment is not my business. I grin, proud of that revelation.

"Zac?" Carolyn says. "Mel told me days ago."

"Of course she did."

"You'll like him; he's hot."

"That's what Mel said. But that isn't what matters." I sound righteous.

Carolyn smiles, "But it helps get the juices flowing, and it does matter if he's only a D appointment." She winks.

"A what?" I lurch forward in my chair.

"A dick date. A sneaky link. Jesus, you're old Sera. A hookup." She exaggerates air quotes.

"Oh. My. Effing. God." I slap my palm on the desk and laugh. "How do you know all these things?"

A grin spreads across her face.

I roll my eyes. "Well, I guess we just put it right out there. Zac is a booty call." I work my pen, *click, click, click.* "Do you know this guy?"

"I don't. I've seen him a time or two, but I don't know him."

"Hmm, that's strange," I say, more to myself.

Marta interrupts our tête-à-tête, calling from her desk outside my office. "Ms. Kincaid, your conference call starts in two minutes."

"I'll leave you to it," Carolyn says.

———————

On the other end of the line, the attorney yammers on about his client, my client, and why can't the two find some common ground and settle. I scroll through my emails.

"I agree," I say, distracted as I await the picture from Zac. "Set up the independent medical examination and my client will be there." I'm not a fan of personal injury cases, but they are good paydays.

The attorney continues about other discovery issues, wanting to take depositions, do vehicle inspections, *blah, blah, blah.* I stop listening when I see the anticipated email pop up. Butterflies fill my belly. Feeling like a groom in an arranged marriage about to lift the veil and see his bride for the first time, or in my case, my for-sex-only partner, I click open the email. An image of three men in golf attire fills the screen. I know through our cyber conversations that Zac is six-foot-three-inches, and has ink sleeves, his words not mine. In the middle of the picture, stands a big man with tattoos running the length of his arms who seems to fit the bill.

My beating heart, I smile at the image filling the screen; *he is sexy.*

"Ms. Kincaid?" the voice on the phone breaks in. "Hello?"

"Oh, sorry, my assistant walked in, and I got distracted. Where were we?"

"No problem. I was saying we need potential dates for your client's deposition."

Hmm, I like his smile, gentle eyes, somewhat mischievous looking but kind. I could be in trouble. I remind myself this is only physical.

"Yes, I'll get you some dates," I say to the attorney on the phone. "I'll have Marta call your assistant. Anything else?"

Please stop talking.

"No. I think we're good."

"Great. Thanks again," I say, still ogling the picture on the screen.

It's my turn to send a picture. I choose one of me in my happy place, hanging out in Puerto Vallarta, drinking a margarita with a straw, and wearing a goofy balloon hat twisted by a local vendor.

His quick email response shows I've passed the visual test, "Text?"

CHAPTER

12

My heart races as I type my number into the email and send it to Zac. In an instant, my phone vibrates.

"Hey, it's Zac."

I send my well thought out reply, "Hi."

What's wrong with you? You sound like a giddy schoolgirl.

A few texts later, and I have agreed to a casual meet-and-greet at the Flying M in an hour.

Holy hell in a handbasket, you had better get a move on, Serenade.

I rush to the bathroom to check my teeth, fluff my hair, sniff my armpits, and pop in a mint. I walk into the M at the precise time we set. I don't want to look overly eager to meet a would-be sex partner.

"Hey Vance," I greet my friend behind the counter, trying to act as casual as possible. "The usual, please."

"No problem, Sera. How's work? Any thugs getting the needle?" He winks, playing coy as he waits for my response and mixes my drink.

"Funny."

Vance knows full well I don't handle capital cases, but he enjoys the banter. I swivel the display case on the counter, loaded with magnets bearing low-brow phrases that elude me.

"What does that even mean," I ask, "party like a pineapple?"

"Oh, honey, I wouldn't have a clue." Vance laughs and waves me off. "Here's your skinny chai latte with a splash of vanilla, hot, like you like 'em." I grin at his double entendre.

He leans over the counter and, in a conspirator's voice, whispers, "That ruffian in the corner's been staring at you since you walked in." He scratches the air like a cat, "Meee-ow. Now that's hot."

I glance over my shoulder. Zac grins and licks his bottom lip. My belly flutters, and my knees nearly give way.

"Yes, he is." I drop an extra five in the communal tip jar and make my way to the back table.

Zac stands and pulls me into him, my head resting on his chest. He wraps his arms around me, leaning down to embrace more than just my head. It's awkward, his height and mine, he's a foot taller, but we somehow fit. Zac smells freshly showered, woodsy, with a hint of musk, all rolled into one tidy package. I release the tiniest, "Mmm."

"Hello," he says when he takes his seat. His voice is deep and velvety. His blue eyes are the color of the Caribbean Sea, and I nearly drown in them.

I blink in disbelief once, twice, and swallow hard, coming up for air, and utter a breathy, "Hi."

"Would you like to take your coffee next door for a bite?" he asks, grinning. I can tell this is not the first time he has experienced this type of flabbergast.

"Tea," I correct. "I thought we agreed—"

He shrugs. "Let's go." He tips his head back, motioning to the door. Before I can answer, he has my hand, his fingers laced between mine, and I am shuffling behind him to the door, neither able nor willing to stop myself.

I look over at Vance who is holding up two thumbs, mouthing, "You go, girl." My eyes widen, and I mouth back an exaggerated, "Oh. My. God."

"You like sushi?"

"Not my favorite, but I can eat a California roll." I smile up at him. I detest sushi but would eat raw squid for this guy.

Zac loves sushi it turns out; its details, the explosion of the different flavors, even the textures are exciting to him. I stare like a child meeting Santa Claus as he talks about his life, his travels, his brief stint in the military, and his job. I nod my head, playing along, too lost in his smell, eyes, and aura to retain much. In less than an hour, he's captivated me, and I altogether forget about the unappetizing food on my plate.

You nailed this one, Mel.

Without a lead-in, Zac blurts, "So, Sera, what's this all about?"

"W-what do you mean?" I stammer, surprised by his directness.

"Come on, cut the crap. Mel said you were fresh out of a relationship but looking for some fun."

"Yes. I split from my partner."

I jump when he slaps the table. "Your partner?" He throws his head back. His laugh, as large as him, booms through the restaurant. "So, are you a lesbian, bi, fluid, or what?" he asks. "Not that any of those bother me, just curious."

I feel all my blood rush to my face.

"I-I'm straight."

"Are you telling yourself or me? Because that's not very convincing."

"No, I am, I just, things are, I haven't been, it's just . . ." I stop, and my shoulders slump. With my chin tucked, I say, "I'm not sure there's just one person for any of us. I'm straight, as far as I know, but I'm also gun shy about men."

"Mel told you I am fresh out of a divorce too, right?"

I nod.

"Well then, I'm gun shy too, about women."

I look up and raise the corners of my mouth. "Okay, here's the deal," I say, lowering my voice as I lean over the table, hoping the other patrons can't hear me. "I have an excellent job, and I can't screw it up by sleeping with every Tom, Dick, and Harry. I have not been, shall we say, successful in my relationship choices. So, until the right person comes along, well, I'm looking for—"

"A booty call?" He finishes my sentence in a voice far too loud for my liking.

I blush hard, and Zac raises an eyebrow and waits for my response.

"I was thinking more of a friend with benefits." Zac doesn't move, eyebrow frozen in place; he's still looking for the right answer. I inch across the table to get as close as possible and just above a whisper say, "Yes, I'm looking for casual sex. But there needs to be some rules."

"Rules?" Satisfied, Zac folds his arms and leans back in his chair.

"Texts only, no calls. I don't have time at work to ramble on about the weather and where to go for dinner. No consecutive encounters, meaning there must be at least one day in between each . . ." I pause, searching for the right word, ". . . tryst."

"Tryst?" Zac chuckles. Seeing that I'm not laughing, he turns serious. "Go on," he says, his tone softened.

"I'm not cuddling afterward," I add.

He looks at me with surprise.

"And no overnights."

"Why no cuddling or overnights?" He looks intrigued, bringing his chair upright with a loud *thunk*.

"I don't want to get attached," I answer, dropping my gaze. "I will still be looking for the-the right one," I stammer.

"And what makes you think I won't be the right one?"

"Mel said you didn't want a relationship, that you were—" My face flushes again, and I avert his stare, adding, "Unsuitable boyfriend material."

"She's right." His voice is flat, hurt, and matter of fact. "Stand up, please."

"What?"

"Please, stand up," Zac repeats, all business.

I stand, and he comes around the table, cups the nape of my neck and the small of my back, and kisses me. His lips are soft when they press against mine. He parts them and I do too. He slips his tongue into my mouth, exploring, playful. I close my eyes and feel my foot come off the floor. Zac pulls back and in a husky voice says, "Your place or mine?"

"What? Right now?" My palms are sweaty and there is a tickle in my panties.

"Why not? Isn't that what this hooking up thing is about? We need to make sure we are compatible, right?" And then matter of fact asks, "Do you have a condom preference?"

"A condom preference?" The flush on my face races down to my navel.

"Ribbed, flavored, lubed?"

"Oh, God," I groan and look around the restaurant. I'm surprised only two people catch my eye, and even they don't seem to pay much attention to what we're saying.

Their judgment is none of my concern.

"Uh, no. I have no preference. But I can't get pregnant." My mouth is dry. "I mean, I'm incapable." I suddenly find a spot on the floor that holds my interest.

"Have you been fixed?" Zac chuckles as if I am a stray dog, and his words slice through me.

"No. I, well, we tried. My ex and me. And I couldn't carry our children." I swallow the sour taste that's come up from my stomach.

He looks at me; gentleness settles in his eyes, "No problem, I'll take care of it, still a good idea against STIs." He throws down a wad of cash. "Meet me at my place. I'll text you the address." I am relieved he doesn't say "deets."

I walk alone to the parking garage under my office to collect my car and my composure.

Out of habit, I push number two on my speed dial. It rings once.

"Carolyn," I yell, "Oh, my God. Oh. My. God."

"What? What is it? Are you okay?"

"Yes, totally. I met Zac."

"Ah."

"Oh, my God."

"I take it that's a good 'Oh, my God'?"

"It's better than good. He kissed me."

"And?"

"And my foot popped off the ground."

"What the hell?" she giggles.

"You know, it just lifted behind me." I giggle with her.

"That's a serious kiss."

I scream, giddy like a high schooler asked to a dance by the hottest boy in class, and repeat, "Oh, my God!" I jump into my Barracuda, the replacement for the convertible Stingray lost in the divorce.

"Well, what now?" her voice is dripping with honey.

"I'm meeting him at his place," I cup my hand over the phone as if others might have snuck into my car and are listening, "We're auditioning," I squeal.

CHAPTER

13

Zac lives in a modest townhome in the coveted area just above the heart of downtown known as the Bench. He has a clear overview of beautiful Boise, the City of Trees. Jitters run from my head to my toes as I walk to his front door. I wipe my sweaty hands down the back of my skirt and moisten my lips with my tongue. I double-check the address on my phone. *Good God, don't get the wrong house.*

I rap on the door and hear the immediate click of the deadbolt. The door swings open, and Zac is standing in his jeans, barefoot and shirtless. My stomach flips: *I am in trouble.* Zac grabs my arm, gently pulls me inside, pushes me against the wall, and kicks the door closed. Pinning my wrists above my head, he holds them with one hand, running the other down my cheek and the length of my side. He leans in and kisses me with the same intense passion he displayed at the restaurant. A soft moan escapes my lips.

Zac scoops me into his arms and carries me up the stairs, lowering me with care onto his bed. His lips brush mine and travel to my cheeks, ears, and neck. He slips his hand under my dress, looping a finger around my panties, sliding them to the floor.

"Open your eyes," he says with a throaty hunger.

I stare at the half-naked stranger looming over me and shiver. His eyes are unwavering, and I ache with anticipation. I bend my head back, tilting my chin toward the ceiling, and arch my back, encouraging him to have his way. His mouth travels down my stomach, teasing his way to my inner thighs. I wrap my legs around him.

Minutes later, lost in my euphoria, I hear the rustle of a wrapper and smell latex. Zac lowers himself on me, taking his time, keeping his eyes locked with mine as we move together until we are both spent.

We bask in silence, lost in the afterglow and our thoughts, him tracing my body with his fingers and me allowing myself to enjoy the moment.

"Will that work for you?" he whispers, breaking the silence.

I nod and smile, scoot to the end of the bed, gather my clothes, and leave.

Two days have passed since I met Zac, and the thought of him consumes me: his smell, his taste, and his way. Every few minutes, I pick up my phone to check if he has messaged me.

"What's up? No word from the side squeeze?" Carolyn plops down two mugs filled to the brim with hot coffee.

"Thanks." I reach for a cup. "No, I haven't heard from him."

"So, why are you waiting? Call him."

"I will not call him." I can smell that the liquid has sat too long in its pot. Afternoon office coffee is never my preference, but it's a friendly gesture, so I oblige with a few sips.

"Why not? He's your booty call. If you want him, just call him."

"We have a no-call rule." I blow over the steaming cup.

"Then text him, smartass." Carolyn smiles over her cup and takes a sip, grimacing at the taste. "Jeee-sus. This is nasty."

We spend the next twenty minutes chit-chatting about everything and nothing until our cups are drained. As the conversation wanes, I switch the subject.

"Since you're here, I'd like to talk to you about something," I say.

"Sounds serious. Shall I shut the door?"

I nod. When the door clicks shut, I continue, "I want to buy a house."

"What? Sera," she says, "that's fantastic. Where? Tell me everything."

"Well, it's downtown, and it's perfect, but there's a minor problem . . ." I can't look her in the eye as she waits for my explanation. "I need some money."

"Go on," she says, now in boss mode.

I raise my gaze to meet hers. "I'm wondering if I could get my bonus and partner's share early this year." I pause and add, "It should be just enough."

Don't blink. She who moves first loses.

I am well-studied in the art of chicken from my days growing up on the prairie. I was excellent at not being the first to veer. After dark, we stupid kids played the deadly game, daring a challenger to drive chicken by moonlight. This meant we would race our cars toward each other without the use of headlights to see who was the least fearful. The first to swerve, lost and dubbed chicken. The loser bought the beer. Since I was poor, I never lost.

"Done," Carolyn says.

"Hello. This is Sera. I would like to see you."

I write out the text and press send, and then wait.

My phone vibrates and lights up with a message, no name, just a number. I thought it best not to add Zac into my contact list, embarrassed in case anyone ever saw it: *Zac–Booty Call.*

"I know who it is; I thought you'd never ask."

My body tingles.

"Where would you like to meet?"

I'm breathing heavy.

"Do you remember how to get to my place?"

"Yes."

"Meet you in 20."

Zac and I begin meeting every other day, almost like clockwork. Within a week, I'd thrown the pacing rule out the window, and now we see each other whenever we can, sometimes as often as five times a week. While his house is comfortable, our desire leads us anywhere that is quick and available: his truck, a parking garage, my office, a dark alley, the stairwell of my building, and even an occasional bathroom. I'm not sure what that is all about, but somehow, it's sexy to me, and that's all that matters.

We have also begun cuddling and engaging in small talk, our conversations easy and enjoyable. I even allow myself to doze next to Zac. The no talking on the phone and the no overnight rules have stuck. Having just purchased my new place at One

Nineteen, I want to get settled, and as much as I hate to admit it, I enjoy quiet time and reading self-improvement books.

———————

The no-attachment rule with Zac is a slippery slope and a challenge to navigate. He may be a self-proclaimed bad boyfriend, but he is perfect in my book, and it scares the hell out of me.

On this lazy Saturday, I break all the rules and lie naked next to Zac asking about his multiple scars on his torso.

"What happened here?" I trace my fingers across the lines in the middle of his chest and stomach. The shiny skin covers an unusual depression, a round mark on his sternum. A rigid scar below it runs the length of his midsection, dissecting his belly into two distinct halves. Between two ribs, he bears a thin, horizontal scar. Its precise margins appear surgical, and my guess is it once housed a chest tube.

Zac remains quiet as my fingers linger on the wounds of his past. I watch a myriad of memories wash over his face as he ponders my question.

"I got shot."

I blink hard at the words spoken by this former Marine.

"You were in combat?"

"Yes. Mogadishu."

"Somalia. I remember the movie about the helicopter—"

"Don't even say it," he says, sitting up, suddenly agitated. "That movie's a bunch of horseshit. A glorified version of what happened. Yes, three pilots died, but what that movie fails to do is honor the rest of the men killed."

"Okay, sorry." My words have struck a nerve, and I lie still, unsure where this might lead.

He must see the concern on my face because he takes a breath, closes his eyes, and in a low, soft voice explains, "I was a foot soldier, a grunt. It was a no-big-deal day. We knew there were combatants in the area, and it was mine and Smitty's turn to run the nighttime perimeter; we'd done it a hundred times. A dozen of us walked in pairs around the base at night, keeping the unfriendlies out and the good guys safe, all snug in their bunks." Zac shifts on the bed and covers his vulnerability, and then mine, with the sheet.

"What people don't know about Mogadishu and Somalia is that it is hot as hell. The temperatures get into the hundreds, and the humidity year-round is eighty. It's oppressive and windy. Haboobs are commonplace." I stare up at him and wait for him to continue.

"Smitty, the funniest guy you'll ever meet, and I sat for a break behind a burned-out old truck, some piece of shit the rebels had left stranded. They'd shoot you in the head, steal your vehicle, modify it to be a technical, mount a machine gun on a tripod, and then leave it wherever it stops."

"Technical?" I ask. My voice is timid.

He nods. "It's a Somalia trademark, first of its kind. It started when the U.N. couldn't bring guards for protection into Somalia, so they got so-called 'technical assistance grants' and hired guards and drivers, who modified pickups with the money, which is where 'technicals' comes from. The government's official name for these homemade killing machines is 'non-standard tactical vehicles,' or NSTVs."

I'm impressed.

Zac rubs his forehead, going back to the place where he and Smitty were taking a break. "Smitty had just finished telling me a ball-busting joke and I'd just finished my smoke. We stood up, and I took one step beyond the front of the gunship—that's another term for a technical—and a round struck me in the chest. Those assholes had a bead on us the entire time. We were sitting ducks."

He shifts on the bed again and then lies down, pulling me beside him and wrapping his arms around me, my back curving into his front. "The vests we wore had plates on both sides of the torso that met in the middle. This was before front and back plates were standard issue. I had my jacket open to get some air."

"Because of the heat?"

"Because of the heat."

I feel him tense and roll over to face him.

"The bullet found its way between the center plates—that's the scar in the middle. The long one down my belly was where they cut me open to fish it out, and the one here—" he says, reaching under his arm to the horizontal scar, "this was where they shoved a chest tube in my lung. That son-of-a-bitch hurt as much as the damn bullet."

"What about Smitty?"

There's a palpable thickness in the air as I wait. Zac's body temperature rises and his muscles twitch. "Smitty saved my life. When I went down, I fell backward, my upper body protected by the truck; my legs were still in plain sight of the rebels. They kept shooting at me as I lay there, choking and drowning in my blood, writhing in pain. Shot after shot. The bullets landed so close that dirt and pieces of shattered rock were flung into my face. Smitty lunged forward to pull me back, and when he bent down, his head caught a bullet aimed at me. It plowed through one cheek and came out the side of his neck. It took off most of one side of his face."

"Oh, my God." I gasp at the visual.

"He lost most of his teeth, the upper and lower part of one side of his jaw, and the better part of his tongue." Zac stops mid-thought.

"Did he . . . is he?" I stammer, woozy and unsure of how to approach my question.

"He lived." Zac sounds as surprised as I feel. "He's all kinds of messed up, never been the same, but he's my brother. I owe him my life."

"Have you seen him since?"

"Twice. He's not the most stable, moves around a lot, and he's reclusive, as you can imagine."

I nod.

"He's threatened to come out here a hundred times, but I'm not sure if he ever will."

Zac rolls me over on my back and kisses my eyes shut. "Enough talk."

CHAPTER

14

My new home is on the sixth floor of the One Nineteen building, the penthouse, but only because it's on the top floor, not because it's the biggest or the most elaborate—the former CEO of Idaho Power owns that one. While not to CEO standard, my place is exceptional, and I couldn't be more excited. It has an open floor plan, two bedrooms and two-and-a-half baths, floor-to-ceiling windows, and an expansive view of the foothills. It is decorated with mid-century modern, dark, matte cabinetry and frosted brassy pulls, combined with stark white walls and gray-hued wood floors; the contrast is breath-taking. But the best part of the building is the young doorman, Stefan, they guy who parted the sea for Vance.

"Good morning, Ms. Kincaid," Stefan greets me as I exit the elevator into the lobby. "Have a lovely day."

"Thanks, Stefan."

Things are good at work. I'm settling into my new place and have Zac. I stop mid-stride when that thought hits my mind; I don't have Zac, and I won't have Zac. He is a bad boyfriend; I need to continue looking if I want a partner.

I hear Carolyn's voice before I see her. "Uh, oh, did you and Zac split?"

"What? No. You keep asking that, but we aren't a couple. He's just out of town." I remain focused on the papers in my lap. My socked feet rest on the corner of the desk. A glass of wine sits next to me.

"It's after hours. What are you doing here?" she asks, toting a glass of brandy into my office.

"I have that Carlton Forstner breathing down my neck in the seatbelt case. He's threatening a motion to compel if I don't get our discovery responses to him by the end of the week; smarmy bastard."

"Are they late?" She glances over top of her glass.

"No. Well, yes. We have an extension, but—"

"Damn it, Sera. Discovery is a requirement, not a luxury."

"Hey, whoa." I hold my hands up in surrender. "I get it. It's covered. He's just a ball buster. I'll do them by the end of the week."

Carolyn stares at me for a moment, her wheels spinning. Then her face softens, and she's again in easy-going friend mode.

"Don't be so quick to sling mud at Carlton," she says, sounding as if she's protecting a friend.

"He's coming to town Monday for two days to inspect the Isuzu." I click my pen. "I'll meet him, and we'll clear the air."

Carolyn shoots me a grin, "Lucky you." Her look and her tone tell me she knows Carlton's worth meeting. "Tell me about the inspection." She's back to business in three seconds flat.

"It's routine. The seatbelt maker and the car manufacturer are pointing fingers at the other. Liability isn't clear." Taking off my glasses, I too put on my attorney hat. "Did the roof collapse cause the belt to give way, allowing the child to fly out the back window when the car flipped? Or did the belt give way regardless of a compromised roof?"

I put my glasses back on and exhale. "I don't care what these buffoons figure out during their inspections. Someone is liable, and it isn't the child."

"Got a videographer?"

"Yeah, I'm calling in Columbo."

"Good," Carolyn sips her cocktail.

Columbo, an unassuming guy named Matt, has a degree in forensic science and a spot-on bullshit detector; he can spot a lie a mile away. This, coupled with his laissez-faire behavior reminiscent of the Peter Falk character in the old television show *Columbo*, makes Matt the best, most coveted gumshoe in Boise.

"Hey," Carolyn says, her eyes sparkling with an idea, "let's call it and go catch a movie. I need a break and a hearty laugh, and there's an indie film at the Flix I've been dying to see."

———

The movie was an excellent distraction, and Carolyn and I had some wonderful laughs. Our sense of humor is similar—dry, cerebral, and often juvenile. I still feel warm and fulfilled from my fun evening with her when I pull up to the Store-More storage unit the following day.

"Sure is gonna be a hot one," the old man guarding the gate says through a whistle in his dentures. "Much hotter than normal this time of year." He shakes his head, wiping sweat from his brow.

"Likely the result of global warming," I say, giving him my two cents. "There will be several others coming to inspect a vehicle. Please let them in under my code." The wrinkled man, who indeed looks as if he's seen enough seasons to know this one is unprecedented, nods and pushes a button. The gate slowly rises.

The large-bellied tow-truck driver, whose shirt strains at the buttons and almost covers his stomach, smiles at me warmly. I can't stop glancing at the exposed milky-white flesh.

"The usual Ms. Kincaid?" he asks as if he's about to make me a latte. I've used his services before, and as in the past, he is punctual, well-mannered, and reeking of the previous night's beer, hangover sweat, and cigarettes.

"Yes. Thank you." Taking a step backward, I lift my hand, breathing through my fingers resting under my nose.

The driver hooks up the car's skeletal remains of a frame, four tires, the steering wheel without its column, which rests on the floorboard, and the seatbelts still bolted to the carriage. The car suffered a blowout when the owners were driving home from a Halloween event complete with a corn maze, haunted house, and a water tank where kiddos bobbed for apples. It veered toward the shoulder, caught loose gravel, and flipped twice, ass over teakettle, skidding on its crushed roof and ejecting my eight-year-old client through the back window. The little boy will never again walk.

A black SUV entering the gate caught my attention. Close on its heels is an old beater—Matt's red Ford pickup truck that is at least a dozen years beyond its reasonable life expectancy.

I shake my head and smile. "Cheapskate."

Matt drives the old clunker not for lack of money but for show, thinking it gives him an appearance of fitting in and that it will encourage people to trust him with their secrets. Honestly, it works. He comes across unobtrusively, a regular Joe, just doing his ho-hum job. He truly is Columbo, minus the tan trench coat.

Two men step from the SUV, the first tall, lean, silver-haired, and clean-shaven, his suit reeking of East Coast prominence. Anthony Spencer from Virginia, I deduce, senior counsel for the car manufacturer. The second man, the younger of the two, exits the opposite side, looking like Mr. Rico Suave. He must be Carlton.

Relaxed, California-cool Carlton wears an understated pair of khakis, a navy-blue polo shirt, and comfortable loafers. The old-school Ray-Bans resting atop of his head date him to 1980. He's done a decent job covering up his status until I notice the far-too expensive Breitling resting on his wrist. Much too flashy to fit into his middle-class impersonation.

This ringer is the thorn in my side. He's the one the defense team will no doubt want me to bond with so that I'll give away our position. They probably think I will succumb to his charm and cave in settlement. *Not going to happen.*

I clear my throat, smile, and extend a hand. "Sera Kincaid," I say. "Nice to meet you."

"Anthony Spencer, nice to meet you as well." The older man grips my hand firmly and gives it a quick pump. He holds my gaze for a moment and then releases both eye contact and my hand.

"Carlton Forstner," Rico Suave says.

I reach out to shake his hand. He grasps mine gently and then wraps it with his other hand. I tense and squeeze, possibly a bit too hard. "Nice to meet you as well," he says, leaning into me. The corner of his right eye makes the tiniest twitch from behind his glasses, and crow's feet appear for a millisecond.

Did he just wink?

I pull my hand free and wipe my palm down my skirt.

The inspection goes off without a hitch; day one is in the books. The tow-truck driver returns wearing a cover-up layer of after-shave but, unfortunately, not a fresh shirt, and pushes the battered vehicle and its secrets back into the storage unit.

"Would you like to come to dinner with us tonight?" Anthony asks as we pack up to leave; his tone is professional and inviting. "Carlton and I are staying at Hotel 43 and will dine at seven o'clock at Chandler's. I'm sure they can squeeze in one more."

I glance from Anthony to Carlton, who wears a lascivious grin. I again see a twitch from behind his sunglasses.

What is wrong with this guy?

"Thank you, but I think I'll call it a day. I'm exhausted," I say, fanning myself and wrinkling my nose, Carolyn-style.

Real professional, Serenade. I immediately chastise myself.

"I promise we won't discuss the case, right Carlton?" Anthony looks at his junior partner. "Everyone has to eat."

I'm not getting out of this. I should use it to my benefit, perhaps glean something about their case strategy.

"Thank you." I give my obligatory acceptance. "Do you mind if I invite Matt to come along?" I need him to listen for any dropped tidbits during the dinner conversation . . . and I will be far less likely to sleep with one of them if he's in our company. Both men smile and nod.

"Great. We'll see you there," Anthony says. I extend my hand first to him and then to Carlton. I look for crow's feet that don't materialize.

As soon as I'm in the car I call Carolyn. "You could have told me Carlton was so full of himself."

"Ah," she says, chuckling, "he is that."

"I can't believe you answered. Don't you have a hearing in front of Judge Tarkon?" I ask.

"Yes. Oh, God, gotta go. My case just got called." The line goes dead.

I suck in a breath through my teeth and send good vibes into the universe. No one, not even Carolyn, wants to incur the wrath of the formidable Judge "don't be tardy" Tarkon, for being late.

I forego the office for home, desperate for a shower, a quick nap, and a glass of wine before dinner. "Hi, Stefan," I call out to the young concierge sitting behind the desk in my building's lobby.

"Hot out there, Ms. Kincaid?"

I pull at the material clinging to my sticky skin and notice my disheveled reflection in the elevator's shiny doors. I take a discreet sniff toward my armpit and then blow upward at the sweat-plastered hair on my forehead. It doesn't move.

CHAPTER
15

Anthony and Carlton are sitting at the restaurant's bar when I arrived. Matt, engrossed in telling an animated story, is standing with hands flailing as I approach.

Anthony and Carlton stand to greet me, offering their hands in a courtroom-style "across the aisle" shake. Leaning into Matt, I give him a polite but not-too-close hug. Over his shoulder, I catch the familiar crow's feet twitch of Carlton's wink.

"Don't leave me alone," I whisper to Matt, who gives me a squeeze on my arm as we part, confirming he's here to gain intel and have my back.

We follow the host to our table; Carlton sits between Matt and me. I reach down to scoot my chair and find Carlton's hand resting there. I look at him, eyebrows raised, and see the corners of his lips curl as he lifts his glass.

A bouncy young server appears. "What can I get you to drink?" she asks me. I'm pretty sure she is forcing her ponytail to swing when she walks. Carlton turns his attention to her, a leering smile replacing the playful smirk he wore for me.

"I'll have a vodka cranberry with a twist of lime and splash of

7-Up, please," I tell her. "Not diet. Thanks."

"One Cosmo," she beams, scratching my order on her pad, her youthful presence annoying, like a fly I want to swat.

"Yes." I close my eyes and shake my head. "And a splash of 7-Up. Not diet. Please."

"Of course." Her tone turns curt. She is blushing. She loses her smile as she takes everyone else's orders and turns on a heel, her hair whipping side to side.

Twit. I turn my attention back to the table.

Vodka is a safer bet when I am out with colleagues. I will sip one cocktail throughout the evening but am apt to drink several glasses of wine without noticing how much I have consumed: an absolute no-no. The female-lawyer 101 survival guide, a unicorn, of course, but an absolute must-follow to succeed in this male dominated career, is orally handed down through the ages by pioneering women and prescribes only one drink while out on business. The mantra being the three Ps: protect yourself, protect your reputation, and protect your career at all costs.

"The three Ps can be boiled down to one," Carolyn had said. "Protect your puswa."

Male attorneys use a different handbook and theirs can also boil down to one P: penis. Their manual appears to prescribe drinking as much as you can and being as obnoxious as you'd like. There is no need to worry about how often or where you stick your penis as it won't hurt your career; it may advance it.

The evening is a surprising respite from the grueling day in the sun, and dinner is fabulous, as expected. My excitement at Carlton's occasional brush of my arm is not. Carlton is arrogant, cocksure (pun intended), and he is an attorney, who is someone

I have always sworn I wouldn't get entangled with; it would be way too competitive to have two attorneys in one household. But I am enjoying the tingle when he leans too close, and I feel the warmth of his breath on my neck. A wisp of my hair flutters under his words and tickles my cheek. I reach up to push it aside and the back of my hand touches Carlton's chin.

He's so close if I turn my head, my lips will be on his.

I stare straight ahead and drain my glass. Carlton gives a sly discreet nod to our perky server, who has held her distance. She sits down a second drink in front of me without a word. I glance to Carlton, who stays focused on another of Matt's stories, his hand finding its way to my thigh; *You're welcome,* it says with a slight squeeze.

I take in a shallow breath.

"You know," he says, pulling back and turning his full attention on me, "our clients know this is our mistake. This isn't about liability; it's about how much they want to be out-of-pocket."

My jaw drops. I look across the table at Anthony and Matt. Involved in a sidebar discussion over cars and motors. They do not acknowledge Carlton's disclosure.

Is he baiting me?

Without skipping a beat, Carlton turns back to the men across the table and tells a story about his son. Pride and joy ooze from his words as if he didn't just breach confidentiality with me. He then speaks with great adoration for his ex-wife.

"She simply couldn't get past my philandering," he says, his hand now resting comfortably on my forearm. "It was the ruin of our marriage."

He's taking accountability. At this moment, he is indescribably sexy, and heat rises from my seat to my face.

"I'm going to turn in." Anthony breaks the spell. "I promised to FaceTime my wife so I can hear the highlights of my son's basketball game." Embarrassed, he lowers his gaze and his tone, "Sharon keeps me up on them when I'm not home."

"That's fantastic, Anthony." I reach out to shake his hand. "More dads should be so involved," I gush.

He smiles, his cheeks flushed with alcohol and emotion.

I look at Matt, who looks back at me. I raise an eyebrow; nothing. I then cock my head with my eyebrow raised, still staring. Matt finally gets the hint.

"I-I need to go too," Matt stutters, and he stands to leave. "I told the missus I'd be home in time for the news."

He shakes Anthony and Carlton's hands and gives me a slight hug. "You got a ride home? You going to be okay?"

"I'm walking, and yes, I'll be fine. Thank you for coming."

"I thought they'd never leave," Carlton says when the men walk out of earshot. "Would you like to come up?" He grabs my hand before I can answer, pulls me off my chair, and walks me out of the restaurant.

"Just for a nightcap," I say, and my stomach flutters.

We step inside the elevator face-to-face. Carlton's eyes bear down on me as the doors close. He lunges forward, his hand on the back of my neck, his lips forceful against mine, hungry. I sink my fingers into his hair and return his kisses. He reaches into my blouse, wriggling his fingers between the buttons, skillfully undoing them and me as the elevator slows and its doors open. I'm grateful there is no one standing there to see my flustered expression and exposed bra.

Fumbling to unlock the room, he keeps his attention on my lips and the tops of my breasts. "You know," he mumbles between kisses, "I'm not complicated. I'm a prick." The lock clicks, and we fall into the room. "I'm an excellent attorney. I don't lose, and I get what I want. I want you."

"This is not smart," I whisper more to myself as I step out of my shoes and unzip his fly.

"Why?" He strokes my cheek, his breath hot on my lips.

"It's not . . ." I pause, lost in the moment, ". . .ethical."

He stares at me, silent, the tips of his fingers tracing my face.

"We shouldn't do this," I say and close my eyes, begging for another kiss.

"Do you want to stop?" his voice is thick.

"No." I grab a fist full of his shirt and pull him to me, kissing him hard and long.

———————

My phone alarm wakes me with a start. "Oh shit," I yell, springing up then grab my throbbing head. I catch sight of the empty champagne bottle and fall back onto the bed, noticing my chest is wet; I am sweating.

Odd.

Carlton sits up and reaches for my arm.

"No. I have to go." Twisting out of his grip, I gather my slacks and blouse and look around for my panties; they are hanging off the arm of a chair. I snag them, run into the bathroom, wipe the moisture from my body, and look at my reflection in the mirror.

"Damn it."

On my way out the door, Carlton calls after me, "Same time tonight?"

I leave in my walk-of-shame clothes without answering and trek the half block to my condo. I need a shower, fresh clothes, and a bucket of coffee.

I am again the first one at the Store-More. I pour myself a cup of coffee—my third this morning—and allow my mind to drift. Carlton is friendly, intelligent, and pleasant to be around. He's also arrogant, no amount of vodka or champagne will cover that, but his success and California hustle-bustle life makes this more understandable. I tick three boxes on my imaginary checklist and mull over his worthiness when my phone vibrates.

I smile. *Cute, he's texting me.*

My phone lights up, and I glance at a number that's become familiar.

The simple message reads, "Good morning."

Zac. My heart skips a beat.

Without hesitation, I text back. "Good morning."

I glance toward the storage gate in time to see the black SUV pull up, Matt's beater truck on its heels.

Timely. I shake my head.

My phone buzzes again. I look down, eager to see another of Zac's messages.

"Last night was fantastic."

I swallow hard. *Jesus.* My face feels beet red. *Carlton.*

"Mmm," I reply, hoping my disappointment doesn't teleport.

"I can still taste you." Carlton's reply shows on the screen.

"Oh my," I text back, deflecting any real commentary.

Another vibration. Zac's text shows on my screen. "I'm back in town tonight. May I see you?"

What are you doing, Serenade? My brain bounces between memories, Carlton's from last night and Zac's from all the other days. I feel a sudden surge of guilt as I reread Zac's text.

Can I see him? *Of course, you can. He's only your booty call, or your d-date or appointment or whatever.* I cover my mouth not to laugh out loud, this hook-up terminology still foreign and silly sounding to me. *You want sex with him, don't you?*

"Sure," I respond. "I can't wait."

I am an addict. Zac is my drug. And like any junkie, I will wage war or climb Mt. Everest to get my fix.

My screen lights up, and my stomach sours as I read Carlton's message. "Looking forward to later."

Shit. I'm supposed to see Carlton tonight.

As the day wears on, my exhaustion sets in, this time accompanied by body aches and a thumping head, which certainly has to do with last night's drinks and festivities. I leave the inspection feeling poorly, but the white lie I text Carlton has nothing to do with feeling ill.

"I'm sorry, I think I've caught a bug. Can't make it tonight."

To Zac I send, "On my way."

———————

"Hey, why don't you come down for the weekend? I could show you around L.A." Carlton's forgiven me for abandoning him on his last night in Boise. For all I know, he hooked up with the pert little waitress. A pang of jealousy clenches my belly, and then I remember my incredible night with Zac. I have no room for jealousy or a feeling of ownership over Carlton.

"We could pick up where we left off?" Carlton continues. "My son is with his mother this weekend. It would just be the two of us. What do you say?"

I haven't told him Carolyn is listening in at her usual spot across from my desk, giving me two quiet, exuberant thumbs up.

After running out of excuses and not hearing from Zac in a few days, I hem, haw, and agree.

"Okay, tomorrow morning it is. There's a flight to LAX getting in at ten-fifteen." I hang up, and Carolyn whoops.

"Oh, my God! You boinked him, didn't you?"

I jump up to shut my office door. "Decorum, Carolyn, please. And who says, 'boinked'?"

"More people should be so lucky. It might help get the stick out of some asses." She points a thumb in the direction of the staff cubicles behind her.

Exasperated, I shake my head, saying, "You're killing me." I cough and clear my throat. "Sorry, I have a tickle." I pat my throat with my fingers.

―――――

I feel nauseous on the drive to the airport. It surprises me how Zac can elicit such a powerful response; no doubt this is guilt eating at me. What if Zac's available this weekend? I would rather be with him than anyone, even though I've heard scarcely more than a 'good morning' from him this week. I'm not sure if it's work or another woman that keeps him at bay, and our rules, my rules, keep me from asking.

It's not your place. I catch myself but cannot stop perseverating. *Is he eager to see me like I am him? Or am I just a roll in the hay, a sexcapade, a tryst?* I wish I'd never said that word the day Zac and I met. *But what if he doesn't think of me? But what if he does?*

I take the airport exit, and Carlton seeps into my thoughts. *Is he the right person? Can I see myself with him, loving him? Is he capable of loving me? Am I so clouded by my lust for Zac that Mr. Right could stand in front of me and I would overlook him?*

I'm restless and exhausted, wrestling with compartmentalizing Zac in my mind and heart, then evaluating Carlton and every other man to see if they pre-qualify for a relationship. I cross off shopping for shoes in the imaginary boxes for both Carlton and Zac, which brings on a wry grin.

Not everything is a goddamn joke. Carolyn's words rattle around in my head.

I turn on the radio for the rest of the drive, doing my best to drown out my thoughts.

There is an open space in short-term parking; I take it, rationalizing I'd rather pay the hefty price than attempt the walk. I'm so out of shape, so easily fatigued these days. I go through TSA and sit at my gate, waiting for the call of business class passengers to board. Three tiny finches perched high on an exposed beam inside the terminal have my attention.

"Hello, little ones. How did you get in here?" I ask them. "Are you trapped?" *Like me?*

Two dull gray females carry on with incessant chirping as one beautiful yellow male sits quietly, his eyes closed, disinterested, biding his time. He puffs his chest from time to time, perhaps exasperated by his female counterparts' endless clucking. Or maybe he is merely waiting for nothing more than his next chance to copulate. Just like humans, these females preen and carry on, trying to draw the male's attention—all in the name of mating.

"Ladies and gentlemen, we will now begin the boarding process for business class on Flight 1746 to Los Angeles, LAX."

I don't stand. *I'll go with the next group.*

I fixate on the majestic little flying machines peeping, caged in this building rather than spreading their wings outside. *Did you fly through whatever door was open, thinking it would be nirvana only to have the door slam shut behind you?*

Carlton is nice, but is he my cup of tea? Do I want a long-distance relationship? Can I trust the self-professed philanderer?

The attendant announces all passengers holding a B ticket may board and then she calls for the C group.

Stand up and get in line.

My legs are heavy and unwilling to move. Maybe this is a premonition. I run through a few scenarios in my head.

Don't get on the plane; it's going to crash.

Is it tsunami season for Los Angeles? Is there such a thing?

I shake my head; I'm losing it, clearly. I'm pining for a man, not knowing if he pines for me in return. Regardless, it's apparent I know Carlton is not the guy for me.

Get on the plane, Serenade. See if Mr. California can give you the life you want.

My heart pounds. I always listen to my inner voice when it uses my full name, but this time I'm not so sure, and that makes me feel meek, unsure, and self-deprecating. I loathe self-deprecation.

The next thought hits me like a sledgehammer. *I'm still falling for the proverbial bad boy.* Presently, that is both Carlton and Zac.

At least there is well-defined rules with Zac; Carlton will simply turn into another heartbreaking shitshow.

My upper lip is sweating, and my hands are clammy. I jump when my phone vibrates. A warm rush courses through me when I read the message.

"I'm home. I'd like to see you."

I grab my things, wish the birds luck, and speed walk to the terminal exit. As I reach the door, I hear over the loudspeaker: "This is the last call for Serenade Kincaid. Your plane has boarded, and the doors will close in two minutes."

After the scheduled departure time, I call Carlton.

"I'm not coming." My words tumble from my mouth.

"What do you mean you're not coming?" he sounds surprised and perhaps a little hurt. "Are you okay?"

It touches me he cares, but I can't allow simple good manners and a kind gesture to convolute what I know to be true; Carlton is not and will never be my Mr. Right.

"I got to the airport, went through security, and sat down." A dam is opened, and a torrent of words follows. "There were these three birds trapped inside the terminal wishing they could be elsewhere. Okay, the birds didn't actually talk to me, this is a metaphor, you get that right?" I inhale deeply and start again. "Anyway, these birds wanted . . . scratch that, *needed* to be free. Like me, they flew through an open door thinking the grass would be greener and now they're trapped. I don't want to be trapped. This isn't right, you and me. I'm not coming, Carlton. I'm sorry."

Relief floods me, and adrenaline drains away. I am spent.

"What the hell are you talking about, Sera?" Carlton yells. He sounds angry and understandably confused.

"Don't you see the parallel?" I ask. "I don't want to be like the birds." I am breathless following my spiel. There is silence on the other end. He doesn't get it; how can he? I am raving about birds when I should have told him the truth; I'm in love with someone else. But I am incapable of curing all my destructive behaviors in one morning, so I say the only thing I can, "I'm sorry."

I end the call and send a text to Zac, "Glad you're home. I'll be over in 10."

CHAPTER

16

My phone lights up with a message, "Door's open."

I gulp at the words on the screen and welcome the familiar flutter in my stomach. My heart races as I walk up to the door, its squeaky hinge announcing my arrival. My excitement and the hair on my arms rise. *Where are you?* On tiptoes, I make my way through the living room, dark from the drawn shades. *I know you're here.*

I scan the room, enjoying the exhilaration of our cat-and-mouse game. Light peeks out from under the bedroom door at the top of the stairs. I climb them and find Zac lounging naked on his bed. He pats the sheets, and I kick off my shoes and curl into his outstretched arm.

"Is everything okay?"

"Everything's fine. I missed you."

I fall into the sea of his cyan-blue eyes. He kisses my lips, my cheeks, my ears. His fingers entwine in the hair at the nape of my neck, tilting my chin toward the ceiling. I roll onto my back, knowing, waiting. Zac touches my belly. My breath is fast, and my legs inch apart.

A throaty whisper escapes my lips. "I've missed you too."

He issues a low growl into my ear, and a tingle runs the length of me. I close my eyes.

———

"Hey, Carolyn, you got a minute?" I call out to her from her office door. Her back is to me, and I don't see she is on the phone. She spins her chair around and waves me in; she is not happy.

"I understand, Carlton, no problem at all. Thanks for the call." She hangs up the receiver, glaring. "What the hell happened?"

"Are you kidding me?" I blink hard. "He called you?" I mutter under my breath, "That spoiled child."

She holds up her hand, stopping me short. "I don't give a rat's ass about your personal life unless it affects your work." Her eyes are intense, and I stifle a chuckle. She's serious. "Carlton said you missed a deadline."

"Well, I didn't. We talked about this, remember?" I clench my hands into tight balls, my blood pressure rising to a boil.

"He said he doesn't want to move to compel but will if we don't respond by close of business," she says. With a dramatic exhale, she continues, "This call was a courtesy."

I can feel my face and chest are red. *That insolent little brat is throwing me under the bus.*

"I take it your weekend didn't go well?" she demands. Fury and curiosity flood her face in a perplexing combination of boss and friend.

I loosen my fists, trying to keep my tone level, emotionless, as I explain, "I didn't want to cross an ethics line, so I opted not to go."

Carolyn raises her brows. *Who knew you can do that with Botox?*

She breaks into a wicked laugh. "Fine time to come to that conclusion."

"Okay, that was a lie." I exhale deeply. "Carlton is not right for me."

Carolyn gives me a half-smile, her forehead back to its unlined resting position, and she says, "That's a start."

"I have an extension. Carlton's lackey," I tap my forehead for inspiration, "the guy that thinks he's funny when he calls me Shera, said it would be fine."

"Lucas."

"Lucas, right," I snap my fingers. "Lucas gave me an extension."

"Did you get it in writing?"

"Of course, I have an email. We have an additional week." I look at Carolyn's phone, "Smarmy bastard."

"It's Zac, isn't it?" Carolyn asks.

"What's Zac?"

She waves her hand in my direction, making invisible scribble lines across my face. "This. The look on your face, the instant flash of defense in your eyes."

What is there to say? It is Zac.

Falling into a chair, I admit, "I can't stay away from him." I stare out the window. "He's gentle and kind but refuses to let it show. I see it behind his eyes, the hurt, the fear. I think he's afraid to let it happen again."

The air is heavy with unspoken words. Carolyn breaks the tension. "Why don't you give it a go with him?"

"Are you not listening? He doesn't want to."

"He doesn't want to, or you *think* he doesn't want to?"

"Mel told me, and Zac confirmed it, he's a bad boyfriend." I use air quotes to drive home the point.

"That's bullshit." Her voice is stern, commanding. "What's up?"

I think for a moment. *What is up? Why can't this work between us? He's not a bad boyfriend. He's wounded, no different from the rest of us. So why can't we give it a go?* Reality drowns me in that instant, and I hear the tiniest voice eke out of me, "I chameleoned."

"How so?"

"It's me. I'm the reason Zac doesn't want me." The sudden clarity of my situation lands hard. I lift my eyes now brimming with tears to meet hers and reveal my truth, "I've sabotaged us."

"How? Why? What?" Carolyn fumbles, not quite understanding.

Tears run hot down my cheeks; I wipe them quickly with backs of my hands.

"At first my rules felt empowering, emboldening me to be in charge of the relationship, to give me . . ." I blink hard, and when I open my eyes, I say the word that has been both my truth and my demise: "Control."

Carolyn is quiet for a moment and then encourages in a soft, caring tone, "And?"

"And without realizing it, I have become what he needs, not what I need, and now I'm in love with him," I say, my voice cracking, and in a squeak, I recite the words my mother once told me: "I'm not his beloved." I bury my face in my hands and sob.

"Oh, honey," Carolyn circles the desk, falling to her knees and cradling my head against her bosom. "It'll be okay, sweetie. He loves you."

"But he's not *in love* with me."

My whimpering and sniveling are the only sounds in the otherwise still room. I'm right. Carolyn knows it.

Minutes pass before I regain my composure, and Carolyn says,

"Things might be different now. It's been a couple of months. I mean, you know he cares for you, and God knows the entire world can see how you feel about him."

She pities me and my situation. I hear it. I see it. A lump rises in my throat.

"I don't need a man to complete me."

She eyes me. "Perhaps. But you also don't do *alone* very well."

Another moment passes, and she slaps her desk, startling me. Standing, she smooths her skirt, "Well, I guess you won't mind meeting a new prospect."

"Wait. What are you up to now?"

"I want you to go to a soccer game with Chelsea. Her husband plays in a city league, and there are scads of eligible men, which would be a far sight healthier than what you've got going with your fuck buddy, Zac."

"There's nothing wrong with my arrangement with Zac," I defend. "You were the one who put Mel up to introducing us." I stand with my arms wide. "Just a minute ago, you wanted me to give it a go with him."

"A minute ago, I didn't know you falling in love with him had turned you into such a pussy."

"What? You can't call me the p-word." Flabbergasted, my mouth hangs open.

"Would you prefer the b-word, or the c-word, or perhaps the d-word?" Carolyn folds her arms across her chest, daring me to choose my character flaw. She huffs at my silence, looks down her nose, and says, "God knows you could land in any of those camps." She cocks her head, assessing me. "You haven't been the pillar of stalwartness."

Carolyn is learned in the art of relaxing her subject with childish insults and then smashing them into tiny bits with a well-timed kick in the teeth. Most of the time, I giggle at this flick-of-a-switch, but not when the jeer is a direct hit to me. I search for words to defend myself against Carolyn's alphabet-soup attack, but I am speechless. She is right; I can be a bitch or a c-word (I can't bring myself to say that word). Or a d-word . . . but does Carolyn mean "douche" or "dick"? Either fit. As of late, my usual state of being is argumentative, sullen, moody, unethical, scandalous, and disconsolate. To say I am out of sorts would be a gross understatement. I have been flying through my days checking off boxes about re-centering my world: stability with finances, proper housing, an abundance of sex, all for the sake of a tick mark. But I'm not happy. I'm miserable. I shut my mouth.

"I see how you yearn for him and how screwed up you are when he's not around. You start lily padding, jumping from bed to bed, and even that doesn't fulfill you." Carolyn's eyes are moist, "Sera, I just want you to be happy."

I walk out, my face wet.

"Ms. Kincaid," Marta calls after me. "I have Chelsea Donovan on the line for you. She says it's personal. Shall I put her through?"

"Yes. Thank you, Marta." I wipe my tears and give Marta a quick smile of thanks and slam my door.

I agree to meet Chelsea and her four-year-old twin boys at Ann Morrison Park, where her husband plays soccer on an over-forties team. Through the throng of people in the park, I spot Chelsea trying to corral her little ones. The sun is scorching, and I am glad to have changed into a casual sundress, sandals, and a big floppy hat. I am not handling the heat well this season.

Maybe I'm menopausal. The thought strikes as if God himself ran a bolt of lightning through me.

Chelsea greets me. "Hi, Sera. How are you?"

I give her a tight squeeze, we air-kiss each other's cheek, and I lie, "I'm good, and you?"

Chelsea brushes back a clump of hair that has come loose from her youthful ponytail. She sighs, looking around with the controlled panic only a mother scanning the scene for her children's whereabouts can possess. Upon seeing them, she visibly settles. She rushes her words as she keeps one eye on the boys: "I'm hanging in there, trying to catch greased pigs at the moment."

On tiptoes, she yells over the crowd, "Boys, get over here."

They know her voice. The precocious urchins stop their play, look at each other, and without a word, run off in different directions laughing—the singular brain of twins. Through clenched teeth, Chelsea acknowledges what I'm thinking, "Yep, twinepathy is a real thing."

"It's okay, Chels, you do what you have to do; I'm fine here."

"Sit," she commands, using a tone learned from four years of motherhood. "I'll be back, and then I'll tell you about William." She points to a blanket covered with children's books, toys, half-full juice boxes, and the remnants of what I guess is crushed pretzels.

I sweep my hand over the blanket to clear a spot and settle in to watch a game I don't understand. A bald man with an incredible physique picks up the ball mid-play, cradles it under his arm, and makes a t-shaped gesture with his hands.

"Time out, red," the referee yells, blowing his whistle.

The men scatter to either side of the field. Chelsea's husband, David, and the man carrying the ball trot toward me, stopping short of the blanket.

"Hello," I say to David, "I'd give you a hug, but it looks like you are a little, well, sporty right now." I shrug, waving my hand in front of my face and wrinkle my nose. *Great, I have chameleoned into Carolyn.*

"No problem, Sera, I am very . . ." He pauses, contemplating the word and then confirms, "sporty." He smiles. "This is William. I guarantee he too is sporty." The three of us chuckle. "I promised Chels I'd introduce you two." David gives William a look as if he's handing off the ball to him, slaps William on the shoulder, and then runs back onto the field. William and I stare after him.

No. This is not at all awkward.

William squats and holds out an upturned hand he's just wiped on his shorts. I lay my hand atop his and blush when he kisses it. I could swoon.

"Good afternoon," he tucks his chin in a polite bow. "My name is William York; it's a pleasure to meet you. I apologize for the 'sportiness' of my hand." He grins.

His smile radiates across his face, lighting it up and showcasing his captivating, twinkling green eyes. I still haven't spoken; I can't seem to form words.

"Are you staying until the end of the game?"

I nod, keeping my hand in his.

"Very good." He looks both pleased and as if he may devour me. "I'd like to make a proper introduction after the game, if that would be alright with you." Still mute, I beam, answering with a full-tooth smile.

William looks to an older man sitting in a lawn chair beside us and touches him on the arm, startling him as if he did not know we were beside him. "Dad, I'd like you to meet someone."

He then whispers to me, "What's your last name?"

This guy's smooth.

"Kincaid," I whisper, finding my voice. "Sera Kincaid."

"Dad, please meet Sera Kincaid. Sera, this is my father, Wil."

"Oh, pleased to make your acquaintance, Miss Kincaid," Wil says, his words clipped in a proper British accent.

"He's got some dementia," William says, his voice low. "His short-term memory is absent most days."

"I understand," I say and hold his gaze, and I do understand.

The referee sidles up to William and blows his whistle. "York, you going to finish this game?"

William again kisses my hand that he's still holding, winks, and touches his father's shoulder, not speaking until the elder Wil makes eye contact.

"Dad, I'm going back out on the field now." William and the referee wait to ensure Wil shows recognition of the words. I can see the referee is familiar with the family situation, and I'm struck by this gesture of humanity. Wil shoos the two as if they are children, and the men run onto the field amid a barrage of catcalls.

"How long have you known William?" Mr. York asks me.

Surprised by his sudden coherence, I quickly answer, "We just met, sir."

"Oh, that's nice." Wil contemplates this, and then I see a fog shroud his face, clouding his eyes. "What did you say your name was, dear?"

"Sera."

Chelsea flits into view, breathless, "I'm sorry to bail on you, Sera, but, well?" Frazzled, she motions to her boys, who have again run off in different directions.

"No problem." I give her a quick hug, and she jogs off, calling above the crowd, "Boys, get back here!"

I wonder what she wanted to say about William.

———

"Would you care to join my father and me for a bite?" William asks between gulps of water following the game.

"I'd love to," I gush, taken by his father's charming, albeit slight, conversation over the past hour of the game, and smitten with William.

———

Baptiste's is a hole-in-the-wall restaurant run by Jean-Paul Baptiste, an enormous man from the Deep South, renowned by local food critics for his authentic Creole and Cajun food.

"Creole is the more refined jambalaya and gumbo," Mr. Baptiste explains when we sit, "Cajun is the blackening and fracases." His accent is thick and requires my full concentration.

"Most people assume they is the same." His soft voice a stark contrast to his size. "But they ain't." He shakes his head. I shake mine in unison.

William orders for the table. "We'll all take the crawfish."

"That'd be with all the fixins?"

"Yes, please. Thank you."

Mr. Baptiste picks up a big tube of brown paper, measures an arm's length, and rips it off the roll. It fits the table perfectly; he's done this a time or two.

"Do you know what all the fixins are?" I look from Wil to William after Mr. Baptiste had shuffled off to the kitchen.

"Not a clue," William laughs. The elder Wil, lost in thought, does not respond.

Twenty minutes later, Mr. Baptiste lugs a hot kettle to our table, his glasses fogged from the steam. He tips the pot on its side, and dozens of crawfish, pieces of corn on the cob, and lime sections roll onto the paper.

"Ah," William smiles, "the fixins," and slips a sly wink my way.

I return the smile.

The men tuck napkins into their shirt fronts, and I tie a plastic bib around my neck. We each try our hand at cracking open the crustaceans. William bites off a head and sucks, "Mmm, sweet." Butter and goo roll down his chin. I make a more ladylike attempt, stabbing one with a fork, trying to pry off its shell with a knife.

Mr. Baptiste lumbers back to our table, winded and shaking his head.

"Y'all never ate these critters before?" he asks.

The three-hundred-pound man plops down on the seat next to me, settling in to give us a lesson.

"Hold the head like this an' twist." The crawfish makes a *crack* as the shell snaps and the head releases from the body.

"You can suck out the juice, like mister do, if ya want," he says, pointing toward William, "or throw it in the bucket for the trash." Mr. Baptiste tosses the head in the empty pail in the middle of the table. It lands with a *plink*.

"Then hold 'em with your thumb and pull out the meat." Mr.

Baptiste holds up a small scrap of meat to his mouth and slurps. He then licks his fingers.

We spend the next hour drinking beer, popping off crawfish heads, and laughing.

"And there was the time—"

"Dad, that's enough," William interrupts. "I think Sera has heard enough stories of me growing up." He winks, grinning over the last of his beer.

"Oh, I don't know. I could listen to your stories all night," I assure Mr. York.

"Sera, this has been a most lovely evening," Wil says, lucid and aware of his surroundings and my identity. "I hope to see you again."

He hugs me goodbye and pecks my cheek. I place my fingers to the kiss, wanting to hold it there. *I miss my dad.* William helps his father settle into the car and walks back to where I stand, waiting, still holding the kiss, wishing the night wouldn't end.

"Thank you for such a fun time." I'm beaming. "I can't remember when I laughed so hard. And your dad, he's so sweet."

"Yes, he is, and so are you, Sera. Thank you for your kindness and patience with him. It can be difficult."

"It was my pleasure." I'm lost in his kind eyes.

"May I see you again?"

CHAPTER

17

I walk the three blocks from the courthouse to the office, huffing to catch my breath. *Jesus, Serenade, you are out of shape.*

"Good morning, Marta." I lean on her desk. "Any messages?"

"Good morning," she smiles, handing me three slips of yellow paper with names and numbers. Marta's old-school.

"What's with all the clatter?" I ask, thumbing through the notes. "Seems like the hens are extra clucky today."

"I think they're impressed with your delivery," Marta confides.

"Delivery?"

"It's in your office," she says in a low voice, nodding toward the door.

"Thanks." I push open my office door to peer inside.

The pungent smell of jasmine on steroids smacks me in the face. It reminds me of death.

An enormous bouquet of rosy-pink Stargazer lilies sits center stage on my desk: bold, tall, proud, regal. My mind fills with memories of the last day I saw my father, which was the day I lost my mother, and tears come to my eyes. There was Daddy, so handsome in his dark-gray suit, lavender shirt, and purple tie—the one

I gave him that Christmas—and there was Momma, no surprise, in a lavender dress.

"Don't you think it will look marvelous with Daddy's shirt and tie?" Her tone bore a hint of giddy. She twisted her hips back and forth, childlike, encouraging the hem to flutter.

She leaned into me, "This would make a lovely photo."

Mom took every opportunity to dress the three of us like Hawaiian tourists and, often to my embarrassment, hang the evidence on the farmhouse walls. But that day, I was beyond embarrassed; I was flabbergasted and standing with mouth agape at her words.

"I think you should wear your lavender dress, too," she said.

This was not a suggestion.

I broke with family tradition, and Mom's suggestion. There would be no family photo.

I held Momma's lavender-covered arm in my black one, steadying her as she leaned down and kissed Daddy goodbye. She whispered something in his ear and then gently touched his cheek, lingering until a line formed behind us, and I eased her back straight. When she turned to look at me, her eyes were flat, void of their usual spark. Death took Daddy and grabbed hold of Momma. A jealous pang ran through me. *I want that kind of love.*

Carolyn startles me out of my memory. "What in the name of Peter, Paul, and Mary?" She snatches the card out of my hand. "Way to go, William." She approves. "Is this why you're late today?"

I grab the card and tuck it into the top drawer of my desk. "No, smarty. I was in court. On time, I might add." I'm happy to give her a little dig for her recent tardiness. "It was my client who was late."

"Holy shit." Carolyn flops onto her seat across from my desk. "He was late? I bet that didn't go over well. Do tell."

"Nothing to tell, really. No contempt, but he got a good tongue-lashing from the judge." I grin.

"No. I don't care about court. I mean this." She waves her hand at the flowers. "What happened with William?"

"Oh, this. William's nice." I smile. "We had a pleasant time."

"A pleasant time?" she mimics. "It may have been a minute since I dated, but I know a reward like this equates to something more than pleasant." She thinks for a moment and asks, "Oooooh . . . Did you give him a blowee?"

"Carolyn!" I run past her and slam my door. "No, I didn't give him a blowee. And no one says that." I laugh, falling into a coughing fit. Tears run down my cheeks, and I struggle to catch my breath.

"Are you okay?" she asks, serious.

"Fine," I clear my throat. "Change of season, slight cold coming on. We took his father out to dinner, that's all."

"His dad? Oh, now here's a story." She rests her elbows on her knees, waiting for something juicy.

"William's a wonderful son and takes care of his father, who has dementia. Wil, the father, keeps forgetting my name. Oh, and he's from England, so he speaks with the most amazing accent and so proper; 'I apologize, dear, what did you say your name was?'" I say in my best Brit voice.

"Does William speak with an accent?"

"Did you even hear me, Carolyn? His father has dementia."

"Yes, and that's too bad," she says, apologetically. "But what about William?" She shifts gears as fast as a Grand Prix racer.

"William doesn't speak with an accent. Well, he can when he chooses, I suppose, or I guess. What am I saying? I have no idea."

"You're flustered." She peers at me over her glasses. "Always a good sign."

"Maybe," I smirk. "Oh, and William's gorgeous."

Carolyn slaps her thigh. "And there it is."

"Don't you have work to do?" I ask, still smiling.

Carolyn sniffs the flowers. "They are stunning."

"You can have them," I say, grimacing.

She cocks an eyebrow. "No one hates flowers, especially a bouquet like this. What gives?"

"I don't hate flowers. I hate those lilies. They're funeral flowers. It's what we had when my dad died, and my mom left."

"What do you mean, your mom left? I thought she was up north?"

"She is. But she's not *here* anymore." I shrug. "She never got over dad's death and checked out when he died. It's like I lost both my parents on the same day; only one is still alive."

Carolyn pauses, and the awkwardness envelopes us. "Well, I love lilies." She grabs the vase and walks out the door.

———

My phone vibrates. I turn it over and smile at the number without a name. "Good morning. How are you, beautiful?"

I shake my head. *You always know when I'm thinking of someone else.*

"Aww, thanks. I'm good. And you?"

"I'm good, baby. Lunch?"

I feel an instant tingle at these words, a Pavlovian response.

"I'd like that."

I close my eyes and can feel Zac's touch on my skin, smell his specific scent, hear his familiar and exciting voice. I fall into a heavy, guilt-laden reprimand. *What are you doing, Serenade, lunch with Zac and dinner with William?*

But I can't say no.

Zac picks me up at eleven-thirty and drives to a parking garage around the corner from my office. He circles the floors looking for the perfect parking spot. He backs in, puts the sun visors in the window to ward off onlookers, lifts the middle console, and pats the seat next to him. I slide over. Zac wraps me in his arms, kissing me long and hard. His hand slides up the inside of my thigh, under my skirt. I breathe deeply and close my eyes, the image of William creeps into my mind.

I fling open my eyes and grab Zac's wrist. With fervor, I unbuckle his belt and fumble with the button, unzipping his jeans.

Blowee it is.

"Jesus," he says, my task complete. His eyes roll back in his head, and he looks satisfied.

"When are you ever going to take me out?" I ask, my head still resting on his lap.

"What?" He sounds groggy.

"Look, we've been at this, whatever it is, for a while, I just thought—"

"As I've said, I'm a shitty boyfriend."

"That's bullshit. If you don't want to date me, just say it." I sit up and adjust my skirt, smoothing my hair.

"What about all your rules?"

"Pfft."

"Sera, I'm not great at relationships." His words are quiet, and he refuses to look at me.

"Again, bullshit. You're great around me. We get along well, and I'm not just talking about sex." I'm whining, practically begging. I'm pathetic.

His hand flies to my thigh, obviously trying to derail the conversation. I push it away.

"I'm serious. I think I'm, I'm . . ." My words fall silent, and I stare at Zac, looking for encouragement, reassurance, reciprocation, which are not given.

He puts his finger over my lips, stopping me. "Don't say it. You don't want to do that with me. I'll just hurt you."

Tears well in my eyes.

"You hungry?" His words are quick and deflecting.

I look up and smile, wipe my eyes, and jump back into my role of fun booty call. "For food?"

He laughs, stroking my hair.

The corner of my mouth twitches, and my chin quivers ever so slightly. "Starving."

———

Carolyn is waiting for me in my office. "So?" she demands. "What did he say when you told him you wanted to date him?"

"He reminded me he makes a bad boyfriend. Whatever the hell that means." Remembering a recent lesson I learned from one of the self-help pages, I take a deep breath before saying with a shaky voice, "He's just not into me."

———

William prepares lamb and sweet chutney for dinner; it's impressive looking with the bones all standing at attention and the meat browned to perfection.

"Thank you, son." Mr. York wipes his lips and chin, cleaning off the bits that hadn't made it into his mouth. "Dinner was spectacular."

Wil then looks at me, teary-eyed, "He takes wonderful care of me." The confusion disappears for the moment. Wil stands and shuffles to his room.

"I'm not sure he remembers who you are, but I can see he is fond of you." William grabs a dish towel; I insist on washing.

"As am I." William leans over and kisses my cheek. His lips are smooth and warm, and I'm attracted, but I yawn. Sleep has overcome me from nowhere.

"Am I boring you?"

"I'm so sorry, William. I'm tired all the time. Age, I guess," I chuckle, knowing full-well my forties are not the age when I should be so tired.

"Would you mind finishing up? I need to run upstairs. There's something I'd like to share with you. Please come up in a minute."

I nod, mutely.

Serenade, why didn't you object? You don't even know him. You can't sleep with him. I know I will.

I think about Zac's comments earlier as I finish putting the last dish away. Then I walk upstairs. Inside the master bedroom, I am somewhat relieved to see the empty bed.

"Over here." William calls for me to join him on a sofa in an alcove on the side of the room.

"This is a Nickelback gig, filmed in Sturgis. It's one of my favorites," William says, pointing to a video he has cued up on the television.

"I love Nickelback."

The opening scene pans the crowd of half-naked bikers, shirtless men, and half-dressed women in Daisy Duke shorts or micro-minis, many of whom are also shirtless. Some wear American flags as shawls, and in every hand is a beer, a joint, or both. The air of anticipation for the band is palpable, even from my chair.

William grabs my hand and squeezes it when Chad Kroeger steps on stage.

"Hello, Sturgis," Chad screams above the crowd. "Are you ready for some fucking Nickelback?" He draws out the words, and the crowd erupts as the band starts. I scoot to the edge of my seat.

William pulls out a small tin and a packet of rolling papers from between the couch cushions. He takes a pinch of pot and rolls it into an impressive cigarette. He takes a drag and hands it to me.

Shit, the good angel who resides on my shoulder says.

Who cares? The devil on the other side chimes back.

I take a small hit, holding in the smoke. It's been since my 3L year with Hank that I've smoked weed, but I like the way it numbs my body and clears my mind of noise. I draw in another long pull from the joint and hold it until I cough; it burns my throat.

Turning back to William, feeling the effects of the pot loosen my inhibitions, I sing along, suggestively with Nickelback: "I like your pants around your feet."

A movement in the doorway startles me. There stands a woman with fists balled, and a fury contorted face.

"I hope you're happy sitting in my chair, *bitch*." She stresses the word so hard I flinch. "You cheating pig," she adds, glaring at William who doesn't flinch; these words are not new.

She turns and disappears down the stairs. And I'm left wondering if I'm stoned or she is real. Nickelback gives way to chaos.

Crash. "You asshole."

Bang. "I hate you."

Thud.

Definitely real.

William and I sit still on the couch through the shattering glass and obscenities. After a brief pause in the mayhem downstairs, William takes a deep breath. "I guess I'd better go see if I can calm the situation. Stay here."

"Not a problem." I hold my hands up in mock surrender, too high to do much more.

The muffled voices of a heated argument drift upstairs, followed by a loud, distinct, "Have fun with the new girl."

I guess that's me.

A door slams, followed by squealing tires.

I meet William on the stairs. "I'm sure you understand." My voice is shaky. I grab my purse and open the front door.

Mr. York peers through a crack in his door, sees me, and says, "Oh, hello, miss," oblivious to my identity.

I pause before leaving, my hand on the doorknob and my back to William. My anger, entwined with disappointment and embarrassment, makes me feel vulnerable, nauseous, and used.

"Who is she?"

"I guess Chelsea didn't tell you," William whispers. "She's my wife. I'm still technically married."

CHAPTER

18

'm not a fan of long weekends. I either work too hard or sulk too much, wondering where Zac is, who he's with, and, more heart-wrenching, what he's doing with whom I assume is another woman. This weekend I do both, bounce between a half-written brief and fantasize about Zac, as well as lick my wounds over the train wreck with William and his wife. I feel queasy just thinking about that mess.

The arrangement with Zac has taken a twist. Now he is only available during the workday hours. Come sundown and the weekend it's crickets. Nothing, finito, nada. Someone is occupying Zac's evenings and weekends, and it isn't me.

The brief needs Shepardizing for proper caselaw citation, and my Zac issue needs investigating; I focus on Zac, of course.

I roll my eyes at myself.

Sitting on my couch, I click my pen, working it with a fever pitch. I open my laptop and start an email to Matt. He will find answers, good or bad. I finish the email and spend a few minutes browsing local charities, looking for a volunteer opportunity.

Through reading and self-reflection, I've realized there is more than physical touch that fills my cup; acts of service do as well. I don't need the actions performed toward me; I need to be the performer. And to my utter surprise, neither the acts nor the services have anything to do with sex.

I take a quick look at my inbox; Matt hasn't responded. I click back to the local hospitals, the food bank, a neighborhood cleanup effort; nothing pops off the page and screams, *pick me.* There is a need at the humane society, but I don't have the stomach for animals in distress; that one's a hard pass.

I try my best to stay away from my long weekend fallback, my fill-the-gap-because-you-are-lonely dating sites, but I can't resist. I click the bookmark I have labeled "Dating for Losers," pour a splash of Irish cream into my coffee and reread my profile.

Gypsy Girl. I sip my coffee, smiling at my moniker that draws on my days traipsing around Europe between college and law school: a pack on my back, a limited amount of Euros, and a headful of dreams. I take another drink and continue to read. *Professional, career-minded, outdoorsy, and fun. I enjoy red wine, ballroom dancing, river rafting, and am a sucker for* I Love Lucy *reruns and a bowl of popcorn. Interested in starting as friends and seeing where things go. Not interested in a hook-up. Felons and alcoholics need not apply.*

Satisfied with my cleverness, I scroll down to the activate button, click, and wait.

Within minutes, the familiar chime of an incoming message fills my quiet living room. Before reading the sender's response, I open his profile. He is Voice Man to my Gypsy Girl; all of us doing our level best to come across as fun, engaging, and original. His accompanying picture shows a stocky man with stringy hair and a bulbous nose. His description reeks of arrogance laced with hints of self-deprecation.

I'm a loner, successful, adventurous, and seeking a relationship, although I'm doubtful of women, as they all seem to be gold diggers.

I draw in a deep breath. The excitement of opening that first message dissipates after reading about this less than enthusiastic man. I click anyway and drain my cup.

"Well, aren't you the all-American? I'm sure you're no different from any other succubus," the message reads.

My cheeks burn. *What the hell kind of opening message is this? And who uses the word succubus—isn't that medieval or satanic or something?* Every fiber in me screams to block this lunatic and deactivate my profile, every fiber except the six-year-old teeny *sooyaapoo* on the Rez. That small, bullied girl is now a grown, badass attorney, and she won't let this go.

"Pretentious prick!" I scream at the screen. "You're lucky you aren't standing in front of me; I'd break your nose."

I shoot back a reply, my fingers flying over the keys.

"I am all those things and much more. I am a dutiful daughter, was a wonderful mother, okay, an average wife, but I never cheated. I am well-studied, in enviable shape, and I would no sooner waste my time on the likes of you than fly to the moon. Perhaps there are some awful women out there, but there are plenty of male douchebags to level the playing field. You, for instance."

Within seconds there's a reply from Voice Man. I touch the black screen to bring up the message, ready to fight.

"Sorry. You're right. Not all women are awful, but most are, in my experience."

"Serenade," I scold, "leave it lie. He's baiting you."

I take a deep breath, knowing I can't let it go, and begin typing. "If you're so great, why are you on here?" I push the enter button and send the message off into cyberspace.

"Touché. I'm on here for the same reason you are: I'm bored. What's your name? I'm Rodney."

"Gypsy Girl."

"LOL. You're funny. What's your actual name?" His responses are as fast as mine.

"Like I need you to know who I am!" I tell the computer, realizing he's right. I am killing time during another Zac-less weekend. I cave.

"Sera."

"Nice to meet you, Sera. What are you doing this long weekend?"

A parlay begins with back-and-forth messages. Rodney's are laced with depressive Eeyore-isms and Stewie Griffin sarcasm. Mine are filled with Hermione wit sprinkled with Maya Angelou goodness. We each bolster ourselves, posturing, as we school the other with random idioms and meaningless crap, common online dating hogwash.

Why do you care so much what this Neanderthal thinks of you, Serenade?

I know the answer instantly. I need approval. I need to be wanted. I need love. And I'll conform to whoever gives it to me.

Two hours and three cups of Irish cream coffee have passed since I sent my inquiry to Matt and began chatting with Voice Man. Things have escalated. He wants to know if we can talk on the phone. And then, as if by design, I receive Matt's reply email.

My breath catches in my throat, and my mind races. *Am I ready to see whatever dark secret Zac is keeping? Is he holding a secret? Maybe he just doesn't want to spend time with me. Perhaps I'm just an idiot, and I need to open the email.*

I click on Matt's message.

"Sera, thank you for the opportunity to assist you with your query. My investigation into Zachary Christopher Marcum revealed the following." As I skim the report, my stomach fills with butterflies, stopping at the highlights and making mental check marks by things I already know or believe to be truisms.

Marines. Check.

Honorable discharge. Check.

Marital status, divorced. Check.

Credit, no bankruptcies or judgments. Good to know.

Arrests, none. Check.

Public records, divorce. Check.

I work my way down the items and come to a line entitled former addresses. Zac's bench condo is the first one on the list. *Matt has made a mistake.*

I scroll down to the next page and pause again. Current address, Floating Feather Road, Star, Idaho. My heart stops. *That's why we haven't been to your place for some time.* The room is spinning. My throat tightens.

I click the next line; other individuals living at this address, Anne Andrews, age twenty-nine.

And there it is: he lives with another woman.

My stomach lurches, and I run to the toilet, bend over, and vomit.

I rest between retching, my face buried in the floor mat, sobbing ugly tears. The irony of being on the bathroom floor because of a relationship, like so many of the self-help authors I have read over the past few months, is not escaping me. This is where broken women lie.

Matt's email confirms there is no *us* in the Zac and Sera equation, and while it doesn't appear Zac and Anne are married, there is most definitely some kind of *them*.

This complete mess is my fault, I tell myself, still curled in the fetal position. *I was the one who set the parameters of our so-called relationship. No calls, no overnights, no attachment.*

"What were you thinking, Serenade? All that sex was going to make him love you?" I yell and pound my fists into the floor until my hands are red.

This moment defines me: I am nothing more to Zac than sex.

I stay on the cold floor until my stomach stops heaving, and my tears and snot have dried. Hours have passed. I'm aching, heartbroken, and desperate. I peel myself off the mat, pick up my phone, and dial Voice Man's number.

CHAPTER

19

The phone rings once, and Rodney answers, "Hello, Gypsy Girl," he says in a rich, melodic voice, its timbre buttery, smooth, and romantic.

"Hi, Voice Man," my voice is husky and tremulous from vomiting and heartbreak.

"Come up here," he oozes. "We can hang out this weekend."

There is expectation in his tone. I'm not registering his words as I grapple with the pain in my heart. Zac has moved on, living with a woman who is a dozen plus years younger than me and likely fertile. I can't compete. I've lost him.

"What do you say, Sera, I promise, just as friends?"

I close my eyes, wrap a thick, fuzzy blanket around myself, and stare out the window into the dark nothingness.

"Sure, why not?"

"That's fantastic. I was hoping you would agree." I can hear his smile. "I took the liberty and checked; the last flight leaving Boise is in about three hours. Can you make it?" He sounds anxious.

"Mm-hmm," I mumble, lost in thought.

"Great, I'll send you the details and see you at the airport. I'll be the one with a sign," he laughs.

I hang up and lumber back to the bathroom, strip, and sit on the shower floor, holding my knees to my chest until the water runs cold, forgoing soap and shampoo. I need to find another path, one without Zac.

Disconnected from my surroundings, I move on autopilot, pull my hair into a messy bun, and slip into yoga pants, a cozy sweater, and joggers. I throw similar clothes, my toothbrush, and sunglasses into a bag, then grab the Oprah book on my way out the door.

"Stefan, I'm going to Seattle for the weekend. I'll be home on Sunday."

"Is everything alright, Ms. Kincaid?" Concern floods his eyes.

Nodding, I stare out the door. Finding my sunglasses, I throw them on and wait for my ride share, refusing further conversation.

The flight to Seattle is just long enough to reach cruising altitude before landing. I sleep hard and wake with my knees curled into me.

An old rattletrap pulls up to the curb, and a man yells my name through the open passenger window, "Sera?"

I guess this is Rodney.

I lift the corners of my lips. I am the tiniest bit disappointed he doesn't greet me with a sign. I've always wanted to walk out of an airport and into the arms of someone so excited to see me they write it on paper.

I open the car door and climb inside, scooting the rubbish on the floor aside, making room for my feet. A heavy sensation weighs me down, and the hair rises on my arms and the back of my neck. Rodney pulls into the lane of traffic and pushes the automatic

144

lock button for the doors; it locks us inside with a metallic *thunk*, heightening my foreboding feeling. My breath catches, and my mind snaps to full attention.

Be careful.

Stay alert.

Keep your phone close.

Stay calm.

"Hello," I give a courtesy chuckle. "I'm Sera."

"I know," he sounds unamused.

This man is neither a chatterbox nor a fashionista. He wears a faded-black t-shirt with the image of an eighties metal band on the front, and an old, cracked leather jacket. He has thin, stringy hair trailing from under a Seahawks ball cap. *A real winner you've got here.*

The ride is quiet, aside from the continuing dialogue inside my head.

Sera, it's just a quick weekend, nothing more.

Have a plan, Serenade, just in case.

It will do you good not to sit at home and stew.

But he's creepy.

Give him a chance, girl. He's just different.

"Gloomy weather," I try another conversation starter.

"Mm, typical," he grumbles.

Does he mean the weather or me?

"How have you been in the past few hours?" I giggle nervously, adding, "I mean since we last spoke."

No response.

We ride in silence for the next thirty minutes. I sneak glances at the stranger lurking in the seat next to me. His aura is dark. I think

I can almost see a cloud around him. I shiver and wrap my arms around myself, both for warmth and comfort.

Rodney fiddles with the temperature gauge and turns up the heat. *He's paying attention.* I shiver again as an eerie sensation walks the length of my body, neck to toe. I start a mental roadmap, just in case.

He turns off the interstate and onto an exit, and I swallow hard. *Remember where you are,* my inner voice tells me, and I plot a few more turns on the chart in my mind.

"Home sweet home," Rodney grins, his silky voice alluring but not comforting enough to relax the hair still standing on my neck.

I am reluctant to follow him, but my well-mannered upbringing wins out over my worried inner voice: *Don't be rude.* I am standing outside his walk-out apartment that abuts the side of a hill. *There's nowhere to run behind the building*, my mind says, and I think that an odd sentiment, my sixth sense has never kicked in like this.

He unlocks the deadbolt and opens the door. I'm greeted by a *whoosh* of stale air that escapes the tight seal as it releases from the jamb. I follow Rodney into the musty room. I notice only one window perched high on the living room wall, covered with bars, and framed in thick drapes—my skin prickles into goose flesh.

My prudish grandmother flashes in my mind, "Never forget where you came from," she said. "You are no better and no worse than anyone."

I had lived better but seen much worse. Where I grew up, some lived with dirt floors, others used towels shoved around drafty windows to keep the cold out and the heat in, and often, there were the skinned bodies of poached deer hanging in garages.

Dish soap was a commonplace cheap substitute for shampoo, and black mold clung to many bathroom ceilings. I have seen much worse than Rodney's humid, dark condo. *Suck it up, buttercup.*

"I have a quick lesson to give, and then I'm all yours," Rodney says, and with a click of the bolt, I am locked inside.

"Can I get you something to drink?"

"That would be great," I force a smile, "thank you."

"Tea?" he hands me a mug, its contents steeping a citrus, herbal blend. I sip it greedily, the heat warm against my chilled hands.

Something's not right. The little voice in my head is screaming, *you need to leave. No,* I tell my annoying inner self, *you need a smoke.*

"Mind if I bum a cigarette?" I ask, grabbing for the pack off the table and helping myself. Since college, I only partake when I've drunk too much or am extremely nervous. And I'm extremely nervous.

Rodney shrugs, and I grab the lighter and my cup before making my way to the door. I turn the bolt on the lock. I feel Rodney's eyes following me. Outside, I take in a long draw and close my eyes, relaxing into the nicotine rush, numbing me like a shot of morphine.

I blow out the smoke and watch the white plume curl as it dissipates into the heavens. It's only been a few hours since my Zac revelation, and here I am, standing outside a stranger's house in Seattle smoking a menthol. I take another drag.

Perhaps I need counseling? Maybe I need to stop looking for men to make me happy. I chuckle at the simplicity of the thoughts that so easily define my feelings' complexity, drain the tea, stub out the cigarette, and pocket the butt. I hate litter.

Rodney ends his call as I come back inside, he's wearing an odd look, almost as if he's relieved to see me. I leave the door unlocked.

"I thought we could stay in tonight," Rodney calls out from the kitchen, "get to know one another. I'll cook if that works for you."

I nod, finding my words caught in my throat. My eyelids feel heavy, the day's events catching up to me. I kick off my shoes and curl onto the couch, pulling my legs underneath me and reach for the blanket wadded up on the floor. Its smell grosses me out, but I am tired, and the thought of resting with a blanket, even one this nasty, is comforting.

Rodney shuffles between stove and refrigerator, unenthused by the task at hand. He seems to carry on a conversation with an imaginary friend, mumbling as he plows through his culinary motions and then pauses as if listening to a response. Occasionally, he looks up, giving his attention to something I don't see. Then he drops his gaze back to the task at hand. He nods in a kind of agreement. The hair on the back of my neck will not settle, and my stomach clenches. Sleepy and exhausted, I fight the urge to run.

You're paranoid, Serenade, I tell myself, *and rude.* Even in my uncomfortable state, my upbringing taught me manners trump everything.

"Tell me about your coaching." My words sound lazy to my ears. "You do have a lovely voice." I smile, feeling groggier by the moment.

Rodney stops his fiddling at the stove and glances over at me; he seems perplexed, as if he's surprised when I speak.

"Do you have many clients?" I ask, stifling a yawn.

"Enough." He turns back to the frying pan, disinterested in chit-chat.

I remain silent, fighting to keep my eyes open.

"Dinner's ready," Rodney calls, producing two plates.

"Thank you," I manage to say through my haze, "but I feel a bit off . . ."

My breathing is shallow, and sleep is overcoming me. Rodney sets one plate on the counter. "It'll be here when you get hungry." He settles himself at the table.

Perhaps I am coming down with something. I am repulsed by the man sitting hunched over his dinner, a protective arm wrapped around his plate, shoveling in food.

Jesus, he eats like a convict. I gulp at the thought and close my eyes, hoping to blot out the visual.

"You like rom-coms?"

How long has Rodney been standing over me? I nod and lift myself onto to my elbows. He puts a disc into an old DVD player, *Sleepless in Seattle*. Of course it is.

"I need to lie down, proper-like," my tongue is thick, and my thoughts disjointed. "Where's my room?"

Rodney gives me a grin. "There's only one room. I thought we could share the bed." He pauses, and then says, "Just to sleep."

"Yeah, sure," I say. *Whatever.*

I walk on wobbly legs toward the bedroom, dragging my bag. I pull on my t-shirt and shorts, then climb into the bed, wrapped in a sinister feeling, and succumb to sleep.

CHAPTER
20

My dreams are fragmented nightmares, visions coming and going in nonsensical, drowning waves. I am center stage, a star. It is cold, and I shiver. A fire burns in front of me, but I cannot reach its warmth. A pungent smell envelops me, metallic and sharp: iron. I'm covered in red paint, sticky and slick. Hairy creatures with pointy fangs dressed in dark cloaks surround me; they are chanting in a drum-like cadence.

"A te disfrenasi Il verso ardito, Te invoco, o satana. Re del convito."

The creatures sway in time, their words rolling over me, pulling me, wanting me to fall into their rhythm.

I fight to clear my thoughts and see I am on a bed. A creature lies beside me. I shake my head. No, it is Rodney next to me and we are sharing a bed, as we agreed.

Wake up.

I wiggle and strain to rise, but my limbs are too heavy. I strain to breathe.

Consciousness ebbs and flows, and I swim in confusion.

What's happening?

I clamp my eyes tight and shake my head again, demanding clarity, but it refuses to show itself.

Get a grip, Serenade. You are in Rodney's house, in his bed, and beyond sleepy. These are the facts I know, and I remind myself of them. And then my mind gets murky again. I am held fast with chains—no, Rodney is restraining me; he's on top of me. I force my eyes open, and clarity springs the truth wide open. *He drugged me.*

Foul, fiery breath in my face rouses me further. "Come with me," I hear, "I have the power of the beast."

Rodney's weight crushes me, and he pins my arms fast over my head.

"A te disfrenasi Il verso ardito, Te invoco, o satana. Re del convito."

Still foggy, I can't understand his words. "What are you saying?" I cry. "What do you want?"

He translates, "To you, my darling, verses unleashed. To you, I invoke, O Satan, monarch of the feast."

"Feast? Get off me. What the hell are you doing?"

My head clears enough to understand these words. Terror soars through me as I jerk my head back and forth and strain against his grip. I kick my legs. "Get the fuck off me."

I draw in a breath to scream. Rodney slaps a hand over my face, and my tooth slices into the soft flesh of my lip. I taste blood.

"Oh, my God, please help me," I beg.

A maniacal laugh erupts from Rodney. "No god can help you," he hisses and continues chanting.

"A te, de l'essere principio immense, material e spirit, ragione e senso."

I wiggle and buck, trying to wrench free from his grip. *You must get out of here.* The voice inside my head is steady, loud, and clear.

With as much force as I can muster, I raise my knee and strike Rodney in the crotch. My blow falls soft, ineffectual. I continue to flail and fight; my efforts free one wrist, and I rake my fingernails across his face, aiming for his eyes, and scream, "Help! Help me!"

Rodney clenches a fist and yells, "You bitch!" With a thud to my cheek, my teeth rattle, and the world falls sideways.

———————

I come to in a haze; one eye swollen shut. My vision in the open eye is blurry from the blow. Rodney lies snoring beside me. I reach beneath the covers, my fingers trembling as they rest on my belly and trail to the tops of my thighs. I am no longer wearing my t-shirt and my shorts and panties are gone; I am naked. I choke on a sob.

Serenade, focus.

I spend a moment retracing the events that led me to this. Zac is living with another woman; I flew to Seattle, drank tea, and smoked a cigarette. I became tired, so very sleepy. I climbed into bed. *Oh, my God. Rodney really did drug me.*

I take in a breath, and a sharp pain shoots through the side of my ribs. I wince and reach my hand to my chest. There is warmth on my skin where the pain lives.

Another thought dawns; the chanting. *He is satanic.* A chill comes over me. I shiver and break into a sweat. *You need to leave, Serenade. Get up and run.*

I inch my body to the side of the bed, lifting the sheet with caution so as not to pull against Rodney and wake him. I reach for the floor, touch it, and pain runs the length of my ring finger. I shove the tip in my mouth; the nail is missing.

Only a few feet to freedom, keep going.

I pull my finger from my mouth and move my outside leg slowly off the mattress until my foot touches the floor. Snake-like, I slither off the bed. I lie for a moment, the cool tile refreshing on my hot, bruised skin.

You're naked. Find clothes.

I brush my hands over the floor using wide sweeping motions, aware of Rodney's breathing on the bed, still rhythmical, in and out. I feel silky lace material. *Panties, mine.* I snatch them up and pull them toward me, holding them wadded in my fist close to my chest.

Belly crawling, I inch toward the closed door, careful not to make a noise, forcing myself not to rush. I pause after each scoot of my body to listen to Rodney's breathing. At the door, I wait, gather myself, and reach up for the handle. I draw in a deep, shuddering breath and ease the knob to avoid any click or squeak, and then I pull.

My mind races, wanting me to bolt, but I'm no match for Rodney if he wakes. I slow my breathing and creep into the living room, testing each step for creaks and pops with my toes before planting my weight. Still holding my panties in a vice grip, I scoop up my shoes and purse lying next to the sofa, checking to make sure my cell phone is inside.

Thank God. Relief floods over me when I feel the familiar thin rectangle.

I grab the musty blanket off the couch, wrap it around my nakedness, and again test each step with my toes as I sneak to the front door.

Please, don't make a sound. Please, don't make a sound.

I see the deadbolt is again locked. I release it with the skilled touch of a safecracker, millimeter by millimeter, until it clicks in my hand.

Almost there. Keep breathing. Go slow.

The door is heavy, and I am weak. I strain against its weight, mustering all my strength. With one hand on the jamb, holding my purse, panties, and shoes between my clamped knees, I turn the handle with my free hand and pull the door. It releases its tight seal with a *whoosh*, and I am met with cold, wet air slapping me in the face.

Run!

CHAPTER

21

I sprint into the parking lot, gulping air into my lungs, my chest heaving in pain, my feet splashing without shoes in the puddles made from the evening rain. My teeth chatter from cold, pain, and terror. Panicked, I scan the lot for someone, anyone.

Hide. The devil might wake up.

I run across the blacktop and fall behind a car. I fumble for my phone. Its light gives away my position. I gasp and peer around the bumper—no sign of Rodney. I scroll to my ride share app, allowing GPS to find my location and accept a female driver.

Five minutes.

Shit, hurry, I beg, tapping the screen on my phone over and over to encourage the driver to come faster.

You can do this, my steady little voice comforts. *Put on your shoes.*

I cram my wet feet, bloody with tiny cuts from the blacktop, into my shoes and slip on my panties. Careful to stay crouched behind the car, I check my phone every few seconds to update my ride's position.

Four minutes. Goddamn it, hurry. Please.

A door slams from a distant apartment. I jump and slap a hand over my mouth to keep from screaming.

Please, no. Oh, God.

Footsteps splash through the puddles. *Are they getting closer?* Disoriented, confused, and shivering, I choke down a sob and fall flat, shimmying underneath the parked car in front of me, scraping the skin from my knees and off my back.

Make yourself as small as possible.

A car door opens and then closes. The car drives away, and I release the breath I've been holding. My phone flashes the word, "arriving."

Thank God. Thank you, thank you, thank you.

I peek out from my hiding spot, looking for the red Hyundai.

The ride share driver, an older woman who looks to be in her seventies, wears a knowing look when I climb inside, my battered face, nakedness, and frantic behavior, a dead giveaway. She stares in my one open eye as I watch waves of sadness, fear, and understanding wash across her face.

"Drive," I command, loudly.

The woman puts the car in gear. She eases out of the parking lot, paying particular attention to the speed bumps, taking them slow.

"Take me to a car rental," I yell and then lower my voice to add, "please."

"Miss, you're hurt. Let me take you to the hospital."

"No. I need a car. I want to go home." My voice quivers, shaking both from fear and chill. I can't board a plane looking like this.

The woman focuses on her driving, and objects. "I have, well," she stammers, "I have a duty, or at least a moral obligation—"

"Your only duty is to your customer, and I absolve you of any obligation other than driving. If you want this fare, take me to the rental car company now, please." I'm near hysteria as the old woman drives along at a snail's pace.

Move your ass, lady, or I'm gonna carjack you. I stare at the gray-haired woman behind the wheel, keeping my thoughts to myself.

"Then the police?" she suggests.

She is spirited.

"No. No police."

She hesitates a moment and then strikes a bargain. "Let me at least get you something to wear, a pair of pants perhaps, and a shirt? I live only a few blocks from here."

I flash a look of distrust, but I desperately need clothes. I decide this woman is not my enemy, and even in my pathetic shape, I could take her. I nod.

"I'm Doris." She sounds pleased with her victory. She smiles at me, her loose skin bunching into dozens of wrinkles. She wears years of wisdom, kindness, heartbreak, and sorrow in those lines. I can't help but like her, and I lift the corner of my mouth, returning a crooked smile.

"Sera." I slur my thick tongue. Washed in shame, fear, and cold, I shiver, burrowing deeper into the stinky blanket. I peek over at the matronly woman sitting next to me and correct myself, "Serenade."

Doris pulls up to a dark little cottage frozen in time, standing proud in its mid-century state on a tiny piece of land amongst its modern neighbors. I follow her down a narrow path cut through wildflowers growing haphazard in the front yard and climb the three concrete steps onto an old porch that moans beneath our weight. Two wooden rocking chairs, well-worn, with smooth seats, rest to one side of the door. They, no doubt, have seen their fair share of visitors. A table nestled between them begs for glasses of homemade lemonade and a plate of cookies. Planter boxes filled with geraniums rest on the white spindle railing, and shutters dress the windows. A large sign proclaiming "all welcome" hangs above the door, and a rainbow sticker clings to its glass. The old bird isn't afraid to show her hospitality or inclusivity; now I really like Doris.

"I always forget to turn the porch light on during these late-night runs," she says, fumbling with her keys and looking over her shoulder at me. I doubt Doris forgets much. She smiles, and I hear a click of the lock. The door creaks, and I am greeted with the smell of fresh-baked bread. Doris opens the door, and I push past her, eager for the safety of her home.

I listen intently for the lock's *thunk* behind me, and my shoulders sag in relief. Doris makes her way through the little house, turning on lamps and pulling shades. She leads me into the kitchen, where she motions me to a chair.

"Let me get something to put on those cuts." Her eyes ask a thousand questions, but she keeps them to herself.

I fall onto a 1960s yellow vinyl chair beside a metal table with a matching yellow Formica top. Like the rest of the house, time has stopped in the kitchen. The old olive-green appliances, a stove with a twist dial clock, a single-handled fridge, and a portable dishwasher make the kitchen charming, familiar to my growing-up years, and almost back in style.

"Here we are." Doris trundles back to where I sit. I'm staring at the loaf of white bread on the cutting board next to the percolator coffee pot. My mouth waters, and I realize I haven't eaten all day.

I am suddenly famished. Doris sits down a brown glass bottle of Mercurochrome tincture, cotton balls, and bandages.

"I didn't know they still made that stuff," I mumble through my swollen, blood-crusted lips.

"They don't," Doris snickers. "I've had this bottle of antiseptic since my daughter was little." She gives me a wink. "Nothing on today's market works as good. It's all gotta be hypo this and non-allergy that. You know, free from dyes and all that PC stuff." I stifle a chuckle at her misstatement, having no desire to correct this angel doting on me with her maternal care. A rush of longing for my mother engulfs me.

"This will sting a little," Doris says, dabbing the bright orange liquid on my cuts. "Would you like a piece?" Doris offers after she bandages the last of my cuts.

"I'm sorry?"

She raises her head to look at me. "Bread."

I open my mouth to apologize for staring.

"It's okay, child, you're thin as a beanpole. And I don't get to share my baking very often." In her element as a caregiver, Doris scrambles to the cupboard for a plate, cuts a healthy slice of the still lukewarm bread, and slathers it in real butter that melts before she hands it to me.

I devour the offering, so fluffy and light it dissolves in my mouth. Doris scampers out of sight, reappearing with a pair of soft gray sweatpants and a man's oversized white t-shirt. She then busies herself putting on a kettle of water, and I excuse myself for the bathroom.

Don't lose it now, Serenade, you still need to get home. I can't bring myself to look in the mirror, so I stare at my hands, evaluating the tiny cuts, swollen fingers, and missing nail. I then allow my gaze to travel to my wrists, where red grip marks and bruises have formed. Looking down at my legs, I catch sight of the fresh bandages Doris applied to my knees; she's mummified my feet, wrapping layers of gauze and tape around them to ease the pain of walking. I didn't realize they were in such awful shape from the pavement.

I inhale a deep breath. There's a stabbing, sharp pain in my side. I move the blanket back and see a well-defined welt on my ribcage. I raise my gaze, forcing myself to look into the mirror and gasp, touching my fingers to my swollen cheek and eye. I don't recognize the person staring back at me with her distorted features, matted hair, and tear-streaked face. I choke out a sob and finger-comb a few knots from my tangled locks with my good hand. It's no use, and I give up, reaching for the toilet to lower myself. I wince as the pee flows over my torn flesh.

I plod back to the kitchen in the borrowed clothes and slide gingerly onto the chair next to Doris. We sit in silence, drinking weak tea. My nerves settle, and the tan liquid no longer sloshes over the side of the mug. I order a rental car; it will be here in an hour, maybe two.

"You mentioned late-night runs," I say to Doris as we wait in the small living room for my car. She avoids my question and sifts through a stack of hand-knitted afghan blankets lying next to the couch. Choosing an ornate pink and green number in an intricate rosette pattern, Doris wraps it around me, tucking the ends behind my shoulders. I study her as she piles the remaining blankets in their stack and scoots a basket full of yarn, rolled into neat balls skewered with long knitting needles, into its place. This is Doris's spot, where I imagine she sits and happily occupies her time.

"Do you always pick up people late at night?" I try again, snuggling into the soft, thick blanket; its heady aroma of dusty yarn, Doris's powder, and fresh-baked bread fills my nostrils.

Doris smiles, looking tired, and says, "Seattle has seen its share of crime, in particular, the rape and murdering of young women." She draws in the breath of someone experienced in tragedy. "I have made it my life's calling to do what I can to help. I monitor the late-night ride requests from female passengers."

"That sounds dangerous."

She chuckles, looking at me as if I am naïve. "I have a system, dear. I only pick up women and only within six blocks of my house. I've lived here going on fifty years; I know every back street and hidey-hole." She gives me a confident wink. "And who would bother me? I'm just an old lady out for a drive."

There was more to this story, but Doris wasn't willing to share. And then a sly grin crosses her face as she says, "I'm not the only one."

"Not the only one?"

"There are others, like me, who pick up women late at night to ensure their safety."

I smile. Doris has a network of angels. Of course, she does.

"Thank you, Doris," I say when my car arrives. "I will never forget you or your generosity." My eye fills with tears, and I want to hug her but can't drop my guard. Fearful if she touches me, I might never stop crying.

Doris respects my body language, grasps my icy hands in her warm, wrinkled ones, and presses my fingers to her mouth, kissing their tips. She closes her eyes, breathes me in, and then places my palms to her chest; I feel her heartbeat. When she opens her eyes, she whispers, "Take care, my beloved Serenade."

Surprised by the word "beloved," my breath catches.

––––––––––

It's early morning when I park the rental car alongside the curb outside my building in Boise and slink inside, grateful to avoid Stefan, engrossed in a tenant matter. I am *not* ready to answer questions.

Inside my condo, I send a single-word text, "Hi." While waiting for a response, I strip off the borrowed jogging pants and shirt, leaving them in a heap on the bathroom floor. Vomit rises to the back of my throat as I slide the soiled panties down my legs, step out of them, and throw them in the trash.

Wash this away. The words roll around my head as I reach for the faucet, turning it as hot as I can stand and for the second time in as many days, step into scalding water, sit on the shower pan, assume the fetal position, and sob until the water runs cold.

An hour later, my phone vibrates. "Hello."

"Can you come over? I need a hug."

Within twenty minutes, my phone lights up with "OMW."

"No questions," I text.

A twinge of anxiety and perhaps guilt flutter in my belly. Why didn't I reach out to Carolyn? Do I think Zac will comfort me better than her? Will he judge me less than her? I can't answer my questions, I only want *him*.

––––––––––

Zac holds me as I lay curled on the couch, my head resting in his lap. I sob as he strokes my hair. He runs his fingers carefully over the top of my skin. Hours pass as I wrestle between fitful sleep and rage-filled awareness, my inner voice chastising me, placing blame on me for my situation. I flew to meet a stranger, agreed to spend time alone with him in his home, all to escape the man who is now comforting me. *You are a fool, Serenade.* My face contorts, and again, I cry ugly tears.

Zac coos in my ear, gentle shushing noises. His voice is tender and reassuring when he speaks, "Shh, Serenade. It's okay, baby, you're safe now."

CHAPTER

22

I wake alone on the couch, covered with Doris's blanket. Zac had slipped out at some time while I slept. I inch off the cushions, my body aching as if I've survived a horrendous car crash.

In the light of day, I reassess my injuries. Lumps and scratches cover the entirety of my arms, legs, torso, and face. A handprint marks my check. A large welt surrounds my left eye, and I can't open it. Bruises of different sizes cover my body in an ugly rainbow of black, blue, yellow, green, purple, and red.

I gently trace a pressure point mark on my wrist with my thumb; an image of being restrained floods my memory. I'm lost somewhere between disbelief and rage, unsure what to do, where to place my feelings, and how to overcome this moment. With the back of my sleeve, I wipe my nose and make my way to the bathroom, my legs heavy. Every step is painful.

Using a compact mirror, I slide it between my thighs and crane my neck to check out my nether region. It is raw, and like the rest of my body, an angry shade of purple. Tiny fissures in the skin show ample evidence of forced entry. Reality overcomes me again, and I sob until my tears give way to a coughing fit that sends searing pain through my chest wall. I gag, nearly vomit in agony, and wrap my arms around my midriff until I slow my breath and stop coughing.

Cracked ribs? I reach for a tissue and notice the clothes I wore home aren't on the floor. I look in the hamper—empty. *Zac must have discarded them.*

Tea. The word comes from nowhere, but I heed it; tea always makes me feel better. I shuffle back toward the kitchen, dragging the knitted throw behind me like a child unwilling to relinquish her security. I turn the kettle on and breathe in another deep whiff of the blanket, which now not only smells of Doris' powder and homemade bread but also of Zac.

I choke on a sob and am met by another sharp, knife-like pain that pierces my side. A mournful noise crawls from my belly up the length of my throat, gathering volume as it travels out my mouth until it is a full-blown, visceral wail. This noise, like the sound I made with each failed pregnancy, is deep and guttural, drenched in sorrow. I hold my midsection, fall on my bandaged knees, and slide face first onto the tiled kitchen floor.

The kettle screams, rousing me off the floor and back to my senses. It's Monday morning, and I'm expected at the office.

"Hi Marta, it's Sera," I mumble when my assistant answers. "I will be out of town this week for an unexpected family thing. I'll call in for messages. Thanks."

Afraid Carolyn might answer if I call, I opt for emailing her a similar message, then shut my laptop and turn off my phone.

"Hey, Stefan," I call down through the intercom, "I'm doing a staycation and refusing all visitors for the week. Thank you."

"Not a problem, Ms. Kincaid. Enjoy your time. Let me know if there's anything you need." *Of course, he doesn't know.*

I turn my attention to my vast vinyl collection. Nestled on a shelf between John Lee Hooker and The Kinks is the smoky contralto voice of Etta James that never fails to lull my jitters and empower my spirit. I drop the needle onto the record and let the soulful words and brass horns envelop me. I belt out the lyrics as best I can with my injuries, knowing where to place each throaty growl and wistful sigh. Together, Etta and I harmonize through the chorus, "Ooh, I would rather go blind boy than to see you walk away from me."

I sway and hum, playing air drums and slide trombone, hitting every beat, and not missing a shift in key. When the song ends, I lift the needle and, with deft precision, place it again between the songs' grooves, its well-worn track scratchy from excessive use.

"Ms. Kincaid, Ms. Kincaid," Stefan bellows through the intercom.

Straight vodka has long since replaced my morning tea, and I stumble around the coffee table toward Stefan's voice. Clear liquid sloshes from the glass, rolls down my hand, and lands on the floor. I lick my wrist, enjoying the liquid burn.

"What is it, Stefan?" I roar. "I told you no interruptions." I take another gulp, leaving Etta to croon the gritty lyrics alone in the background.

"Ms. Kincaid, I'm sorry, but Ms. Carolyn is insisting on coming up. She won't take no for an answer."

"Of course, she won't," I mumble. "Fine, send her up." My words a mixture of slur and snarl. I unlock the deadbolt, crack open the door, and turn my attention back to the window.

Singing at the top of my lungs, Carolyn slips inside and stands by the door. I catch her reflection in the window. She stares back at me, looking flush with concern. My disheveled hair stands on end, Medusa-style; I'm still holding Doris' blanket with one hand and the half-empty glass of vodka in the other. I sway with the music and drink, making no apologies for either.

"What do you want?" I screech when I turn around. My raspy voice is as unrecognizable as my face.

Carolyn gasps, her hands fly to her mouth, and she steps toward me, stopping short to my upheld hand.

"My God, honey," she eyes me up and down, rooted in place. "What happened?" She looks desperate to wrap her arms around me and take away my pain.

Throwing back the last of my drink, I say just above a whisper, "He raped me."

"He who?" Carolyn takes a slow step forward, placing her hand gently on my arm. I don't object, and she pulls me to her, nestling me into her. I keep my arms by my side, not ready to breakdown.

"Voice Man."

"It will be okay," she murmurs. "We will get through this together."

————

The doctor confirms a cracked rib. She also found a loose tooth I hadn't noticed, and a punctured eardrum she thinks will likely result in permanent muffled hearing. I chalk it up to lifelong penance for my stupidity. The x-rays of my face and eye socket show no fractures. The physician writes a prescription for a sedative and a pain killer then hands me a pamphlet to a support group.

I work from home, afraid to go outside. Fearful of people, darkness, strangers, noises, and shadows. I use my face and its gruesomeness as my excuse to hole-up, except for Tuesday nights where, like clockwork, Carolyn shows up, harasses Stefan, and accompanies me to the Emanuel Lutheran Church basement. She sits alone in the foyer, holding vigil for us victims who meet behind closed doors and tell our sordid stories to other victims of sexual assault.

"Someone mugged me in the park," a young girl says and shrugs. "It was dark, and the park was closed. It was my fault, being there so late. I guess I deserved it." She's rail-track thin and pasty, with scabs and infected pock marks on her arms and face, and her leg bounces nonstop as she speaks. There is no doubt she's an addict. But I don't judge; I have my own issues.

Others jump in. "It's never your fault," they insist.

"But it is. I shouldn't have been there. It was late. I was, well, I was trying to score some dope. This is on me." She weeps into her hands, humiliated, defeated, broken.

"I feel the same way," I whisper.

"What?" the woman who's sat next to me for the past several weeks asks. "Say that again. Louder."

"I feel the same way," I speak up. The room falls silent. I've never before spoken in these meetings.

"My rape was my fault. I was an idiot," I say, keeping my chin tucked to my chest. "I flew to his house, a stranger, and thought I could stay there, you know, just as friends, that's what he said; I believed him. I had never met him before, didn't look into his past, and he—he hurt me." My voice trails off, and tears fall onto my lap. Splash. Splash. Splash.

"I can't seem to reconcile this or forgive myself."

The bruises and physical signs of the event fade, and my rib has healed. The swelling in my face has dissipated, and my eye is back to normal. My ear still rings, I'm still sick with a nagging cough and fatigue, and my mind continues to be fraught with guilt and self-loathing. I keep my phone off, refusing to see anyone other than Carolyn, who is so forceful I can't keep her away; I've tried. I don't see Zac. I need time to rest, recuperate, and reset.

"Sweetie," Carolyn says on the drive to a Tuesday meeting after my breakthrough, "do you think it's time to go to the police?"

I shoot her a look of disbelief. "I-I can't. You know that."

"No, you can go if you're ready. You need to, and you know it." I know what she means. This can't go unpunished.

"No. I mean, I can't. There's no evidence. I showered, there are no clothes. I will open myself up to mockery by the police. No one will believe me. It will be his word against mine. I can't go through that." I cough as I hyperventilate and focus on taking deep breaths.

"Shh. It will be alright. No one will mock you. They will believe you. And there is evidence." Her lips turn ever so slightly upward, and I see a gleam in her eye.

The crease in my brow deepens. "What are you talking about?"

She pulls into the church parking lot, puts the car in park, and turns to me. "Doris, the lady who picked you up that night, remember her?"

I nod, incredulous. "How could I forget?"

"Her late husband was a homicide detective. She knew to keep the blanket from that night."

"Are you serious?" I stiffen and come to full attention.

Carolyn nods and grins. "She also snapped a picture of your

face when you were standing in the bathroom. She gave me the entire rundown about a certain angle where the mirror reflected your face to the hallway where she could stand unseen and take it with her phone. Blah, blah, blah."

"How did you find her?" I interrupt.

"She found me. Well, she found you. It's not that difficult, your name hangs on a very prestigious firm, and the internet is a powerful tool. I've been fielding your calls at work, and Doris called the firm." The edges of Carolyn's mouth lift again.

"Wow, Doris." I drift back to the memory of the sweet, ride-share granny.

Carolyn's voice lowers, "She wanted you to know that several years ago, her daughter was a victim of a serial rapist. He murdered her. She told me this would answer your questions."

My jaw fell slack.

"There's one more thing," Carolyn said.

I raise my eyebrows. "More?" I'm not sure I can handle any more surprises.

"Zac saved your clothes from that night, including your panties."
That's why they were missing the next day.

"After Zac didn't hear from you for a few days, he came by the office and gave them to me, sealed in a bag. He said he didn't think you would ever want to do anything about it. He said you would blame yourself." Carolyn pauses and then whispers, "He checks in on you, through me, of course. Nothing creepy."

I pay no attention to her last comment as fresh, grateful tears fall. "I've felt so guilty for not doing anything. I've wondered about other women." My words fade. "But since I figured it was my fault—"

"Stop it. The animal raped you. It doesn't matter if you flew there or what the circumstances, Rodney attacked you. Violated you, drugged you, beat you. He can't do that. This isn't on you."

We sit together in the quiet for a long time.

"Let's go."

"Go?"

"Yes, let's do this. Take me to the police before I change my mind."

Without hesitation, Carolyn puts the car in reverse and drives me to the local station. A portly, middle-aged female detective with sober, caring eyes waits for me to tell my story. Her voice is airy and soft when she speaks, reminding me of a cloud. I like her instantly, and I trust her.

"Whenever you're ready, Ms. Kincaid," the detective says in her smooth, feathery voice.

I sit mute, wringing my hands, my throat as dry as the Sahara. I fill an empty glass from the pitcher that sits in the middle of the table. My hands shake, and water dribbles down my chin when the glass meets my lips. I empty it in one gulp and refill it. The story comes back to me, disjointed and childlike.

I went online.

Rodney was such a jerk.

I went to Seattle anyway.

I only drank tea.

So tired.

He was on top of me.

I said no.

There was chanting and demons.

He hit me.

I woke up without clothes.

"I was raped."

———————

The next day I walk into my OB/GYN clinic to see my friend Megan Delane from my IVF days, when Clint and I were trying to get pregnant. My period is late.

"Sera, she's ready for you," calls Tia, Dr. Delane's nurse.

I stand and follow Tia. My mind whirls, and my pulse is rapid. I haven't felt well for some time, and now the lack of period. I figure I must be pre-menopausal.

I undress and cover myself with a gown, and then climbed onto the examination table. The paper covering the vinyl crinkles, reminding me of my breast ultrasound.

"Hi sweetie," Meg says, bending down to give me a soft hug. "I read your paperwork. First, I want you to know, this was not your fault. Next, whatever we find out here today, we can get through it, okay?" I nod. "Okay," she continues, "lie back and let's get started."

She talks me through everything she's doing. "I'm going to touch your left foot and help you put it in the stirrup, okay?"

"Mm-hmm."

"Good. Now, I'm going to touch your right foot and put it in the stirrup, okay?"

"Yeah," I mumble. My lower lip quivers.

"With the back of my hand, I am going to slide up the inside of your thigh, okay?"

"Yes." I eke out the word as tears roll out the corners of my eyes. I jump when Meg's skin touches mine.

"It's okay, Sera." Her tone is assured. "You're doing great."

Meg does a thorough exam, including STI swabs, a pregnancy

test, and an ultrasound; I tell her I've been having belly pain.

"I'm going to step out so you can get dressed, and when you are ready, Tia will walk you down to my office, okay?" Meg asks.

I look from her to Tia, who stands smiling, always prim, always proper. Tia's an excellent sidekick to the occasionally brash doctor.

I dress and open the door. Tia leads me down the hall to Meg's small, private office. I notice a white orchid sitting on the desk.

"Close the door, please," says Meg.

Tia complies, and I'm left sitting across from Meg.

"Sera, there's no easy way to tell you this. You have had a miscarriage."

I gasp and cover my mouth with both hands.

"Given the date of your attack, the pregnancy looks to correlate with the rape. I'm so sorry, Sera. We need to do a dilation and curettage, a D&C, to scrape out the remaining tissue."

"Pregnant?" Surprise and grief overwhelm me. I conceived a child.

"You *were* pregnant. You understand you are no longer pregnant, right, Sera?" Meg stresses her words and nods to encourage me to follow suit.

"Yes," I whisper, "but I *got* pregnant." I stress with equal importance.

Meg smiles, her beautiful, freckled face lighting up at the thought. "Yes, Sera, you got pregnant."

I look down at my flat belly, and my smile fades as I lay my hands on top of my stomach; no bump will form. My shoulders sag.

CHAPTER
23

The drive to my hometown is long enough that I don't want to drive it too often, scenic enough to keep me from sleeping at the wheel, and curvy enough to cause motion sickness. It never fails; I roll down my window for fresh air as I come out of the canyon and into Riggins. A few miles more, and I can roll it back up, about where the bridge crossing over the Salmon River bisects the state into Mountain and Pacific times.

My replacement for the 1960 Stingray I'd lost in the divorce is a 1966 Plymouth Barracuda, hardtop fastback with the signature first-generation wraparound back glass. It is aftermarket bumblebee yellow with black racing stripes over the hood and down the side panels, and boasts a 426 Hemi, dual quad motor under the hood. It set me back a pretty penny.

It's been only a few weeks since I saw Meg and had the *procedure*. I can't bring myself to say the word D&C or even think about it. I am doing better now, at least I think I am, and this road trip feels like excellent medicine.

An hour into the Pacific Time zone, I turn off US-95 onto Johnston Road, the shortcut that shaves seven minutes off "going the long way" through the outskirts of Grangeville. At the end of the short-cut, I turn back onto US-95 for half a mile before turning onto Old Highway 7. Only twenty-two minutes to my old stomping grounds.

I push my foot down firm on the peddle, feeling the thunderous shimmy of the Hemi in my seat. I smirk at the sign on the side of the road telling me I'm traveling much faster than posted and let out a squeal. I whiz by, having traveled it hundreds of times. *I own this road. Hell, I can navigate it by moonlight.* I know this to be true, having turned off my headlights once on a dare.

A calm comes over me as I traverse the hilly terrain. It's peaceful here and gives me time to think, to clear my head. The D&C was awful, but knowing that I could get pregnant was exhilarating, even if the circumstances had been unimaginable.

Spent crops surround me as far as I can see. They take me back to my childhood memories. Harvest is over and the fields are being turned by gigantic tractors coupled to plows and harrows. Life is simple on the prairie, albeit sexist and antiquated, and all but prescribed from birth. Boys grow up to inherit the land and become farmers; girls grow up to marry a farmer. Most, anyway. I push down the memories of my mother's disappointment when I left for grad school. "Are you sure you don't want to just find a nice boy and settle down?" she had asked.

At the bottom of the hill where the Greencreek turnoff tees with the old highway, I stomp on the gas. Faster and faster, I drive up the slight incline, the last hill before reaching the canyon. The speed limit sign demands I slow down. I ignore it and instead scan the road to my right. To my good fortune, there are no cars; I will cross the intersection without the need to slow. With the crest of the hill only a few yards away, I take in a deep breath, brace my hands on the steering wheel, lock my elbows straight, and pin the peddle. The car's nose dips, and there is the sharp sound of metal scraping pavement. The vehicle's front rises, and I let loose an invigorated scream as the tires lift off the road. I've caught air.

The car lands with a bounce; its shocks moan.

"Woo-hoo," I yell and immediately apply pressure to the brakes. The first corner of Lawyer's Canyon is upon me.

I drive this portion of the twisted road and hairpin turns at the prescribed speed of twenty-five miles per hour. There's no room for error here. I glance to the canyon walls, lost in nostalgia, as I always am during this part of the drive, checking out the fresh paint that covers most of the rocks along the side of the highway. The graffiti, markers of the local right-of-passage, spell out the names and initials of the current high schoolers in my hometown who, each year, sneak out here, climb the canyon walls, and paint their names. Most names get covered over. Some, however, are sacred, and left to stand the test of time. *Who are these youngsters?* I wonder reading the mostly unfamiliar names. I know if I carefully peel back the layers of paint, I will find my father's name written here, and possibly that of his sweetheart, my mother. It strikes me for the first time that this is reservation land, and defacing it seems wholly disrespectful, but somehow its accepted.

My car continues as if on autopilot, and my thoughts race to catch up, and then both slow at the spot in the road just before the last winding stretch. I strain and search through the freshly painted names, looking for the familiar faded words. I am almost at a standstill, wondering if this group of names I'm searching for has finally been covered, when I spot the scrawl in silver-white spray paint: Jen, Jill, Kate, and Sera. Next to the names is the designation *Wax Sisters* with a circle around the whole of it. I tear up, nod to the people and times gone by, and continue the drive in silence through the canyon and onto the gravel road named after my great-grandfather.

I see the house in the distance, rising from the fields. It seems more significant and statuesque in my memories. I am surprised each time I see it up close, how it gets a bit more rundown than the last time.

I should have visited more often.

"Momma," I call out, opening the tall, windowed door with my key, "I'm home." I pause. No response. "Mom," I yell louder, "It's Sera."

"Hi, Sera," the nurse says, coming down the hall, Mom's elbow cupped in her hand.

"Oh, hello, dear," Mom says, but I'm not sure she recognizes me, so I reintroduce myself, "Hi, Mom, it's Serenade."

"Well, I know *that*," she scoffs, wafting her hand with little conviction, then falls into a fit of hacking. Her years of smoking haunt her. "Do you think I'm ignorant?" Lack of a verbal filter, her caregiver calls it; an unfortunate byproduct of dementia says her doctor.

"No, Momma, I don't think you are ignorant." I hold her by the shoulders and kiss the smooth, paper-thin skin on her cheek. I linger a moment, drawing in her familiar smell. "What are you doing in the old bedroom?" I ask, noticing she's come from the room she once shared with Daddy before he passed. Last I knew she had taken to sleeping in the front bedroom.

"Just looking for your father, dear," she says, sounding matter of fact. "I can't seem to find him."

"Come on, Momma, let's sit down." I change the subject. From my research and conversations with her team, it's clear that people whose memory fades need redirection, not chastising or reminding of their lapses.

"How are you feeling?"

"Well, I'm good, dear," she croaks. "How are you?" She looks up with childlike eyes filled with wonder and amusement. "How long will you be staying?"

"Not long, Momma," I sigh. "Do you remember the big house we looked at?" The term I use for the care facility.

Nothing.

I try again, "The one where they play Bingo and Skip-Bo, and lots of people live there?"

Her face is still blank. She does not know what I am saying. After a time, she blinks and says, "But this is my home."

"And it will always be your home, Momma," I say, "but it's time for you to stay at the other home."

"Don't lie to her," the doctor had said. But how else could I get her to leave this house without duct tape and a sedative if I didn't tell her a little fib?

We sit in the living room, and Momma drifts in and out of sleep. Her mouth falls open on one side, the side of the stroke, and I look for anything to distract me from the obvious. *She's gotten so old.* I look at the walls covered in years' worth of family photos, my gaze landing on the parakeet-green year. *What a God-awful color.*

I leave Momma to rest and wander about the house, filled with its generational pictures and memorabilia, handed down from owner to owner, great-grandparent to grandparent to parent, and now to me. But this is where the buck stops. I won't be handing anything down. The family tree has ended. After today, there will be no more Kincaids living here. I've rented the home to the farmer who leases the farmland.

I pack Mom's bags into the trunk of my car, wake her, and with her nurse's help, assist her into the car. I take one last look at the house I called home, the place my father and his father before him called home—the house my grandfather's father built in 1895. I sigh and wave goodbye to four generations of Kincaids and their ghosts; give a nod to the family burial plot on the hill, then climb into the seat behind the wheel.

Mom is fearful on the drive, gripping the door handle with all her might.

"What if we hit a big rock?" she asks with the randomness of one not paying any attention to the road or its surroundings. "I think you're driving too fast. Perhaps I should drive," she offers when I pass a slow-moving farm vehicle.

"Are you sure you know where you're going?"

"Why are we leaving home?"

"Have you seen your father?"

"Are you my new nurse?"

I field her questions as best I can, but after a while, saddened and exhausted, I leave them to fall unanswered as if dealing with a two-year-old. The memory care facility will be the best place for her. The seasoned staff is expecting us, and they greet us on arrival, help mother out of the car, and show her to her room. She becomes stressed, frightened, and agitated.

"I don't want to stay here."

"You can't make me."

"Have I been bad?"

"Serenade Jean, you wait until your father gets home."

The charge nurse takes my arm and leads me into the hallway. "This is common. People with dementia don't always understand what's happening, but it's apparent your mother needs around-the-clock care and surveillance. You're doing the right thing for her."

"I know," I say, my voice catching, "but she's, my mom." I stare at the frail old woman with the blank expression who has replaced my fierce, feisty mother.

The little girl inside me, who needs her mommy, asks, "She won't remember me when I come back, will she?"

"Probably not."

CHAPTER
24

On my way back from the courthouse, I debate how to respond to a text. It's been a while since the words *good morning* lit up my phone. Lost in the excitement of seeing the greeting, I don't see the rise in the sidewalk, trip, and spill my files, creating a sea of paper.

"Here, let me help you," a man squats and starts scooping my papers into his arms.

"Thanks, I've got it." I scowl. Frustrated with myself and this do-gooder, I snatch papers from his hand as quick as he gathers them. I glance up and see a pleasant smile worn by a handsome man in a cowboy hat. Cowboy hats are a weak spot for me. I blame my childhood.

As if in a movie scene, I'm frozen, mid-grab, smiling, and locking eyes with a modern-day John Wayne. If he calls me ma'am, I may swoon. I gather myself and say, "Thank you."

Take a stab at human interaction, Serenade; it's been a while.

I draw in a deep breath. "I never could walk and chew gum. Not sure what I was thinking trying to walk and text."

"You're mighty welcome, ma'am."

There it is. I grin. *Will he tip his hat?*

"You're lucky you only dropped your files and not your phone. Those things are downright expensive to replace." He almost twangs when he speaks. Or maybe I'm just hoping for a drawl.

"I'm still old school." I waggle my relic Android, its age apparent.

"Yes, ma'am, that's a dinosaur." His smile lights up his face. "Someday, you'll need to cross over to the dark side."

"Excuse me?" A chill runs up my spine, and I inch back.

"Join the masses?" he is quick to explain. "Get an iPhone like the rest of us sheeple; cross over to the dark side." He gives a reciprocal wiggle of his phone, showing he's already crossed over.

I chuckle. "Ah," is all I can muster. "I hadn't thought of it like that."

"My name is Cary," he says, still smiling, "as in Grant."

"Your mother must have had a wonderful sense of humor."

"Yes, and no. My name is Thompson, not Grant."

I don't laugh, still flustered by his previous reference.

"May I be so forward as to ask your name?"

My breath quickens, and my palms are suddenly moist.

I wipe my hand down my skirt before placing it into his. "Sera."

"Nice to meet you, Sera." He gives me a moderately firm handshake. I jerk my hand back in ownership. "Buy you a cup of coffee sometime?"

I stare at him and feel the color drain from my face.

"Oh, I apologize. Did I cross a line?" Cary stammers, and I work to gain my composure.

"No, you didn't cross a line." My cheeks are hot. "We could meet during the day for coffee," I add quickly, setting firm, clear boundaries. "But I'm buying. A thank you. For helping me." My words come out falteringly.

He studies me with curiosity, pauses, and then says, "Okay, great. Coffee before the sun goes down, and you're paying. May I get your number?" His caution shows me he understands any sudden movements around this feral cat might make her spring straight off the ground.

"Yes." I smile, reaching into my bag and digging out a business card, another sign of my old-fashioned ways. "Here's my office number."

"Serenade Kincaid of Wetzstein Yates Toll & Kincaid," he reads. "Are you the Kincaid in that list of names?"

"I am."

"Very nice," Cary's impressed. "I'll call your office, Ms. Kincaid." He leaves me with another kind smile but without a tip of his hat.

My phone vibrates in my hand. Still grinning, I again see the number without a name.

"Hello? Is everything okay?"

Does it bother you I haven't yet replied? Yes, Zac, everything is fine, but you live with another woman and my booty call days are over. Oh, and I just met a cowboy.

Emboldened for a moment in my thoughts, I am pulled back to reality by the familiar tug at my heart and the tickle beneath my skirt when another text populates the screen. "I miss you."

I sigh. *I miss you, too.* And then I text, "Yes, hi. I'm fine. Thank you for checking."

"May I see you?"

My belly flutters, and my fingers tap their reply before my brain can stop them. "Yes, please." As soon as the message is sent, my mind races. *Am I ready?* The hairs on my arms rise with my thoughts.

"Meet me at the Riverside Downtowner, Room 124."

A hotel? My throat tightens.

I nearly drop the phone when it vibrates again, flashing Zac's answer to my unspoken flurry of fears, "You're in charge."

A smiley face emoji is the best I can do, as I'm flooded with anxiety, excitement, and trepidation.

Before I know it, I am tapping on the door of room 124, and it opens immediately. Zac steps aside, allowing me to decide to enter. Willing my foot to lift, I plant it across the threshold. Zac places his warm hand on my arm. "Are you alright?"

I nod.

"May I close the door?"

I nod.

He guides me with a hand on the small of my back into the open space that serves as both sitting area and bedroom. My feet freeze at the end of the bed.

Zac touches my chin's underside with the knuckle of a curled finger and lifts it gently until I look into his eyes. With incalculably slow movements, he bends down to meet my lips.

"Ms. Kincaid, I have Cary Thompson on the line for you. Shall I put him through?" Marta's pleasant voice interrupts my daydreaming. Zac had held me for hours on the hotel bed where we lay fully clothed. His fingers gently slid up and down my arm, occasionally reaching up to my face and touching my cheeks and lips. He never made a sexual move, and after a while, I relaxed and breathed.

"Did you say, Cary?" I come back to Marta.

"Yes. He said you met last week on the street when you dropped your files." She pauses and adds, "He sounded like he wasn't sure you would remember."

"Yes, please put him through. Thanks, Marta." I clear my throat and answer the call.

———————

"Hey, Sera." Vance beams and comes around the counter, lifting me off the floor in a full-on bear hug. Settling me back on solid ground, he pulls away and holds me at arm's length.

"I have been so worried about you. Sweetie, are you okay?" he asks, drawing out the honey-dipped words for emphasis. He pulls me back in for another hug. He holds me so tight I think I feel his backbone.

"Thank you, Vance." I cough and catch my breath. He prances back behind the counter. "I took some time off, but I'm back now." I glance around, take a small step away from the man in line behind me who's crept into my personal space.

He means no harm, I remind myself. *He's just eager to get his coffee.*

"Stefan told me about . . ." Vance stammers, embarrassed. "He wasn't gossiping, he's just concerned—we both are—I'm sorry."

"It's okay. I'm fine. Are you and Stefan still together?"

"We are." Vance juts out his finger, displaying a band. "We're engaged."

"Oh my gosh," I trill, "congratulations."

"Thanks, love. We're so happy. Come by, and we'll tell you all about the plans. And we have a special favor to ask of you," he says, winking. "What can I get you? It's on the house."

"The usual would be great. Can you make it chilled?"

"Can do," Vance calls out the order. "It's a scorcher out there." He hands me the drink, and I turn around, spotting the cowboy sitting in Zac's usual seat by the window.

Cary stands swiftly, suggesting his manners the other day were not just for show. "May I?" He opens his arms, gesturing a hug. I squint slightly and then nod. He greets me with a much lighter hug than the bone-crusher from Vance.

"Great to see you again," he says, settling back in his chair. Chuckling, he adds, "You must be a celebrity around here. I didn't get near the warm welcome."

"I've been coming here for years but have been MIA for several months. Vance and I have known each other since he was in high school and started working here. Now he's engaged to my doorman." I take a sip of my iced drink.

"Ah." Cary sounds uninterested in my friend's joyous news. I give him a pass, not wanting to judge him too harshly on our first date.

Cary and I spend an hour people watching and getting to know one another, both of us cautious about what we reveal. I feel safe at the M, and it's nice to be without Carolyn lurking; she's hardly left me alone since Seattle. But I'm careful not to go into personal details with Cary. I don't want this charming stranger to know where I live or my routine. Cary is also hesitant, although no doubt for different reasons, revealing little more than he works mostly out of town and loves God, country, and family in that order. He dodges most of my questions, with aloof answers, volleying his responses back to me as questions.

I make a mental note to have Matt check him out.

"I need to be getting back to my office," I say, checking the time on my phone.

"Right, I should too." Cary reaches out a hand to help me stand. I look at his upturned palm and pause before placing mine in it. He leans down, giving me another gentle hug. "I would like to take you out on a proper date if that's alright."

I swallow hard. "I would like that." A rush of nerves fills my stomach.

On the way back to the office, I text Matt. "Please do a personal and professional search on Cary Thompson. Around forty-five, tattoo, left forearm, U.S. flag. Sorry, that's all I have." I attach a covert picture Vance took for me and add a smiley face emoji for good measure. I then send a second text, "And he's a cowboy."

My phone vibrates with Matt's quick response. "That's helpful, NOT."

I chuckle and busy myself at the office, waiting for the intel, which comes in short order.

"Ms. Kincaid, Matt's on the line," Marta says, pleasant as always. "Thanks."

"Hey, Matt. That was quick. What did you find out?"

"Well, a lot, and not much. Your guy, Cary, is a bit of a ghost. He exists, and he *is* real, but he is not on the radar if you get my drift."

I don't. "I'm sorry, Matt, care to explain?"

"There is one blip I can find on the guy, which leads me to believe he is a contractor, perhaps a Department of Defense type of contractor. It would appear he's stationed both in San Francisco and North Carolina. He also works here in Boise for a tech firm, which is not only unusual but weird."

"Again, Matt, what does that all mean?"

"It means your Cary Thompson is a bit of an enigma. It appears he can be in three places at once."

"Are you sure it's the same guy?"

"Yes, I'm sure." His words are terse, taking my question as an insult.

"Thanks, Matt," I ooze, hoping the words act as a salve.

"Oh, Sera, one more thing," he says as I'm about to hang up.

"Yeah?"

"He's clean. Squeaky. It's like everything about him is fake or erased, witness-protection style. The only people who can do that are mafia and the government."

I wonder if Carolyn told Matt about what happened to me or if I'm reading into it.

"Thank you."

CHAPTER

25

It takes a few more times for me to be comfortable enough to be alone with Cary, insisting we meet in group settings and public areas instead. He is gracious and patient, and never pushy as I vet him. Without being told, he seems to understand my hesitation. He handles my timidity with kid gloves, placing a hand on the small of my back as an escort, waiting until the second date before asking to hold my hand—never more than a goodnight peck. But there's a controlling side to Cary that lies hidden just below the surface; I can feel it. I can see it smoldering, ready to rear its head, but he's very self-aware and pushes it back into its neat little cage. I chalk Cary's ugly side up to his mysterious life.

"Going away for the weekend with Cary?" Carolyn bolts into my office. She's back to her old self around me. I'm thankful, although sometimes I miss the days when she was more subdued and worried about my sensitivities.

"Yeah, he's taking me to Pendleton. He has friends in Oregon with a ranch, and we're going riding."

"So, you're now a cowgirl?" Carolyn asks.

"I guess." I dismiss her comment and continue kneading the back of my neck.

"Are you okay?"

"Yeah, just stiff."

"Are you going to be with other people?" Carolyn does her best to disguise her worry with a false tone lacking interest.

"Carolyn," I snap, "you don't know him. He's magnetic and powerful, mysterious, and elusive, and he makes me forget about Zac," I gush before I can stop myself.

The corners of her mouth lift. She sucks in a long breath and nods; she doesn't have to remind me that everything and everyone revolves around Zac.

———————

"How long have you known Cary?" one of his friends asks when we arrive.

The hair prickles on my neck. "Two months."

A smile passes amongst them, a look like that of the stable hand when we picked up the horses. He, too, gave me a sideways grin and avoided eye contact as I effused over how Cary and I met and how splendid things were going between us. I wonder now if I am but a mere blip on an otherwise roaming radar.

In our room, I take a deep breath and ask, "Why do all your friends ask me how long I've known you and then give me the eye?

"The eye? What's that?" Cary's tone is condescending and makes my gut tighten.

"Don't be smug. They look at me like I'm the village idiot. As if I'm the only one who doesn't know something. They look at me like a joke."

"Sera," his voice booms, "I refuse to defend myself to you or anyone else." I feel relief when Cary ends up too drunk for sex. I don't reveal I was going to sleep with him for the first time this weekend.

I bring up his behavior again when we leave Oregon.

"Cary," I say, my voice shaky and small, "I didn't appreciate the way you spoke to me yesterday."

"Oh, is that so?"

The nerve of this man. But I'm uncomfortable angering him, so I keep my thoughts to myself.

The ride to Boise is quiet, and Cary drops me at my door without so much as a "thanks for coming with me."

Cary's behavior is unpredictable, bouncing between happy and gloomy, secretive to transparent, which makes my life a rollercoaster of high-highs and low-lows. His gentle touches and wooing words around one corner and unexplained absences and dark moodiness around the next. One minute I am on a cloud of euphoria, then hurling toward the ground from insults. Cary is relationship suicide, yet I seek him like a moth to the light.

What is wrong with me?

———————

"Do you think I need Botox?" I ask Carolyn one evening as we share a bottle of red.

"What the hell kind of question is that? Is that Cary talking?" she says, outraged, as if she would never dream of such a procedure, although I know that's not the case.

"Well, yes, but maybe he's right." I study my brow in the living room mirror and trace the space between my eyes. "There is a line there."

"You're an attorney. Of course, there's a line in your brow."

"Maybe I should get bangs instead, to detract from the wrinkles."

"Okay, enough. This guy's a dick. I've seen Cary. Perhaps he should consider liposuction and hair implants," she snorts.

"Carolyn!" I try to act shocked, defensive for the man I'm dating, but wind up slapping my leg and laughing until tears run down my cheeks and I fall into a coughing spell.

"Seriously, though, what the fuck?" Carolyn says when my coughing subsides. "He can't change you, and you shouldn't let him. And where's Zac?" A strange bitterness seeps from her words.

"There's a first," I say, taking a sip from my glass. "Since when do you care about me and Zac?"

"And when the hell are you going to get that cough looked at?"

"Cough?" It's become such a part of me I stopped recognizing it as abnormal. But Carolyn is right about one thing, *where is Zac?*

———

Cary's gifts and comments begin to show their true strings-at-tached meaning, symbolic of what he thinks I needed to change. A few days ago, he handed me a glasses case. "These Versaces are a far cry better than those," he said, waving a hand and scoffing at my knockoffs resting atop my head. Then he told me, "Viv, at Nordstrom will outfit you more appropriately for our dates. My card is on file."

Another time Cary said, "I bought you a membership to a twenty-four-hour gym. Now there's no excuse." Cary was cunning with his insults. *Maybe Carolyn's right*, I think, running on the treadmill contemplating my new iPhone. I have yet to activate it, having reservations about using a digital device gifted from Cary. I don't put it past him to bug it or use it as a tracking device.

Cary had become cruel, mocking me in public, ridiculing my dress and the character lines on my face. He picked me up when I was insecure, scared, and lonely, and then reshaped me into what he wanted. Throwing my insecurities back at me is his power play. But I bought it all, hook, line, and sinker, just like the chameleon I am.

You need to bring this up in counseling, demands my rational self.

My demeaning counterpart replies, *and then what, give up Cary? No one else is here for you.*

I opt not to talk about Cary's changed behavior in counseling, and I stop revealing much to Carolyn. I want to be wanted. And strange as it is, I am falling in love with him.

Cary is out of town, not unusual for him, and I expect his call. Instead, he texts. "Meet me at the pub. I need to tell you something."

Dressed in a slinky, braless number Viv picked out, I order myself a vodka cranberry.

"And please bring a Pendleton, neat," I say to the bartender, hoping to please Cary with his favorite drink and my new attire, even though I thought it made me look a bit like a prostitute in the sports bar. I sit at a table and wait, feeling more vulnerable with each minute.

He's never late.

"Where are you?" I text when an hour passes.

No reply. I wait, nervous.

Is he going to tell me he loves me? Oh, God, am I ready for this? My leg jumps under the table. *Yes, I'm ready. I love him too.* The admission sends nervous tension through my innards.

Ten minutes later, Cary strolls in without apology.

He kisses the top of my head like my father used to do and walks past me to an empty table. He sits down, turns around and looks at me, waiting for me to follow. Embarrassed, I pick up our drinks and walk over to his table. He hands his untouched Pendleton with a smarmy look to the skinny little server with the pert ass and the high breasts.

I feel my ire rising.

"Have you heard of a Dark and Stormy?" he asks her.

She shakes her head and giggles.

Oh, God, to be twenty-one again. I roll my eyes and stew. *Am I now old and irrelevant?* I sip my vodka and swallow my jealousy.

Cary explains it is dark rum and ginger beer. He then turns to me and says, "I met a woman at the hotel bar last night who was drinking one. I asked if I could try it. Now I'm hooked."

I can barely breathe. "You tried some woman's drink? Did you even know her?" I ask, shocked at what I am hearing. My stomach sours.

Cary leans in and hisses, "Do not use an accusatory tone with me." His pupils are pinpoints. He leans back, smiling for the benefit of the bar patrons.

Stunned and terrified, I recoil and rage in silence. *I don't hear from you during the week, and now you tell me you're trying another woman's drink. What the hell?*

We eat and finish our drinks in relative silence. Without warning, Cary blurts, "I can tell you love me." He stares at me long and hard, "I could make you cry right now." He then stands abruptly and walks out the door.

But why would you want to? I watch him leave. *You love me, right?*

Like a dutiful, whipped puppy, I follow him back to his house. I've become accustomed to staying with him on the weekends. When I arrive, Cary is quiet and avoids me. I busy myself in the bathroom getting ready for bed.

"Sera," Cary's voice calls from the kitchen, "Did you forget to dry the sink?" he asks, pointing to the water droplets in the basin.

"Oh, sorry, I must have forgotten when I got a glass of water," I apologize, padding in from the bathroom.

"I've told you, if you don't dry the sink every time, you can't get the water spots out later."

"What the hell? Why are you treating me this way?"

"I'm going to bed," he says, turning off the lights, leaving me alone in the dark kitchen. I tiptoe into the bedroom, feeling my way, and slip under the covers. I chew at my lip, fuming.

———————

"I need to run. I have some work to catch up on." I gather up my things and toss them into my overnight bag. My eyes burn from no sleep. "And I feel flush. I think I may have had a fever last night." That part is true; I woke up in a sweat.

"That works. I need to pack and get ready for the week," Cary says. "Would you mind taking your saddle down to get the stirrup fixed? Here are the keys to the trailer." He hands me a wad of keys, ignoring the fact I just told him I'm not feeling well. Drawing me in, he looks deep into my eyes.

Do I see remorse?

"I need to tell you something," he says.

I hold my breath; *this is it.*

"Thank you, for everything." Cary lets out a long exhale and kisses me hard.

Disappointed and confused, my reply comes out as a question, "You're welcome?"

I dial Marta on my way to court. "After the hearing, I'm heading out to the Swenson's to take some photos. If Cary calls, please message me."

"Will do, Ms. Kincaid." I hope she doesn't hear the distress in my voice.

"Why aren't you answering my calls and texts, Cary?" I ask, looking at my phone, void of incoming texts and calls.

Sleep doesn't come that night as I toss and turn. I wonder about Cary's absence and his strange behavior over the weekend.

Why did he thank me instead of telling me he loved me?

I send him another quick text. "Hey babe, how are you?"

By Thursday, and with no responses, I call Cary again, this time trying a more formal approach.

"Hey, Cary, it's Sera. I'm not sure where the trailer is, so I can't pick up the saddle to take it to the shop. I hope everything's okay. Call me." I wince at the whine in my voice.

The weekend is long and painful. I vacillate between crying fits and rage, mystery fevers, and coughing spells. *What have I done to earn this silence? And how have I caught the flu in the middle of summer?*

In the wee hours, somewhere between late night and the crack of dawn, I realize I will never be enough for Cary. Just like with Hank, Clint, and even Zac, it seems. Though all those situations are different, they are completely the same, and it is so simple. No amount of changing clothes or sunglasses, getting Botox, a new haircut, learning to ride a horse, or even having a child will make me enough if I wasn't already enough. And I must be real with myself: Cary doesn't want *me*. I sob and like an addict reaching for his kit to shoot up; I grab my phone.

"Hi."

By mid-morning, I receive a response. "Hello."

Ah, the familiar nameless number powders my screen like cocaine.

"How are you?" I message back, impatient but understanding the parlay; it's been a while.

My phone vibrates. "I'm good. How are you?"

"I'm okay. Want to have lunch?" Lunch, of course, code for sex.

"Duh, LOL." The response is quick. "I'll swing by at 11:30."

———

I meet Zac for lunch in the parking garage, no food on the menu. I need to feel wanted and desired without explaining myself; Zac is the only person who can do that.

Curled into him in the backseat, warm with afterglow, I aimlessly trace the outline of a tattoo on Zac's arm. "So, how have you been?"

"Funny you should ask," he says, clearing his throat before continuing, "My roommate has asked me to be her Lamaze coach."

"What?" I jump as if hearing a rattlesnake, and twist around to face Zac. I grab my clothes and pull them to my chest, suddenly too vulnerable. "She's pregnant?" Bile burns my throat, and I cover my mouth, afraid I may vomit.

"It's not mine," he chuckles, as if that makes it all better.

I fumble with my blouse, feeling blotches of heat speckle my face. "I need to go back to work."

"Look, I'm sorry. I wanted to let you know, but it's not a big deal."

I freeze, "You're right, Zac, it's not a big deal. It's an enormous deal."

CHAPTER

26

C ary ghosted me. It had been almost two months since our last weekend together and it was time: I pull the wad of keys he had given me from my purse and stuff them in the back of a drawer in the kitchen, shutting them away with his memory.

———

"Excuse me, Miss, you dropped your tomato," a voice next to me interrupts my meandering.

"Thanks." I shake my head, trying to clear the cobwebs. *A bit of depression,* I rationalize making a note to check back in with my counselor about all this brain fog.

"Those little suckers are quick. They can jump right out of your basket, can't they?"

"I'm sorry?" I stare blankly at the stranger, not entirely understanding his humor and reach for the Roma in his hand.

Mister tomato man is small, with a petite build and sharp features. He's not handsome but not unattractive; I guess he might even be cute in a quirky sort of way. With his dark, angular features, he reminds me of a rat, but a cute one. I laugh to myself.

"Can I help you?" the rat asks. "You look a little lost."

"Oh, no thanks. I was just wandering the produce aisle."

"Well, I'm a frequent flyer here at the Co-Op. So, if you need anything, I'll be over there in the bulk food section." He points behind him as he walks backward, still staring and smiling at me. When he reaches the bulk foods, he hollers, a bit too loud, "My name's Phil."

I glance around and shrug at another shopper glancing in our direction.

"Nice to meet you. I'm Sera." I call out, weighing whether this is boyish good-nature or pure childishness—the former being okay, the latter not so much. Phil holds his hand high in the air and waves.

Yes, I see you. I return the gesture with a slight lift of my hand.

Oh, God, you are a juvenile—strike one.

I catch glimpses of Phil playing a game of hide and seek throughout the store, poking his head around corners and ducking behind end caps. His stalker behavior feels more sophomoric than threatening.

Loading my items onto the belt at the checkout stand, Phil sidles up behind me and whispers, "Looks like we meet again."

"Hmm, why am I not surprised?" I flash the cashier a catty grin, avoiding Phil's gaze. Then I mock, "Are you following me, sir?"

"Only a little," he replies and holds up a finger and thumb with an inch of space pressed between them. "I came here to shop. But since you dropped your tomato, I've been monitoring your movements in case something else drops, and you need assistance."

He puffs his thin chest, arms akimbo. His slight Superman stance causing both the cashier and me to roll our eyes.

I tap my card on the reader to pay for my groceries, pick up my bag, and walk away. Phil calls after me, his voice too loud for my liking, "Can I get your number?"

"I think not." I feign distress, the back of my hand to my forehead. "I don't know you or your intentions." I walk out the door and load my groceries into the white wicker basket on the front of my old Schwinn cruiser and begin the half-mile ride to my condo. Within minutes, a voice behind me calls out, "Miss, miss, you dropped your tomato!"

Laughing, I stop my bike and wait. "You're a hard lady to keep up with." He wipes imaginary sweat from his brow. "I would like to see you again, perhaps outside the produce aisle. Can I get your number?" He thrusts his phone toward me.

I pause and stare deep in his eyes, then take the phone, type in "Sera-Tomato" and my number, and make a mental note to reach out to Matt for some recon on this guy.

"You'll be hearing from me."

I know.

Within the hour, my phone pings and wakes me. The five-block ride from the Co-Op left me exhausted, a debilitating type of tired where my jaw fell slack. I left the groceries on the counter and curled up on the couch for a nap.

"Hello, miss. I have tickets to the Bare Naked Ladies at the Botanical Garden tomorrow night. Pick you up at seven? We can ride bikes. Phil."

God knows I need something in my life. With Zac now playing Lamaze coach to the roommate . . . why not?

"Thanks," I text back. "I'm at Building One-Nineteen" and add a second message: "As friends." I sniff the milk left out on the counter, shrug, rationalizing it's only been a little while, and place it in the fridge with the rest of the groceries.

———————

Matt's investigation of Phil uncovers him to be a drinker, convicted of a DUI seven years prior, a minor-in-possession ticket from the way-back days, and two dropped charges for being drunk and disorderly.

Okay, he likes to imbibe. Let's hope he's matured.

Seven o'clock comes and goes, then seven-thirty. By eight, I put on my reading glasses, curl up on the sofa, and start answering work emails. At eight forty-five, I call it a night.

Netflix and fuzzy jammies it is.

"Ms. Kincaid," Stefan buzzes, "I have an inebriated Phil here to see you. I'm not comfortable sending him up." Stefan sounds like an overprotective father.

So much for growing up.

"Thank you, Stefan. I've been expecting him. Please send him up. Oh, and Stefan?"

"Yes, Ms. Kincaid?"

"If I'm not down in five minutes, please come up and check on things."

"Already noted."

Phil pours in reeking of alcohol and cheap cologne; no doubt attempted cover-up. He looks like he's slept in his clothes.

"Hello, Miss," his words slur and he leans to one side,

counterbalancing by tilting his head the opposite direction. He blinks hard. "I apologize for the tardiness. I had a few beers and then fell asleep." I catch the gist of his garbled words; he still wants to go to the concert.

"Never keep me waiting like this again." My voice is low and steady. I point a finger in his chest, "And sit down before you fall. I need to change, again."

The two-mile bike ride to the venue in the brisk evening air gives me time to cool down. It also causes immense muscle fatigue.

We miss the two opening acts but catch The Bare Naked Ladies, a fully clothed group of five middle-aged men out of Canada. *Who knew?* The music is catchy, some of which I recognize from the radio, but most of the concert is a blur. I'm so tired that I lie next to Phil, passed out on a blanket, and sleep.

I wake as the concert wraps up, and rouse Phil, who jumps to his feet, clapping and whistling through his fingers as if he'd just witnessed the entire concert.

He's an odd one.

The bike ride home is quiet. Still drunk, Phil rides ahead of me, swerving from one side of the street to the other.

Is he doing that on purpose, or is he that piss drunk?

As quickly as the thought comes to my mind, Phil slams head-long into a parked Subaru. With a dull *thump*, he lands on his belly, splayed out on the car's hood, and skids over the roof, ending up in a crumpled heap in someone's front yard.

His bike bounces off the car and careens at me, its wheels entangling in mine. Arms outstretched I fall to the ground. Gravel digs into my palms and knees as I slide across the pavement, my cheek scraping the road. The handlebar strikes me dead center between the eyes. "Goddamn it." My eyes fill instantly with hot, furious tears.

"Miss, are you okay?" Phil stumbles to stand over me. Blood is pooling under his nostril, his hair tousled and there is a tear in his shorts. Swaying, Phil reaches down and grabs both sides of my head, steadying himself.

"Don't touch me," I snarl, batting his hands away. "And stop calling me, miss." I growl, wiping tears from my cheeks. "Just how many beers did you have?"

"Fourteen."

"Christ."

"My place is just around the corner," he slurs. "You can clean up there. I'll look at your bike," he says. The front wheel is bent. There is no riding it home.

"Fine," I huff, "but you are pushing it." I thrust it toward him, and he wrangles both bikes.

I limp behind him. Regardless of wanting to clean up, I need to pee and won't make it home. We come to a rundown doublewide with a dilapidated carport. Phil opens the low, chain-link gate leading into the unkempt yard and walks up the steps.

Serenade, what are you doing? I reach inside my cross-body bag and feeling the cold cylinder, wrap my fingers around it: pepper spray.

I will use his bathroom and leave.

"It's a little messy," Phil says, opening the door. The stench of cat urine and rotten food slap me in the face. Was it just me, or did Phil's goofiness suddenly turn twitchy, rodent-like? I step inside.

Good God, my little voice yells. I put my hand over my nose as a filter.

A lamp in the corner casts shadows over heaps of laundry on the couch. *Clean?* The kitchen counters overflow with mountains of food-crusted dishes and curdled milk-coated glasses. A beer tap rises out of the counter.

"What is that?" I point, my curiosity getting the better of me.

"Oh, you like? That's a kegerator." He sways and pulls his shoulders back proudly. "I installed it myself."

"A kegerator?"

"Yeah, a mini keg is cheaper than dozens of cans or bottles. My dishwasher used to sit there." He shrugs.

That explains the dishes.

"I need to use the bathroom," I say and shiver at the thought of what I'll encounter.

He turns on a heel, without a word, and walks to the back of the trailer; I follow. We pass what at some point I assume was an actual bathroom. Now, it looks more like a storage room filled with boxes and bags, and more piles of clothes. The smell of a filthy cat litter box and gym socks assault my senses, *a meth lab?*

"Do you have a cat?"

"No cat." He shakes his head and continues down the hallway. "Just me."

What the hell are you doing?

At the end of the trailer was the master bedroom suite, a stark contrast to the nastiness upfront. It's clean and modern with a king-sized bed, a love seat in front of a big-screen television, a computer desk and chair, and a mini-fridge. I am a little surprised there isn't a second kegerator.

I walk to the bathroom, and Phil calls after me, "The door doesn't lock; I don't believe in locked doors."

"Well, I do, so please stay out."

I twirl the lock mechanism in my fingers. It does not latch. I grip the pepper spray and hover over the seat.

Mid-stream, the doorknob jiggles and Phil flings the door open, falling inside.

"What the hell?" I yell.

"No locked doors," he says in his stupor.

"Get out."

"It's okay, miss, I can wait." He folds his arms, deliberately crosses one foot over the other, doing his best not to fall.

"Are you kidding me?"

"Nope. Relationships must be open, one-hundred percent." His words slur, and his thin lips curl: he has no intention of leaving.

"Relationship? Seriously?"

I look at the paper holder, its cardboard tube picked clean. I yank my panties up, forgoing the drip dry and the hand wash.

You need out of this creep's house, right now! Did you learn nothing in Seattle?

I shove Phil and push the pepper spray in his face as a warning. His small, drunk body folds easily into itself. He lands on top of the counter with a grunt. I sidestep him and bolt down the hall, past the stinky bathroom, the beer tap, and the pile of laundry on the couch. I am at the front door in record time, swing it open, manage the steps, and hobble for home, leaving my bike by the front door.

CHAPTER

27

I have a goose egg the size of Texas in the middle of my forehead, and dark, purple-black circles around both eyes. My face looks like a raccoon and unicorn mated; it's not pretty. I dab concealer around the bruises and throw on my most giant pair of sunglasses.

"Good morning, Miss Kinca . . ." Marta's voice trails off, and her smile wanes. I walk past her and into my office. When I reach my desk, I look at my phone to see both Marta and Carolyn's lines illuminated.

I slip off my sunglasses and count, "Three, two . . ."

"Oh, my Gawd!" Carolyn drawls as she runs through the open door.

"One."

"What in the name of Peter, Paul, and Mary happened to you?" Carolyn cups my chin, turning my head from side to side, inspecting the damage. "Are you okay?" her voice heavy with anger and concern.

"I'll be fine." I put my glasses back on my face.

"Who?" She pauses, resets, and starts again, "Did someone?" She is trying to remain calm.

"No one. I went to a concert with some guy—"

Carolyn flies into a rage: "Un-fucking-believable. Who is this dickhead?"

"I met him at the Co-Op."

She takes a breath to calm herself. "Did he hit you?"

"What? Oh God, no. No, nothing like that. He's an ignoramus, a complete drunk, maybe even a meth manufacturer, or a cat owner, I'm not sure which, but not an abuser. At least not that I'm aware. Not that Matt found out, no." I take a breath and clear my throat. "He was drunk as hell, rode his bike in front of me, and caught my front wheel with his. Nothing more, promise."

Carolyn stands with her fists on her hips, studying my swollen face. She narrows her eyes and purses her lips. "You are not going out with this guy again," she says, stamping her foot for effect. "Right?"

"I would have, maybe, probably, if I hadn't seen his house," I say, feeling compelled to be wholly honest, and then immediately regretting it.

"Are you kidding right now? You went to his house? And did you say meth dealer?" Her tone incredulous.

Marta shuts the door.

"Have you lost your mind?" Carolyn continues. "I mean, seriously, are you that dim?"

"I had to pee, you know, after the accident."

"You can't fix stupid." Disgusted, Carolyn huffs, "You need to call Zac. He'll get this idiot out of your head."

"Wow! Again, with Zac? He's *her* Lamaze coach."

"And?"

"You are joking."

"He told you it's a favor, it's not his, and they apparently aren't a thing, so why not Zac?"

"Look," I clench my teeth, "you think you know what's best for me, but you can't keep trying to run my life."

"Well, someone needs to take care of you."

"Fuck off."

"Brilliant."

There's an uncomfortable pause as we both stand our ground.

"Okay, here's the thing." Carolyn takes a deep breath, and I wait, assuming she'll apologize for her comments. "You need to get this out of your system, whatever *this* is." She flashes jazz hands. "If you can't be with Zac, then go screw a sailor, a guitarist in a band if that's your fancy, maybe a college boy would scratch your itch, whatever it takes, get it handled. But you can't just keep doing this. Haven't you been through enough?"

"Get out of my office." My tone is venomous.

Carolyn stands firm, red-faced, and proud.

The vibration of my phone ends our stalemate. The screen lights up with familiar words and no name. "Good morning."

And on cue, here you are.

I exhale and without thinking text an immediate, "Hello."

"Thank God for Zac," Carolyn says over her shoulder.

"How do you know it's Zac?" I ask defiantly.

"No one else makes you look like that," she says, wagging a finger in my direction. And like the blustery storm she is, Carolyn blows out of my office.

"How are you?" the message flashes on my screen.

Honestly? I'm awful. I have again picked a loser, have a golf ball growing out of my forehead, I have a chronic case of flu, and

I spend most of my time sitting around pining for you.

"I'm good. How are you? Had a baby yet?" I text, hoping I sound nonchalant.

Ten minutes pass before his reply. "Yes. A boy. Lunch?"

My heart falls to the pit of my stomach.

Why does he want to see me? Are they done? Are we? Do I give him farewell sex?

"Sure. When?" I can't avoid my drug.

"I'll pick you up downstairs. 11:30?"

"Great."

I pull out a mirror from my side drawer and look at my face. There is no way to cover the swelling or bruises. I will have to suck it up if I want to see him.

I run to the bathroom, gargle some mouthwash, and sniff my armpits—all good.

My phone vibrates. "Here."

"Marta, I'm off to lunch. I should be back before one." Nerves flutter in my belly as I hurry past my assistant's desk. I haven't seen Zac for some time and given that our relationship is one without definition or convention, I'm never sure where I stand with him. Not a girlfriend, yet more than just a friend with benefits. But to what degree this means, I have no clue. And now there is an Anne, and a baby.

What am I doing?

I push open the door to the building and relax at the sight of the familiar truck waiting for me.

"Hello, darlin'," he says as I climb into the lifted pickup. Shock washes over his face, "What the hell happened? Are you okay?"

"Bike accident. I'm fine." While my words sink in, I glance at his

214

left hand as discreetly as possible; *still bare. Is he a ring-wearing kind of guy? Would he take it off around me?*

"Mexican?"

"Sure."

We drive in silence to a place we once agreed was our favorite, back when I thought there might be a chance for us. It's a dingy, hole-in-the-wall in the basement of a haughty nightclub. The nightlife's stench weighs heavy in the seat cushions and velvet drapes, but the food is authentic.

"How have you been?" Zac asks. "I mean besides the bike accident."

"I'm good, really." I give what I hope is a convincing smile. "Now, what about this little guy?"

Zac beams. "He's healthy and ugly as hell. All babies are," he laughs. "Cries all the time, but it's an amazing experience." He speaks with the far-off awe I've seen in other parents' eyes as they gush about their children.

Zac seems pensive, as if he wants to tell me something, but he takes a bite of his deep-fried chimichanga instead and fills the awkwardness with polite conversation.

What is it, Zac? I beg in silence. We eat and chat as my tension grows.

"I need to use the restroom." I say at the end of the meal, leaving Zac to settle the check.

The door squeaks as I'm flushing the toilet; there are heavy footsteps approaching, and a jolt of excitement thrills me as I see the familiar male shoes stop outside my stall. I unlocked the door, and Zac pushes it inward. He wears a mischievous, wanting grin.

He leans down and kisses me with intensity, the back of my head rests in his palm and he laces his fingers through my hair, pulling my head back to expose my throat. He runs his tongue up my neck and onto my lips, licking them, feather soft. His breath burns hot on my skin.

"We shouldn't," I whisper into Zac's neck.

He looks disappointed. "Why not?"

"B-but, what about . . ." I can't seem to say the words, *Anne and the baby*.

He reads my mind. "I've told you, it's not what you think."

Then tell me what it is, I silently beg.

He pulls me playfully by my wrist, ushering me to the sink, and lifts me onto the counter. I rest on my elbows as he crouches, lowering on top of me; excitement and fear of being caught rush through me. "Jesus," he mutters, kissing my lips, "I've missed you."

CHAPTER

28

This weekend is my turn to host Carolyn. Since the Seattle event, we've taken turns staying with each other on the weekends; unless, of course, either of us are on a date, which lately isn't often the case. I found a funny movie to watch and plan for us to hit the Saturday farmer's market. Sunday, my agenda is to spend time with Vance and Stefan to discuss any last-minute touches for their wedding. As their "best person," I want to ensure nothing is overlooked. I'm just finishing warming up the takeout dinner when Carolyn pops in; she no longer needs Stefan's blessing, since I gave her a key.

"Hey girl," she sits down with a bottle of wine in her hand, "what's for dinner?"

"Brick 29," I take a deep breath and add, "Take out. I know it's where you and Jeremy used to go when you were . . . when he was . . ." I stumble, hesitate a moment, and then continue, ". . . in the good old days." I say the words gently. Jeremy is still a painful subject for Carolyn, even months after their breakup. "I know it's your favorite," I continue, "and you need to move beyond this weird food hang up; it wasn't the food, or the place that, well . . ."

She squints her eyes, and I can see the Jeremy subject is off limits and closed.

"And before you ask, I'm still reading those self-help books. I am trying, on all fronts, including being a better friend."

"What's the occasion?" she asks, a forced-happy tone in her voice. "For the food, I mean."

"No occasion, just goodwill." I keep my smile and wait, holding two plates.

She looks up at me and whispers, "Thank you."

We eat and drink, and as always, our conversation comes around to men. "So, let me ask you," I say, then take a healthy swallow of wine, "how did you come to date your professor?"

She shrugs. "Easy, I needed to pass my contracts class. He was handsome and I was between guys, and that was that."

"Well, that's boring as hell."

"Okay, your turn." And so began a rousing "never have I ever" game of dating confessions.

"Did I ever tell you that Phil had a kegerator in his kitchen in place of a dishwasher?" I divulge, biting the side of my bottom lip.

"Now, which one was Phil?"

"Mister tomato?" I'm a little disappointed the impact of my statement is getting lost in the minutia of Phil's identity. "Ratface?" I offer.

"Oh, right. The alleged meth dealer."

"Manufacturer," I correct. "And probably not."

"But that's not shocking, the kegerator thing. He was the biggest drunk."

"You're right."

There is a pause and then Carolyn says, "Jeremy and I did it in the back of a horse-drawn carriage, riding through Central Park."

I squeal, "Shut up. That's hot."

We laugh, clink our glasses together, and drain them. I walk into the kitchen and uncork another bottle.

"Oh, I've got one." I pour Carolyn another glass. "Guess who I saw when I went to the horse track the other night?"

Carolyn looks blank.

"Cowboy Cary." I gulp my wine, and then cough into my elbow.

"Shut the hell up," Carolyn says. "The ghoster? Did you punch him in the face?"

"No. But I wanted to."

"I would have." I see her wheels turning. "Did he look good?"

"Yes, wearing his perfect boots and his perfect jeans and that damned hat."

"You loved the hat."

"I know." Sighing, I take another drink and clear my throat.

"So, what about him?"

"Who?"

"Cary. You just saw mister almost-perfect, whom you were mad for, that usually equates to you starting up again with that person." Carolyn's voice has a sour edge to it as she waits for the details.

"There's nothing to say. What Cary did was unacceptable, and I'm worth more than that." Tipsy, my words come out slow and deliberate, making them seem weightier.

"I'm glad to hear that."

"Thanks," I whisper, wondering if I am worth more.

"So, are we good?" Carolyn asks, sounding hopeful.

"We're good. You're right. I'm a mess."

"You aren't such a mess anymore." She swirls her glass,

watching the wine roll. "You're much better." And then she offers, "How's Zac?"

"He's unavailable this weekend."

"Oh, with the roommate and the little guy?"

"He didn't say. I didn't ask." I drain my glass and clear my throat.

"I made an appointment for you," Carolyn catches me off guard.

"You did what?" I ask. "Why? With whom?"

"Your cough, and with Meg." She holds up her hand to stop my impending missile launch. "Hear me out. Unless you have tuberculosis, you shouldn't have had a cough this long. There's something not right. I called Meg, and you see her Wednesday at ten." She sounds sheepish, almost afraid of how I'll respond.

I draw in a breath, careful not to take in too much in case I cough and prove her point. "Thank you for looking out for me, but I feel fine. It's just allergies. And, why Meg? She's an OB/GYN doctor."

"She's the only one I could get you in with at short notice; I pulled the friend card." Carolyn looks even more sheepish.

"I just saw her."

"You did? When?"

"Jesus, Carolyn."

"Look, I'm worried. You've had this cough for months. When did you see Meg?"

"After the—well, you know . . ." My voice trembles at the memory of Rodney. "She ran blood work and said I was fine." I lie. Meg had not run blood work.

"I didn't know you saw her after that." Carolyn sounds hurt, as if she's the last to know a secret.

"I don't tell you everything," I say, grabbing the remote.

"I suppose not."

I see disappointment in her eyes, and I avoid them, saying, "I was pregnant."

Carolyn jerks and then places a hand on mine, "What?"

I nod. "I lost it."

"Oh, honey."

I pull my hand back slowly, and we sit in silence. I focus on the shadows from the streetlights filtering into the room.

"I'll go to the appointment," I say after long minutes, and push the play button on the remote. I reach out to touch Carolyn's wrist gently. "Thanks."

———————

I roll out of bed on Monday morning, nauseous and clammy after another night of sweats.

Damn menopause.

"Good morning, Ms. Kincaid," Stefan says as I step from the elevator into the lobby. "Early day at the office?"

"I thought I'd walk over to the M, grab a coffee, and catch up with your soon-to-be hubby."

Stefan blushes and gives me an excited, full-teeth smile. The mention of his upcoming nuptials causes an immediate shift from polite, restrained concierge to giddy child. "Just a couple more weeks." He claps his hands and starts doing some sort of run-in-place dance.

"It will be beautiful." I smile and walk to the door. "Have a great day, Stefan." I step outside and shiver, pulling my sweater tight. The weather forecaster called it a "temperate" day, but it feels chilly to me.

Vance meets me at the door of the M. Like Stefan, he does a happy dance at the mention of his upcoming wedding. "Oh. My. God," he says, beaming. "It's so close."

Thrilled, he grabs me by the shoulders and pulls me into him. I fall in time with his jig, pull back to catch my breath, and start a fit of coughing—Vance's demeanor shifts on a dime.

"Sera Jean, when are you going to the doctor?" he demands, standing over me with his hands on his hips.

"How do you know my middle name?" I ask, more concerned about this than his meddling.

Vance dismisses my comment with a *pfft* and a flick of his wrist. He walks me to my favorite table, telling its inhabitants, "I need you to move." His face sincere, he says, "This is an emergency." Vance shoots me a look, and on cue, I cough. The patrons scoop their mugs from the table and leave in disgust. Vance and I sit.

"Well?" he asks, snapping his fingers toward the young barista behind the counter who scurries over with a glass of water.

"I see Doctor Meg on Wednesday." I sip the water and dab at my face, feeling flushed.

Vance puts the back of his hand to my forehead, then leans in, kissing it the way my mother once did. "No temperature, but you don't look well."

Damn mystery fever.

"I don't feel well, Vance," I confide.

I rest a few minutes, order two coffees to go, one for me and one for Carolyn, and make my way to the office, stripping my sweater to cool off.

At my desk, scrolling through the barrage of morning emails, my cell phone vibrates, lighting up without a name, "Lunch?"

"Who's that? Zac?" Carolyn asks, flopping into her usual chair. She grabs the coffee and a pen and begins doodling on a sticky note.

I contemplate, but only for a second. I'm feeling better now, so I text, "Sure. Where?"

"What did you end up doing Sunday?" Carolyn asks, still drawing.

"Oh, not much, just watched reruns of *I Love Lucy* and ate popcorn."

Concentrating on her masterpiece, Carolyn doesn't see the deceit on my face; I had slept all day.

"Any new prospects?" Still, she doesn't look up from the paper.

"Nope."

"Lunch with Zac?" She stops her drawing and looks at me as if she just read my text exchange.

"Maybe." I smirk and clear my throat.

She laughs. "Girl, why don't you just stop this charade and get on with him? You two are already in a quasi-relationship."

"I can't." My tone is more bitter than I want it to be as I add, "He's living with the hairstylist and her baby; you remember the Lamaze girl?"

Carolyn snorts, "He's got a hairstylist?"

"For hell's sake, Carolyn, we've been over this. Yes, Zac has a hairstylist." My tolerance wanes.

Carolyn stops laughing. "They're living together? That's an enormous deal."

"Yeah, that's an enormous deal."

"How did you find out?" she asks.

"Matt. A while ago."

"Why didn't you tell me he was living with her?" Carolyn sounds hurt.

"I knew you wouldn't approve if I kept seeing him."

"Do you?" she counters.

I shake my head.

Carolyn shrugs, "Can't be too serious if he hasn't married her. He's not married, is he?"

"I don't think so."

"Jesus." She's quiet for a moment, and then I watch a devilish grin spread across her face. "Well, enjoy what you've got. You get good sex without having to put up with relationship crap."

I wouldn't mind relationship crap.

She stands to leave. "See you after lunch. I want details."

So much for our file review.

The vibration of my phone and its message make me smile. "Meet me in the stairwell at 11:30." My knees go weak. Zac may be unhealthy for me, but he's always exciting. The mere thought of him causes a tickle in my panties.

I futz around the office, anxious for our rendezvous. At eleven twenty-five, I rush into the bathroom, check my breath, sniff my armpits, and confirm there's no food in my teeth. I spritz my hair with eau de toilette and add a dab of pink-tint lip gloss.

"Marta," I say, walking toward the exit sign leading to the stairwell, "I'm out for an early lunch."

I push the door open, and my pulse quickens. We've played this game before, an adult version of hide-and-seek. I look for him as he hides, ready to grab me, scoop me up, and ravish me.

Do I go up or down? I listen for any movement, but the only thing I hear is my heart pounding. A gum wrapper lies on a step leading toward the rooftop. I take it as a sign and climb the stairs. One flight, two flights; no sign of Zac.

My pulse races, and it crosses my mind that I need to hit the gym. I have zero stamina. A large, familiar hand covers my mouth, stifling my excited yelp, interrupting any other thoughts. Another hand scoops me up by the waist and pushes me gently against the wall, facing away from him. I feel the rough, scratchy brick on my cheek. The safe, familiar scent distinct to Zac fills my nose. He reaches under my skirt, his breath hot on my skin.

"Mmm," he mumbles between nibbles and kisses on my neck and shoulders. I know the feel of his purposeful stubble. I hear his zipper, feel his warmth, and our bodies begin to move together.

The sound of an opening door freezes us. We hold our breath and wait for the metal to bang shut, its echo filling the stairwell. The sound of footsteps lessens. The intruder has left. I let out a nervous giggle. Zac pulls my panties up and my skirt down and whispers, "Don't turn around."

My legs wobble as I gather myself. When I turn around, Zac is gone. I make my way back to my office and find a takeout bag from Mazzah's, my favorite Greek restaurant in Boise, sitting on my desk. Inside is a chicken gyro (he knows I am not a fan of lamb), three dolmas with tzatziki sauce, and a side of hummus and pita chips.

Marta shuffles in, "I'm sorry, Ms. Kincaid, he left this too," she hands me a note that reads, "Thank you for lunch. Now eat; you've gotten way too thin." At the bottom of the words is the letter Z.

CHAPTER

29

Wednesday morning, I call Marta on my way to my doctor's appointment. "Hi, Marta, I have a girly exam today." I can hear her blush through the phone. "I'll be in before lunch."

"Hi Sera, good to see you," Meg says, walking into the room flanked by Tia. Meg leans in and gives me a friendly hug. "How are you doing?"

"I'm good, thanks, Meg. How are you?" I nod a quick hello to Tia, who gives a little wave in return.

"Oh, I'm doing great," Meg says, warming up her stethoscope between her palms. "Same old thing, delivering babies and looking at coochies." We all laugh at her pet name for vaginas. Meg then turns all business. "So, how are you, medically speaking? Anything we need to talk about?" She looks over the top of her glasses.

"I know Carolyn called you," I say, feeling and sounding defensive. "I have a cough. It's allergies."

"I'll be the judge of that," she says. "Still seeing Zac? Using condoms?"

"Yes. No. Sometimes."

"Anything ever going to come of that?" she asks, putting the stethoscope to my lungs. "Deep breath," she pauses, moves the device, and says, "Again."

"Zac? No. He's now living with the Lamaze girl. Do you remember me telling you about that?" I pull back and suck in a deep breath through my teeth. "Oh, God," I say, my eyes big as saucers, "did you deliver her baby?"

"Yes. What? No," she babbles at my string of questions. "Yes, I remember the Lamaze story. And now he's living with her? Damn." Meg shakes her head. "And no, I didn't deliver Zac's non-baby momma." She leans in and whispers, "I didn't tell you that."

Tia's shoulders shake as she stifles a giggle.

"The situation isn't all bad," I say with a non-convincing chuckle. "I don't have to put up with any relationship crap, and I still get to have great sex with him." My chuckle causes a coughing spell, followed by a round of throat clearing.

"How long has this cough been going on?" Meg asks.

"A few months, maybe more," I tell her, sensing it crucial I be honest.

Meg flattens my tongue with a depressor and, peering into my mouth, exclaims with utter surprise, "Holy hell, girl, those are some big-ass tonsils."

I pull my head back and stare, dumbfounded, terrified. "I had my tonsils removed when I was a kid." The air grows heavy. I feel queasy.

Meg reaches for the metal stool reserved for doctors, sits down, and places her hands on my neck, palpating up and down, front, and back. "Swallow," she instructs, her fingers pressing both sides of my throat. She stares over my shoulder at a random point on the wall, concentrating on the flesh beneath her fingers. "Do you have tightness or fullness in your throat? Difficulty swallowing, feeling like food gets stuck?"

"Yes." I attempt to minimize the symptoms and their severity with a Carolyn-style wrinkle of my nose.

Meg's fingers palpate the soft tissue beneath my chin, the length of my throat. A pianist running scales up and down my neck, spreading her fingers apart, taking expert measurements without a ruler, calling them out to her scribe, Tia.

"Half a centimeter left quadrant, two o'clock position." Pause, more palpating. "One centimeter, left, three o'clock." Meg's fingers run over the same area just behind my ear once, twice. She takes a deep breath, turns to Tia, and says, "The left chain is wholly involved." Meg turns back to me, the corners of her upward curved lips failing to mask the dread in her eyes.

"What?" I ask, my lower lip quivering.

"Shh," she says, closing her eyes, drumming out a tune on the back of my head and the soft spaces between the side of my neck and my clavicle. "Lift," she instructs as she palpates one armpit and then the other.

She's close enough to feel the heat of her breath and smell her familiar essence, an unusual combination of sweet musk and latex gloves. It both comforts and puts me on edge. The quiet room grows small, and my anxiety intensifies. The pounding of my heart drowns out Meg as she calls out sizes and locations: "One point five centimeters left clavicle, zero point nine, mid-position, left axilla."

Meg completes her examination of my body and addresses me, her words deadpan, almost accusatory, "How long have your lymph nodes been enlarged, Serenade?"

She used my full name. My mouth is instantly dry and my tongue sticky. I whisper truthfully, "They're new . . . ish," and add a qualifying, "A few weeks . . . ish." I swallow, "It's not allergies?"

I stare at Meg, willing her to dispel my fear. She remains silent.

"I figured it was the high pollen count or something." My eyes brim with tears.

"Why didn't you call me?" Meg scoots the stool back, holding my hands in hers. Fear and hurt flood her face.

"I didn't want to bother you." Hot tears are now streaking my cheeks, and I wipe furiously at them. "You're a lady doctor—you know, babies and coochies."

"Sera," Meg's tone is void of its usual vibrato, "I'm not just a doctor, I'm your friend. You can call me. You're supposed to call me." She's gentle with her chastisement. She throws a nod in the counter's direction and asks, "Anything else? Nausea? Fatigue? Night sweats?"

Tia hands me a tissue as the dam breaks. I swallow hard, "Yes," I mouth, "all the above."

"Tia," Meg leans into her nurse, "please order a CT for Sera, head and neck." Meg's voice is calm, doctorly. "Stat, please."

"Meg, come on," I beg. "What's the big deal?" Tears continue to rain.

"Sera, you have night sweats, fatigue, and nausea. You have multiple swollen lymph nodes, several over one centimeter, and your thyroid feels wonky. None of this is normal."

"Wonky?" I cling to the word, avoiding the others. "Is that a clinical term, doctor?" My words come out snarky, desperate.

"It means I'm not sure. Your thyroid is different—atypical, to put it clinically," she says, sounding perturbed. "It might be nothing. Maybe an infection or a thyroid issue, but you're presenting with unusual symptoms. I also want to draw some labs, a full panel, check your white blood cell count and thyroid function. We'll get that done now and do the CT within the next day or two. Once I have all the results, we'll get back together to go over everything. Okay?"

Dazed and unable to speak, I sit mute and nod.

"Tia will call you to set everything up. Okay?" She pauses, holding my stare, and then lightening the mood, says, "Now, let's check out that coochie of yours, make sure everything's good downstairs." She smiles, a failed attempt at reassurance. I dab my eyes dry and lie back on the paper, its crunching noise reminding me of my breast cancer scare and my recent miscarriage. I put my feet in the stirrups and stare at the empty ceiling.

—————

My appointment over, I step out of the building's elevator and into the medical complex.

Where do I go now? Do I call someone? Who? Carolyn? No, she'll drive me crazy with too many questions. Zac? I laugh when his name pops into my head; *he's only your hook-up*—my inner voice sounding bitter to my ears. Mom is out of the question. *You rely on yourself.* The robust, comforting voice in my head is my dad's; he's with me in the shadows.

My feet sense my inability to decide where to go, take control, and walk me in the opposite direction of my office. I wrap my sweater tight around myself and shiver in the ninety-degree heat. Aimless, I walk down Idaho Street and cross the busy intersection onto Warm Springs Avenue with the historic, colonial-style homes where I once dreamed of raising a family. I am numb. Has my body betrayed me and allowed something sinister to take up residence? I keep walking.

The vibration of my phone startles me, and I realize I am lost on a side street. Tia's sweet voice on the other end tells me matter-of-factly, "Your scan is tomorrow morning at eight-thirty."

There is another vibration and I look at the screen; it's Carolyn. "Well?" I close the message.

CHAPTER

30

The lady sitting across the desk at the imaging center greets me. "May I help you?"

"I'm Serenade Kincaid. I'm here for a CT." My mouth is suddenly void of spit and my words come out tacky and clipped.

"Yes, I see you here," the receptionist says. She is standoffish but not unpleasant. "Please spell your last name and tell me your date of birth."

This annoys me because she can see these details on her computer screen; but I comply.

"Thank you," she says, still looking at the screen.

"Did I pass?" I ask. I sound sarcastic and somewhat bitchy.

"Have you had a CT before?" she asks, unfazed, still wearing her much-too-practiced smile.

"No."

"Okay. Someone will come and get you in a few minutes and explain the entire process to you. Do you have your insurance card?"

I hand over the card, wait for her to scan it, and then find a chair apart from the others in the waiting room, willing myself not to make eye contact, fearful of their conditions, worried about mine, overwhelmed and alone. My phone vibrates. Carolyn has reached out six times since my appointment yesterday, and I have yet to respond with much more than a "Busy. Nothing definitive to report. Will call later." I just can't do Carolyn right now.

"Serenade?" A kind-looking young man in scrubs who doesn't seem old enough to be carrying the clipboard, calls for me. "Hi, my name's Austin. I'll be taking care of you today. Please spell your last name for me."

"K-i-n-c-a-i-d, and it's Sera."

"And your date of birth?"

"I just—"

I begin to complain, but this man stares at me, his sparkling blue eyes demanding an answer. I avert my gaze and tell him my birth date. He's got the type of face romance novelists obsess over: square-jaw, clean-shaven, and young enough that the woes of the world haven't yet knit his brow. In any other setting, I would have thought him handsome.

"Great," he says. "Please use one of these changing rooms. Take off anything with metal, including your bra if you have an underwire, and put on these scrubs." Austin hands me a well-worn, faded blue top and matching bottom that smells of disinfectant.

"Once you've changed, please have a seat out here," Austin points to the two rows of chairs outside of the dressing room. I watch him disappear through a large, thick door emblazoned with giant red letters stating the words RADIATION, AUTHORIZED PERSONNEL ONLY. Dizzy, I pull the curtain, swallow hard, and change into the old pajamas.

My naked reflection in the mirror is startling. *How long have I been this thin?* My belly is concave, and my ribs pronounced; I run my fingers up them. I turn away, grab the shirt, and pull it down to cover my nakedness. *You're just stressed.*

Outside the curtained area in one row of the chairs sits a disheveled, unkempt man with a scruffy beard, whose head looks too heavy to hold up on its own; he cradles it with both hands. Opposite him, a haggard, hunched woman struggles to breathe through a nasal cannula attached to a portable oxygen tank. Both are disinterested in me and more focused on their woes and their own survival. I sit next to the man. *Good God, is this my future?*

The seconds are long, and the minutes creep. The unpadded chair is uncomfortable, and my tailbone wants to cut through my skin. I shift like an impatient child. An attendant takes away the man next to me, leaving me to endure the woman's wheezing—her struggle a reminder that things could worsen.

Thank you, God, that my health is better than hers. I immediately reel with guilt.

"Serenade?" the square-jawed Austin calls. "Come on back." He sounds like a game show host. "This way." He waves his hand toward the door with the big red lettering. I follow.

"It's just Sera."

He smiles dismissively. He has no intention of personalizing this. "Have you ever had a scan?"

"No." I'm nauseous. *Maybe I should reschedule.*

"Okay. No need to worry. It doesn't take long and is painless." The young man's perfect smile cannot calm my nerves. "We're doing a head and neck CT today, correct?"

I release a nervous chuckle. "Yes, but this is all a mistake. There's nothing wrong with me."

His smirk tells me he has heard similar desperation.

You can leave, Serenade. Just stand up and walk out the door.

"I need to start an IV to push dye through during the second half of the scan, okay?" Austin wraps the tourniquet around my arm and thumps at my vein, not waiting for my response. "Tiny stick," he says. I take in a small breath and turn my head.

"Dye?" I'm overwhelmed and incapable of forming a complete sentence.

"For contrast," he says, finishing the IV and covering the entry point with sterile tape. "It will give a better picture for the doctor. It won't hurt," he reassures me, "but you will feel some heat in your throat and a sensation as if you have wet yourself."

"Wet myself?" My eyes open to their widest.

"Don't worry," Austin says with his kind smile, "it will only *feel* as if you wet yourself."

"I'm not sure that's comforting."

There's still time. I contemplate ripping the needle out of my arm and running out.

"I'll talk you through the entire process; no surprises, I promise. Questions?" The young man pauses, still wearing the unwavering doll-like smile.

Questions? I repeat in my head. *Yes,* I want to scream.

Why am I here? Seems an excellent place to start.

What have I done to deserve this? A great follow-up.

Want to run away with me?

Keeping my thoughts to myself, I inch to the edge of the table, poised to escape. Through my haze, I hear my name repeatedly called.

"Serenade? Serenade?" My gaze leaves the door and, following the voice, I track the room until my vision focuses on Austin. Concern has replaced his perma-grin.

Has he been speaking to me?

"I'm sorry, yes, I mean no," I gush, "I have no questions." Austin helps me back onto the metal table lined with paper, *always crinkly paper*. He tucks a warm blanket around me.

"I'll be on the other side of that window," he says, pointing to what looks in my world as an observation window to an execution.

The machine begins its rotation with a whir.

Alone, my thoughts race, looking back to when I first noticed my cough, throat clearing, exhaustion, and fatigue. *How long have I been feeling ill? How long has my body been failing me?* The whirring comes faster, like a turbine engine ramping up, ready to take off. *Whir, whir, whir.*

"Lie still." Austin's voice booms over the intercom. "The computer voice will tell you when to hold your breath and when to breathe. Here we go."

My heart races as the bed slides into the tube. An automated voice, cold, sterile, says, "Do. Not. Breathe." I hold my breath. "Breathe," it commands, and I exhale. A few more times, I am instructed to hold my breath and then breathe as the whirring, thumping, and spinning continues around me.

The table slides out from its tube, and the machine slows. "Almost done," Austin says through the microphone. "Now, I will push the dye. You'll feel warmth in your throat, and you'll get that sensation I told you about, as if you are peeing."

The bed moves back inside the tube, and I am greeted with a warm, liquid sensation that floods my nether region and lights my throat afire.

Oh, my God, I've peed.

I gasp.

Austin's voice fills my ears. "You're doing great, Serenade. Don't move."

The computer drones, "Do. Not. Breathe."

My panic reaches a fever pitch; I need to call out to stop the machine. *There is a problem—my throat hurts. The device is malfunctioning, the red laser light is searing through my neck.* I expect to smell burned flesh.

"Breathe." The flat tone instructs. I exhale, panting, trying to regain my composure. "Do. Not. Breathe." I hold my breath, and tears slid down my cheeks, pooling in my ears.

"You're doing great, Serenade. Fifteen more seconds," Austin's voice soothes.

Hurry, hurry, it's burning me!

"Five, four, three, two, you're done. You can relax now, Serenade." The table slides out from the tube. The intense pain in my throat and the peeing sensation dissipates. I reach up to my neck and down to my crotch: no wounds, no urine.

"You did the right thing by coming in," Austin says, unhooking the IV. "There are remarkable advances in medicine, and we are here to help you." He walks out, leaving the door open and his words hanging.

What the absolute hell?

CHAPTER
31

My phone is face down on my desk, ominous. It seems an eternity since I lay terrified on the metal bed, listening to the whir and thump of the CT machine. I flip the phone over; only three hours have passed, still no word.

The results will come when they come.

Marta buzzes in, jolting my frazzled nerves. "Peter Landry is here."

"Thank you. Please show him to the small conference room."

Peter is a sweet, older man who made quite a fortune making and selling homemade candies and is here to get his affairs in order. Mr. Landry loves his children and his third wife but wants to protect them from each other and themselves. That's why he's hired me.

After my meeting, I drop the Landry file in Marta's in-basket, complete with my cryptic scribbling on a yellow sheet of paper clipped to the top. I pause, struck by the thought of how astute Marta is in interpreting my chicken scratch. I'm overcome by a sense of clarity, as if seeing Marta for the first time. My unflappable, skilled, and kind assistant.

Have I ever really noticed her? Do I thank her enough for her exemplary performance? Only a few hours have gone by since my surreal event, but something's changed within me. A perspective shift—there is more to life than just *me*.

"Thank you, Marta," I say, "for all you do."

She looks up at me, confused. There is an uptick to her words, "You're welcome?"

———————

At my desk, I stare at the backside of my phone, my hand trembling as I turn it over. The glow of the red light shows a missed call. I reach back for my chair, the blood draining from my face. I touch the voicemail button, take a deep breath, and say a quick prayer.

"Hi Sera, it's Tia. Can you please call me when you get this?"

"Shit," I mumble.

"Shit, what?"

"Jeee-sus," I draw out the word as I catch my breath. "Can you knock?" I yell.

"Whoa, what's going on?" Carolyn stops short.

"Nothing."

"Oh, really, miss snappy pants? What are you not telling me? You see Meg yesterday and avoid me with any update, and you're out this morning, and now you're gloomy and barky as hell."

"I don't know. Nothing. Maybe something. I had a scan today," I blurt, clicking my pen at a blistering pace. It feels good to say the words.

"What?" She rushes to the door and slams it with a bang hard enough to rattle the pictures. "Why didn't you say something?"

"What am I supposed to say, that Meg thinks there may be something wonky with my thyroid?"

"Wonky?" Carolyn smiles wryly. "Okay, so, now what?" she asks, serious again.

"I have a voicemail from Meg's office."

"And?"

"And what?"

"And what did the voicemail say, Sera?"

"I don't know." I lower my voice and give a more succinct answer, "I'm supposed to call Meg's office."

"Oh, for fuck's sake. Let me see that." Carolyn snatches the phone out of my hand. "What's your password?"

"I'm not giving you my password." I grab my phone back. "Damn it. You're such a pain in my ass."

I tap a few random places on my screen, as if I have a password.

I dial Meg's office and ask for Tia. Carolyn pantomimes her request to have the call put on speaker; I oblige.

"Hi, Sera," Tia's voice echoes through the phone. "We got your CT results back. Dr. Delane, Meg, would like to see you at three-thirty." Her tone clearly says this is not a suggestion.

"Yes." Carolyn leans over my desk and into the phone. "She'll be there."

Tia pauses. "Sera, are you there?"

"Yes, Tia, I'm here. That was Carolyn."

"Oh, hey, Carolyn. It's been a while."

"Hello. Yes, it has." Carolyn replies, disinterested in chit-chat.

"So, three-thirty works?" Tia asks.

"Yes," I answer.

"I'm going with you," Carolyn announces as I end the call.

"No, you're not."

"I'm going. You don't have to want me there, and you can drive alone if you'd like, but I'll be there, even if I sit in the waiting room." She storms out, leaving me alone to wonder about her huffiness.

———————

I walk into the clinic and check in, seeing Carolyn sitting in the waiting room, flipping through a magazine.

I sit next to her.

"Hey," Carolyn refuses to raise her eyes, thumbing through the pages anxiously.

"Good articles?"

"You can be so stubborn," she flings the magazine on the side table next to her.

"Why are you so pissed?"

"I'm not, well, maybe a little. I get that you are a strong, independent person, but I'm your friend." Carolyn's eyes are watery, "I'm mad because I don't want to lose you like I lost my mom."

"And I didn't say anything because I didn't want to dredge up everything you went through with your mom."

"I want to be here for you, Sera."

"Thanks. I want you here too." I give her a smile.

"I wouldn't have missed it," she whispers, placing a hand on my knee and giving it a light squeeze. "I love you." She sounds almost put out by the words, as if they might be used against her in the future. She wipes the corner of her eye with her thumb and picks up the magazine again.

"Sera?" Tia calls from across the waiting room.

I look at Carolyn. "Shall we?"

She nods and stands, then follows me.

"Have a seat. Dr. Delane's just finishing up." Tia is formal as she directs us to sit across from Meg's desk; the door clicks closed behind her. We sit in silence. The tension is thick and palpable.

There's a tap at the door and Meg walks in. "Hello, Sera." Seeing Carolyn, she gives her a quick smile. "Carolyn, I'm glad to see you."

I wonder why she is "glad."

Meg sits in her chair and clasps her hands together on top of her desk. Carolyn stares straight ahead, fumbling for my hand and, upon finding it, pulls it into her lap and grips it tight.

"Sera, your scan isn't good."

Carolyn's gasp is audible. My eyes widened but remain unblinking.

"Your thyroid is, in fact, wonky."

The corners of my mouth involuntarily turn up at the silly word, too silly for the severity of the situation. "And you have several enlarged lymph nodes in your neck. This is not my area of medicine, but I have scheduled you for an ultrasound and biopsies of your thyroid and one of the larger nodes. We'll get this done in the next day or two and then see you back with the results. We'll go from there. Okay?"

I am catatonic. *Why does everyone keep asking if things are okay? Things are obviously not okay.*

"What does this mean, Meg?" Carolyn asks.

"I'm not sure. But it isn't normal."

"Do you think it's cancer?" Carolyn asks in her unwavering, lawyer-steady voice.

"Likely," Meg says to Carolyn. "The biopsies will confirm things."

"Isn't it true the thyroid can be removed if cancerous?" Carolyn sounds hopeful in her cross-examination.

"Well, yes, with certain types. Again, this is not my area of practice."

"Don't give us the disclaimer bullshit. We wrote that policy," Carolyn snaps. "Sera is our friend, Meg, don't pull any punches."

Still paralyzed and mute, I can do nothing more than wait for Meg's response.

"I'm not sure. It's something, but what, I'm uncertain. I would prepare for a less than positive outcome on the biopsies. I work closely with MSTI and can get you referred as needed."

"Who's Misty?" A stranger's voice comes out of my mouth.

"Sorry, I mean the Mountain States Tumor Institute," Meg says.

I'm unaware Carolyn is still holding my hand until she squeezes it.

"We'll get through this. I promise." Carolyn says the words for my benefit but glares at Meg, waiting for her confirmation and reassurance.

"We will," Meg agrees.

"I need to go," I say, standing.

"Tia will call you with the appointment."

"Thank you," Carolyn says on her way out.

Walking past the bathroom outside Meg's office, I turn back and rush to the toilet, fall to my knees, and vomit. Carolyn follows and kneels beside me, stroking my face and holding my hair back, as the contents of my lunch fill the bowl.

"Shh, it'll be okay," Carolyn soothes. "I'm here for you."

What the hell is happening? My eyes search hers.

I clamber to my feet and move on autopilot. My footsteps echo in my ears. I sense others around me, pregnant women with their partners, glowing, laughing, and happy. Baby doctors hand out pleasant news, not death sentences. This is the worst place to be given this news.

Do they know? I wonder, walking past women with swollen bellies. *Do I look like—cancer?* There was the word that had sucked the air out of Meg's office and left me in a stupor.

Step, step, step.

I stop at the reception desk to check out and watch the receptionist's mouth move, *blah-blah-blah.* I cock my head, and my eyes glass over. Carolyn encourages me to move.

Step, step, step, I'm walking again. Suddenly we are in the parking lot.

"And then we'll shave our heads and wear big earrings and bright lipstick and . . ."

"What?" I whisper, turning to face Carolyn. Like the lady at the reception desk, Carolyn's lips move, but I cannot comprehend her words.

"Nothing. I was just rambling. Sweetie, you go home. I'll take over at the office for the day."

"No. I want to go back to work." Then I tell her, "And don't you dare tell a soul, no one. Understood?"

She nods her head, and I climb into my car.

———

"Hi Sera, it's Tia again. We have you scheduled for nine tomorrow morning at St. Luke's downtown for your ultrasound and biopsy.

You won't need a driver. Okay?"

And there it is again, the damned "okay." Do these people even understand what that word means?

"Yes, thanks, Tia."

CHAPTER

32

A soft rap at my door and a turn of the lock announce Carolyn's arrival. "Hello," she says, returning the key to her handbag. "Ready to go?"

"Just a minute," I call back. I take a deep breath, gather my composure, and smooth my blouse.

Let's do this, I tell my reflection in the mirror and step out from the bedroom.

"You're wearing a suit to a biopsy?"

I look down at my silk blouse, pencil skirt, and matching jacket. I see nothing out of place. "I have work to do afterward. Besides, this is all going to turn out to be nothing. Meg's just overreacting."

Carolyn shakes her head, exasperated, and follows me out the door.

"I've meant to ask," I say in the elevator, "how did you know when my appointment was?"

Carolyn shrinks and grimaces. "I talked to Meg."

"You know that's a HIPAA violation?" I growl.

"Not when you checked the little box listing me as your emergency contact."

I had forgotten I'd chosen Carolyn for this role after my divorce.

The journey to St Luke's is a blur. Before I am ready, we are at the hospital registrar's desk. I spell my last name, give my date of birth, verify my insurance, and receive a hospital admission wristband. It feels featherlike against my skin but weighs me down like an anchor.

Carolyn sits next to me, silent, and reaches for my hand. I steal a glance. She keeps her eyes fixed straight ahead. I can see a tear in the corner of her eye. It slips out and rolls down her cheek, more following in its trail, and they drip off her jaw. She reaches up with a knuckle and dabs under her lashes.

"Serenade?" a pleasant, stumpy old man calls. His nametag announces him as a volunteer.

"It's just Sera," I say, maybe for the hundredth time.

He winks. "A beautiful name for a beautiful girl. I'll be showing you to the imaging center."

"Thank you. It's kind of you to volunteer," I add.

"Oh, not at all."

I run-walk to keep up.

"My wife was treated at this hospital throughout her cancer. I wanted to give back for all the care they gave her," he explains.

"How is your wife doing?" I ask when we reach the reception desk under a sign that reads Diagnostic Imaging.

He smiles at me in a way that tells me all I need to know.

A pain shoots through me. "Oh . . . sorry for your loss."

The man finds and squeezes my hand. "Best of luck, dear. I will keep you in my prayers."

"Last name?" asks the gatekeeper to the biopsy suite.

I spell my last name and knowing the next question, give my date of birth. Carolyn and I sit and wait.

Moments later, a young nurse calls for me and then runs me through the name and birthdate rigmarole. I give Carolyn an exasperated, sideways glance, and she smirks. I recite for the third time in thirty minutes my last name and date of birth.

I'm prepped for the biopsy. I try not to overthink the crinkly paper, sterile sheet draped over my chest, and warmth of the blanket that covers me. I focus on a spot on the tile in the ceiling.

"Hello . . ." The doctor squints at my name on the chart. "Serenade? Hmm, unusual name," he muses, as if I'm not right here. "I am here to take biopsies of your thyroid and lymph nodes."

He explains there are to be sixteen needle sticks in total. My pulse quickens.

"That seem excessive."

The doctor ignores me and continues, "The needle makes a loud click when it takes the biopsy. It will feel like a pinch, a bee sting, and then you will hear a scraping sound while I get the sample. Okay?" The doctor snaps on a pair of latex gloves and smiles at me with his eyes, his mouth covered by a mask.

I nod, loathing the word "okay" more than ever. This does not sound okay to me.

"Do not move. Do not swallow," he commands.

My breathing becomes rapid.

"Let's begin," he says to the technician, who places the ultrasound wand on the opposite side of my neck to guide the procedure. Standing over me, with the needle primed on my neck, the doctor squints at the screen and, in an incredulous tone, asks the tech, "What is that?"

"*That*, doctor," the technician hisses through clenched teeth, "is her thyroid." The tech glares at him as if asking, "Are you stupid?"

Holy shit! It is wonky.

I grab the doctor's hand. "What's going on? What's wrong with my thyroid?" My words flood the room. I shove him away, sit bolt upright, pull the paper off my chest, and begin hyperventilating.

Carolyn leaps from her chair and stands toe-to-toe with the doctor, her nose inches from his. "What the hell is wrong with you? Don't they teach you *anything* in medical school? Like, how not to be a complete *asshat*? What kind of lame-brained, ludicrous question was *that*?" Carolyn eviscerates the young physician, taking another step forward until her breasts are inches from his chest. He steps backward.

"You don't know shit from shine-ola." She pokes a finger into his chest, making contact, and unleashes her days of pent-up fear and frustration. "You and your God complex, thinking you can say whatever pops into your head!" More steps, more jabs as Carolyn leads the veritable dance. "She's a person. Her name is Sera. She's my friend. And that, doctor, is her *thyroid*!" Hot tears fall down Carolyn's cheeks for the second time today. The doctor, beet red, now standing in the doorway, turns on a heel and flees the room.

An hour, a sedative, and a different physician later, the biopsies are complete.

"What a cluster fuck," Carolyn says in the elevator on our way back to the main floor.

Monday morning, Carolyn and I are once again sitting across from Meg. It is me this time who reaches for Carolyn's hand as I hold my breath.

"I'm sorry, Sera, there's no easy way to say this; your biopsies show you have non-Hodgkin lymphoma, suggestive of mantle cell. I am referring you to a blood cancer specialist, a hematology oncologist at the tumor institute. They will follow your care from here, okay?"

Her rip-the-band-aid spiel sounding more like she just wiped her hands of me, off her plate, out you go.

I'm not breathing. Not *okay*.

"What about thyroid cancer? I thought she had thyroid cancer?" Carolyn asks as if I'm not sitting beside her and in need of CPR.

"No, Carolyn, she has lymphoma," Meg says. "The lymphoma is in the lymph nodes and has spread to the thyroid, not the other way around."

"So, is surgical removal of the thyroid an option?" Carolyn demands.

Still here. Still in need of resuscitation.

"Carolyn, she will need to see a specialist."

Then back to me, "Sera, I am referring you to MSTI, okay?"

"No, Meg, it isn't okay. Please stop asking if it is." My voice cracks, and tears pool in my eyes.

Meg falls silent, my harsh words hitting their mark.

Then she says, "I'm sorry, Sera, really I am." Her expression shows she too feels the weight of the diagnosis. "Go home and rest. We'll let you know what's next."

"Thank you, Meg." Carolyn's words are gentle, a whisper. Reaching under my arm, she assists me to my feet, steadying me as we shuffle out of Meg's office. I wait this time, until I get home to vomit.

Sleep overcomes me. When I wake, I dress in an off-white linen pantsuit, lavender blouse, and strappy sandals that add a couple of inches to my stature. I shove a pair of dangle diamond earrings into my lobes and clasp a two-carat solitaire pendant around my neck, a graduation gift from Dad. I take a deep breath, put on my best smile, and tell myself, "Tonight is about Vance and Stefan."

CHAPTER
33

The wedding is stunning. Both Vance and Stefan wear black tuxedos, Stefan in top hat and tails. Their dress shirts match my lavender blouse, and their suit jackets sport a single white rose. I carry a beautiful bouquet of white lilies and stephanotis down the aisle, their heady smell of jasmine intoxicating. Vance's brother officiates in a venue filled with friends and family; parents, aunts and uncles, nieces, nephews, and cousins, all of whom are gathered to share in the couple's joy. I am both happy and jealous.

Following the ceremony, there is to be karaoke, dancing, food, and drinks. I will sing, cut a rug, and imbibe, all to excess, and no doubt crawl into bed in the small hours, exhausted and happy for two of my dearest friends who have just vowed to care for one another through sickness and in health. For now, I think only of my sickness and how there will be no partner caring for me.

The following week finds me checking into a multi-story building in the heart of downtown emblazoned with the words Mountain States Tumor Institute, the mysterious MSTI to which Meg referred.

Funny, I've lived in this city for decades, working only a few blocks away and have never really seen *this place.* I give the pleasant lady at reception (Amy, her nametag tells me) my name, spelling it out, and offer my birth date.

"Thank you," Amy smiles and adds, "I think you have a friend waiting for you." She points to Carolyn. "She's been here a while."

I sigh and turn to see Carolyn sitting in a chair, again feigning interest in a magazine.

"Hi." Carolyn stands and envelops me in a hug, and we sit together and wait.

"I didn't know you were coming."

"I already told you, you're not doing this alone."

I don't argue.

"How was the wedding?"

"I think I'm still drunk," I scoff.

"Serenade?" a young aid calls.

I look at Carolyn; terror gripping me. She stands, reaches out her hand, and helps me to my feet. She is still holding my hand as we walk through the double doors. Passing the aid, Carolyn says, "It's Sera. Make a note."

The aid takes my temperature, blood pressure, heart rate, and weight; 43.9985 kilograms. She looks at me and I see her swallow. "What is your normal weight?"

"Um, I don't know. I'm always thin, maybe one-ten?" I look to Carolyn for confirmation.

"A week ago, she was down to a hundred and three," Carolyn

leans into the assistant. "I'm sorry, I don't know metrics. How much is this?" Carolyn points to the digital readout.

"Ninety-seven pounds."

There is a heavy silence as I witness Carolyn and the aid hold each other's gaze.

———

Dr. Z, whose name sounds Polish and starts with a silent C, is a rotund, balding man with smart-looking readers he wears at the end of his nose, giving him ample room to peer over their rims. He speaks in a gentle, thickly accented voice, "Hello, Ms. Kincaid. May I call you Sera? I understand that is your preference."

I squint, reserving judgment, nod, and huddle next to Carolyn in a chair against the wall, refusing to sit on the exam table; it makes me feel singled out, put on the spot, sick.

"You may call me Dr. Z, if you'd like, most of my patients do, my name being somewhat difficult to pronounce and to spell, I'm told." He chuckles at his humor.

"And who are you, miss?" He directs this comment to Carolyn, who seems taken by the smooth talker.

"I'm Carolyn Scott, Dr. Z," she says, appearing quite relaxed given the circumstances, almost smitten. "I'm Sera's best friend and caregiver." I'm not sure which shocks me more; her previously unspoken proclamation as my BFF or identifying herself as my caregiver. I let both titles stand.

"Very good," he says, looking to his nurse, who jots down a note. "Sera," Dr. Z addresses me again, "Would you be so kind as to sit on the table so I can examine you?"

There's no demand in his tone, and he seems to have all the time in the world as I contemplate his request. Weighing my options, I climb onto the loathsome paper-covered exam table. The doctor washes his hands, leaving them to linger in the water to let me know he is warming them. And then, like Meg did days before, Dr. Z palpates my neck, running scales with his fingers over my throat, clavicle, underarms, belly, and groin.

Finished, Dr. Z reaches out his hand and helps me sit up, saying, "I've reviewed your chart and read the results of your tests. I am afraid we have confirmed Mantle Cell Lymphoma." My ears burn, and a ringing fills my head, drowning out most of what follows. I only catch an occasional word. The rest, reminiscent of my rafting trip with the one-eyed pirate, are lost to me. I hear "aggressive," "terminal," "stage four."

I watch his lips move as he draws a diagram of the lymphatic system on a paper towel he's extracted from the dispenser above the sink. He then draws two chromosome chains, side-by-side, and writes the word DNA above them. Next to one chain, he writes the number eleven, and beside the other chain, he writes fourteen. He draws two arrows between the two DNA strands, each point to the other chain, and then writes the word "translocate."

I understand. My numbers eleven and fourteen have somehow gotten switched, resulting in my cancer. I sit rooted and dumb.

"We need to start with the heaviest chemotherapy we have, R Hyper-CVAD, nine drugs administered over a consecutive five- to seven-day period. It's inpatient, eight rounds are standard." Dr. Z's speaking to Carolyn; I've checked out of the conversation.

"That sounds excessive." Carolyn is white as a sheet and sounds as shocked as I feel.

"It is," he agrees. "It's the only chance she has for extending her life. We call it the nuclear bomb."

"Will it reverse the chromosomes?" I ask stupefied.

"It will not," he breathes. I make my way off the exam table and curl up in the chair next to Carolyn, tucking my feet under myself and holding my sweater tight. I wish it were my mom beside me. Carolyn wraps an arm around my shoulder, pulling me in tight.

"Will I lose my hair?" Again, I speak from somewhere down deep.

"Yes."

"How sick will I get?"

"Very sick."

"What's the prognosis, Doctor?" This is Carolyn's voice. I shoot her a look. Dr. Z looks at me for confirmation.

"Do you want to know, sweetie?" Carolyn asks me.

I swallow and turn to the doctor, my heart pounding. I can tell Carolyn wants to know. I nod.

"It's grim, Sera, I won't lie. It's quite advanced. The average prognosis is around five years, but it's difficult to predict how a person will respond, and if it turns blastoid . . ." He pauses before adding, "Well, that's another story altogether. We should just start with the treatment and hope for the best."

"That's a far cry from an answer, *Doctor*." Carolyn's emphasis of "doctor" bites. She is suddenly less taken by him. "Could you be more specific? A week? A month? A year?"

Dr. Z stares at Carolyn and then speaks to me, "I wouldn't wait to get your affairs in order."

———

I stop Carolyn at the entrance to my building.

"I'd like to be alone."

She opens her mouth to object, closes it, then says, "I'll pick you up Monday morning and take you to the hospital."

Inside my condo, I toss the keys onto the credenza, kick off my shoes and slide down the wall to the floor. Out of tears, I stare across the room, reevaluating my life, taking stock, checking boxes of all that I possess, have done, and missed out on.

Pity and anger well to a boiling point. I am weary, broken, enraged, and sad. The bug inside me is growing like a fast-moving wildfire. Pounding my fists, I rage, scream, and tear at my blouse until it rips open, scattering small buttons across the floor, bouncing on the hardwood, and traveling to far corners and under chairs. I yank hard at my hair and yell, "Just leave already. You're going to anyway, just like everything and everyone." I lose myself and go mad. Guttural noises emanate from deep within and swallow me. A rap on my door halts my mania, and a man's voice calls out, "Miss, are you okay in there?" It's my neighbor, the older man with the *real* penthouse.

I scream, feeling the heat of my fear on my face, "I have cancer, and I'm dying." There's silence on the other side of the door, followed by quick, retreating footsteps.

"You're smarter than this, Serenade," I say aloud. "Figure this out."

My mind races with ideas on how to eradicate the disease. Drinking a caustic agent, acquiring leeches for bloodletting, and voodoo are the first three options that pop into my head. As there's no way I'm swallowing bleach, and I don't know where to find leeches or a witch doctor, I grab my phone and start searching for homeopathic cures for blood cancers.

A suggestion to the efficacy of ingesting blue scorpion venom is intriguing, but I would need to travel to Cuba, and that's not happening; I only have a weekend. Another claim touts drinking tea extracted from the bark of the poisonous Devil's Club plant, found predominantly in Alaska; no time for that either. And then I strike gold: essential oils. Cancer thrives on inflammation, toxicity, and stress, or so I have read. If I can reduce or eliminate these issues, perhaps I can cure myself, or at least stave off the need for chemotherapy, I deduce.

I stand and sprint to the cupboard that holds my oils. I have them all: cinnamon, lavender, Frankincense, chamomile, ginger, thyme, eucalyptus, bergamot; I even have helichrysum, whatever that is, and dozens of other fragrant oils. I remember the boyfriend who got me into aromatherapy and say a little thank you. For once, chameleoning is going to save my life.

What was his name? I think for half a second, shake my head and say, "Who the hell cares?"

Using veggie gel caps I still have from previous attempts to cure whatever ailed me, I drop oil into the caps, doubling, tripling, or quadrupling any suggested dosage. It's life or death over here. Drop after drop I fill the capsules—two drops of this, three of that, and so on until I've filled multiple caplets totaling thirty-one drops of every kind of anti-inflammatory, stress-relieving, and antioxidant-touting oil in my quiver. *I've got this.*

I uncork a bottle of wine and throw half of the capsules into my mouth. "Down the hatch," I say to the little pills and take a drink of wine. Then I take the other half and drink more wine.

I drum my fingers on the countertop, wondering how long the results will take, unsure how I'll know if it's working. I push down the inkling I may have been a wee bit irrational.

I stride to the bookshelf and run my hand across the exposed spines of my self-help library, lined in alphabetical order by author Angelou, Brown, Chapman, Doyle, Gandhi, Gilbert, Winfrey. I've learned a great deal from these people. Their pearls of wisdom have not fallen on deaf ears. I am more self-reliant and have better boundaries. I enjoy volunteering more than I did before, and I do more beyond-self thinking. I've learned it's okay to love more than one person; I love both Zac and Carolyn, and each fulfills a need the other can't. Zac, physically and emotionally, sort of, and Carolyn through friendship and companionship. And this is okay.

Sharp pain in my stomach brings me back from my bunny trail; the oils must be working. I take the wine, still drinking it straight from the bottle, and make my way to my closet, pulling down bins of mementos and photographs. It's been years since I've gone through these boxes, but it seems appropriate now to revisit them. Save some, give some, and destroy most.

I force myself to pause at the photo of my wedding; me in a knee-length dress and flower crown, barefoot in a meadow overlooking Payette Lake. Clint stands beside me, his little girls, Hailey and Elise—the only children I will ever know—smile beside him, each dressed like mini-me in a nod to my mother and my upbringing. I hold the picture to my chest, breathe deeply, and lay it on the floor, placing my divorce decree on top of it. This is the burn pile.

My high school photos make me smile. I was small for my age, a chipmunk-cheeked girl fighting acne. Most of the pictures capture me squinting because of my defiance against wearing glasses. "They make me look like a geek," I would scream to my mother. "Sera Jean," she would say, "you *are* a geek." I know now Mom was trying to tell me it was wonderful to be a geek.

"Mom," I say to her memory, "you will never understand I am sick." I sigh, heavy with remorse of her mind-stealing disease. Another sharp pain in my belly causes me to gasp and grab my side.

"Holy crap," I breathe through the wave. When it subsides, I go back to the boxes, finding trinkets from my multiple trips to Puerto Vallarta, coming across a copy of my airline ticket from when Steve and I went there for the first time over spring break. I make a mental note to visit Steve and Marin before . . .

My shoulders sag. Still holding the ticket stub, I close my eyes, gulp from the bottle, and say, "Before I die."

The sharp, stabbing pains come faster, closer together as if labor pains. I'm panting, sweating, and sleepy. I curl into a tight ball on top of the photos and baubles strewn on the floor. Holding my knees to my chest, I rock and moan. It strikes me that I've poisoned myself.

I scan the floor, searching for my phone, remembering I left it by the front door. A puddle of drool has formed beneath my cheek. I roll to my side, still holding my midsection, and will myself to my knees, crawling and dragging myself toward the living room. I grab the phone and push speed dial.

"Help."

CHAPTER
34

hemotherapy on day one is mostly just paperwork, calls to the insurance company, and lengthy waits. I am grateful Carolyn is here to slog through the minutia; filling out consent forms for me to sign, inquiring why this is taking so long, and offering ideas on how the staff could better perform their jobs to maximize efficiency.

"Hurry and wait," a bald woman dragging a pole laden with chemo bags says to me wryly as she shuffles past. She seems to be an expert.

A shiver runs the length of me. *Oh, God. That's going to be me.*

"Looks like we're ready for you, Serenade," says a fresh-looking young woman with a bouncy ponytail. She grabs the overnight bag from my clammy hand. "This way."

"It's Sera," I tell the back of her head.

Carolyn and I walk behind the nurse. She has not yet spoken directly to me following my essential oil overdose. When she arrived at my condo after my desperation call, I forbade her to take me to the hospital, fearing admittance to the psych ward.

Carolyn learned from poison control that nothing could be done unless I fell into a coma or stopped breathing. She stood me up and enlisted the help of Stefan and Vance. The three of them helped me *walk it off.* Right or wrong, I'm here now, and still have cancer.

We make our way down a long hallway, passing several rooms. I peer in through the slightly open doors, anxious and curious to see other cancer patients. There is a broad array of men, women, young, old, but no children, thank God; they are cared for elsewhere. Some moan in obvious pain, others sit playing cards or chatting with friends and family. One stares blankly at a dark television screen. I quickly avert my eyes.

"This is you for the week," the spirited nurse says, waving me through the door. My name is on a whiteboard above the bed; Carolyn's name and phone number is beneath it in smaller print. I now know why Dr. Z had his nurse make a note of Carolyn's name.

Carolyn, still not uttering a word to me, reaches up to the board and erases the last half of my name with her finger.

I lift the corners of my lips in thanks.

"Put your things in the closet or the drawers. This bathroom is for patients only," she addresses Carolyn. "We monitor all the output."

Carolyn leans in, her first words to me are, "You have to pee and poo in a hat."

"Is that true?" I'm mortified.

"I'm afraid so," the nurse admits.

"I can't do this." I turn to Carolyn. "Let's just leave."

Carolyn, who had read the pamphlets given to her at Dr. Z's clinic, says to me in a calm, deliberate voice, "All decisions from here on out are yours. If you want to leave, we are out of here." She smiles, adding, "But I think you should try it. We both know the homeopathic route didn't have a great outcome." She holds my gaze, not batting an eye.

I turn back to my happy-pants nurse and nod my desire to continue.

"Why don't you get yourself comfy, and I'll be in to access your port. Can I bring you a warm blanket for now?"

Always cold, I jump at the offer.

My port was installed the day before my appointment with Dr. Z, and it remains dressed in Steri-strips. It's painful to the touch, and I can't imagine how bad it will hurt to have it "accessed," a term that terrifies me.

I change my clothes as Carolyn steps out to find the coffee machine and public restroom. The nurse comes back, wraps me in a blanket, and helps me into the bed.

"Are you ready?" she asks. "Deep breath, one, two, three, poke." She sticks the three-quarter-inch needle into the middle of my port, my first access. I am right to have worried.

The days blur into each other, Monday into Tuesday and then Wednesday, bag after bag of chemicals hang on the tree beside me. Each drip courses through the plastic tube and into my port designed to kill my nemesis and save my life.

I smell that Carolyn has walked into the room and open my eyes. These days, she smells of fabric softener and sweet perfume, no doubt an expensive blend: lilac, amber, a woodsy smell I can't quite place, and she smells of fear. It's a strange, subtle aroma, a type of ammonia-laced sweat. I know she's aware of it, too. I've caught her applying extra deodorant and washing her armpits when she thinks I'm sleeping. She's worn the new scent since she sat next to me in Meg's office.

"Good morning, sunshine," she sings, walking to the window and opening the blinds just a smidge to let in a bit of light but not too much because my eyes hurt; they're sensitive now, and she's aware of it.

"Hey," I say, lolling my head from its usual position, staring at the bag of chemicals. "Thanks for coming."

"Don't be a silly goose," she chides, sounding girlish. "I'm not going anywhere." She reaches down and draws me into her arms for a gentle hug and then kisses my cheek. "Anything I can get you while I'm up?"

"Nah, I'm fine, thanks." I'm tired, having been up a good portion of the evening alternating between dry heaves and diarrhea. My hands and feet ache, engorged by retained water. The bed scale shows an eighteen-pound weight gain since I first lay on it three days ago. Lasix, a drug designed to keep water weight off thoroughbreds, is my new best friend; it makes me pee like a racehorse. *Oh, the irony.*

Carolyn scoots the metal legged chair next to my bed, positions her laptop and phone atop the extra rolling table she had brought in, and begins checking her emails. A wave of nausea takes hold, and I push the call button.

"What can I get for you, Serenade?" The voice crackles through the built-in bed rail speaker.

"I'm nauseous," I say, my mouth dry, "and it's *Sera.*"

Carolyn jumps up, nearly toppling the table, "What do you need?" she asks, handing me a barf bag and a Styrofoam cup filled with water and a straw.

The nurse enters with a needle and pushes its liquid into my IV. I drift into a sleepy haze; grateful I've lost the urge to hurl.

Two hours pass, and when I open my eyes, Carolyn is sitting next to me in the visitor's chair. Her suit coat drapes behind her, and she has kicked off her shoes, resting her feet on the bed next to me. She is plunking away at the keyboard and, without looking up, says, "Feeling better?"

"Mm-hmm," I mumble. I have no energy for chitchat.

Dinner comes soon after, and I pick at the rice and bland chicken. I drink part of the artificially flavored smoothie and eat two slices of canned peaches. My immunocompromised diet consisting of nothing fresh or uncooked.

"Can you please try another bite or two?" Carolyn begs.

I shake my head, defiant, and push away the tray. I turn onto my side and curl into myself. Carolyn lifts the blanket and slides in beside me. She strokes my hair and whispers into my neck, "I'm right here." Silent, weary tears roll from my eyes and onto the sheet. She stays next to me through the night.

The graveyard-shift nurse comes in to take my blood pressure and temperature, and we share a smile. Unable to sleep, I had snuck out of bed and now sit in the recliner, doing a crossword puzzle by the light of my cell phone. Carolyn remains asleep in my bed. The nurse finishes her chores, pulls the blanket under Carolyn's chin, and creeps out the door.

———————

Time passes after treatment with me spending the bulk of it sleeping. I'm twelve days out from my first treatment when I shuffle out of my bathroom to find Carolyn standing in my kitchen, frying ground beef, and making macaroni and cheese, the only two foods I can stomach. Dr. Z explained my craving for red meat may be because of my iron deficiency. No one has a reason for the mac and cheese, but all are glad I'm eating.

"Can I ask you a favor?" I climb onto a bar stool. I'm dressed in my fuzzy pajama bottoms and a loose cotton top and run my fingers through my thinning hair.

"Of course, anything." Carolyn sits the spatula down, giving me her full attention.

"It's time." I hold out hair clippers.

"It would be my honor," Carolyn says, taking the clippers from my hand. She turns the stove off, leaves the half-cooked meat and boiling water to cool, wraps a towel around my neck, and says, "Do you want to video it?"

I chuckle, "For posterity? Sure, why not?"

With the phone recording, Carolyn announces, "It's time, ladies and gentlemen, the big reveal." She grins, and I squeal, covering my face with my hands then peeking through my fingers at the camera. Carolyn leans down and whispers, "Ready?"

I nod, and she runs the shears down the middle of my head. We laugh until I cough. Carolyn pushes pause, waits until I regain my composure, and then she taps the record button again.

To my surprise, the finished product is liberating. I make my way back to the bathroom and stand in front of the mirror, running my hands back and forth along my scalp. It's prickly yet soft, and reveals my face as I've never seen it, as the focal point. My long mane, a lifelong security blanket, is gone, leaving nothing to hide behind. I decide my new hairdo goes great with my hazel eyes; I had given up my brown-colored contacts at the hospital.

I apply bright pink-red lipstick and huge loop earrings, slip out of my hospital garb and into a sundress that hangs limp and oversized on my skeletal body. I walk into the living room, posing for Carolyn.

She draws in a breath, clasps her hand to her throat, and whispers, "You look beautiful." She snaps a picture with her phone.

"I need to ask another favor."

Carolyn nods, on the verge of tears.

"I want you to help me become a better person." I lift my hand to stop her, not wanting to hear a programmed response of what a good person I already am. "I want to go through this with grace."

She nods again. A tear crawls down her cheek.

"I read those books, you know," I said. "I hated that you brought them to me, but they were so poignant and powerful. I'd like to use their wisdom and your help to become a better version of me while there's time. I want to leave a lasting and positive impact for others when I'm no longer around." I hold my hand up again. "I can't fix the world, but I can do a few good things for a few good people."

"And what does that look like?" she chokes.

"I have some ideas. Oh, and I want to throw a big party."

"A party? Why not?" Carolyn says, and I can feel the mood in the room lift. "What's the occasion?"

"A celebration of life, my life, and I want to be there for it."

CHAPTER

35

By the second week at home following round two of treatment, I finally feel human again.

"Let's take a road trip," Carolyn says one afternoon. "I'll drive. But we can take your car. Deal?"

"Any place in particular?" I ask, shuffling to the closet to throw a clean pair of fuzzy pjs into a bag.

"I was thinking Lewiston," she says, holding my gaze.

Carolyn's right. I need to see my mother and try to explain, perhaps even say goodbye. I choke at the thought.

"Lewiston it is," I agree.

Carolyn packs the car, putting in our overnight bags, several water bottles, my necessary medications, and two sleeves of soda crackers to stave off my nausea. She tucks a puke bag in the glove compartment, puts a pillow on my seat, and wraps me in a blanket.

"Ready to go?" Carolyn calls out. I smile, admiring what she calls her road trip clothes: linen Capri pants, silk blouse with its sleeves rolled in crisp folds to just below her elbows, and a pair of deck shoes, white and without a scuff.

"Yes," I say, and with the help of Stefan, I load my pajama-clad, slipper wearing, blanket-wrapped self into the car.

We stop often, since the Barracuda guzzles gas and my bladder is weak—a side effect of one of the chemo drugs. The drive north is otherwise uneventful. We rock out to seventies disco when my head and ears can handle the noise, with an occasional Etta James and requisite Pat Benatar—because no girls' trip is complete without "Heartbreaker."

"Detour," I call out. "Take old Highway 7. I want to show you something."

Carolyn follows my directions, keeping to the posted speed.

"Faster," I blurt. We are at the bottom of a hill where the intersecting road sign reads, Greencreek 6 miles. "Go faster."

"I'm driving at the speed limit."

"Just do it."

I see Carolyn push the peddle down slightly.

"Faster."

Carolyn jerks in her seat, and I see her foot press toward the floor. The speedometer surges. I scan the upcoming road for cars: all clear. "Pin it," I yell.

"I am."

"No, you're not. Pin it." I reach over and place my hand on Carolyn's knee.

"Are you trying to kill us?" she screams, swatting at my hand.

"We have to be going as fast as possible when we reach the top of the hill."

"What?"

"Trust me. It's a Thelma and Louise moment."

"We're driving off a cliff?"

"Drive," I scream at the top of my lungs, laughing and coughing and whooping.

"Oh, what the hell," Carolyn yields. "Dibs on Louise."

I shrug. "Works for me."

Near the crest of the hill, I draw in a dramatic breath and stare at Carolyn. She glances at me and follows suit, her cheeks puffed. I grab the door's armrest and reach for Carolyn's hand; it's clammy. She's nervous.

The car's nose dips, and I let loose a loud, "Woo-hoo."

Carolyn's hand tenses in mine, and she releases an even louder, "Oh, God!"

The familiar scrape of metal as the car bottoms out causes me to release a crazy, knee-slapping, Thelma-like laugh as the wheels inch off the road.

The Cuda lands with a stomach jolting *thud.*

"Brake," I command, my tone stern, controlled, and unwavering. "Hard."

Carolyn obeys. The thunder of the Hemi subsides and the car bunny hops until it slows enough to take the first curve.

"Oh. My. God." Carolyn laughs and screams, "You're crazy! Woo-hoo!" She shakes her head, her mane swishes around her face. She looks happy, beautiful. "I think I peed a little."

"I know I did."

We laugh.

"Now mind the speed limit and hold your lane, it can get dicey here if you meet a car and you're over the line."

Carolyn sobers, expertly navigating the canyon. I stare at the painted rocks, lost, as always in memories.

"Stop."

"What's wrong? Are you okay?"

I reach for the handle before the car stops rolling. "Here." My door swings open as the car comes to a stop. "Help me out, please."

Carolyn huffs and puts the car in park, rushing around to my side. "Are you mad?" She looks franticly in both directions. "We're stopped in the middle of the road."

"It's fine. We'd as likely see a turtle cross the road as another car."

She helps me out, and I walk across the pavement and stand on the gravel shoulder, looking up at the rock wall. Carolyn stands next to me.

I point to the faded circle and explain. "Me and my three closest high school friends, too afraid to become blood sisters, dipped our fingers in the bottom of a burning candle and became Wax Sisters." I close my eyes to the memory. "We wrote that in the days just before one sister died."

"I'm so sorry," Carolyn whispers, wrapping an arm around my shoulder. She pauses and then adds, her voice loud in the empty canyon, "Wax sisters? Really? That's ridiculous, and absolutely precious. You're fortunate, you know. I'm a little jealous."

"I am lucky; they really were like actual sisters to me."

"Would you like me to take a picture? I'll angle it up to catch the words."

"Yeah, thanks."

She clicks the photo with her phone, and we are back on our way, not meeting another car until we pull into my hometown, population four hundred.

"Do you want to stop?" Carolyn asks as we creep through the sleepy downtown.

"No, I've said my goodbyes here." I close my eyes for the next forty-minutes of the drive.

Just outside Lapwai, another small town in the reservation's heart, I say, "Please stop at the next station."

"Sure, but we'll be at your mom's place in Lewiston in fifteen minutes if you can wait. We have enough gas," Carolyn adds, checking the fuel gauge.

"No, I'd like to stop first, gain my composure, put my head on right." This will be a difficult visit.

Carolyn pulls into the gas station, which has a convenience store attached. She hops out and comes around the car to help me before pumping the gas. "May as well top her off," she says.

"I've got this." I shrug off her help. "You go ahead."

I shuffle into the store, opting to go au naturel, sans headscarf. I wait in line to ask the clerk for the bathroom key, standing behind a tribal police officer paying for a soda. His sun-kissed skin and jet-black braid are both familiar from my youth. His single feather tucked in his plait tells me he's not only an officer but a warrior.

"Sammy?" I ask when the man turns. My voice is shaky from medication, nerves, and excitement. "Sammy Red Feather?"

"Sam," he replies. "Sheriff Roberts. Can I help you?"

"Hi," I whisper, "It's Sera. Kincaid. From school." I choke the words out as Carolyn slips in beside me.

"Teeny *sooyaapoo*?" He's clearly shocked.

I nod, and Carolyn gasps, "Is he . . . ?" Her words trail off; she's heard most of my stories.

Sammy and I nod, and he chuckles.

"Look, I never apologized," I start.

Sammy holds up his hand to stop me. "No need, we were kids."

"How are you? How have you been?"

"I'm good. I'm sheriff on the rez, as you can see." He smiles and points to the patch on his sleeve. "I married Brenda, and we have two sons. If I'm not getting my comeuppance." He lowers his gaze, thoughtful.

"Wow, that's great."

"You have kids?"

"No," Carolyn answers for me, her hand resting on my shoulder. She's taken charge to protect me.

"How's the younger brother?" I ask, recalling Sammy relished being two minutes older than his twin.

"Paul? He's chief now." Sammy beams with pride.

"What? Oh, I'm sorry for your loss." I know that the only way Paul is chief is that their father has passed.

"It's alright, been a few years now, but thank you. He had—" Sammy pauses, looks into my soul, and says knowingly, "he had cancer."

I nod, my eyes filling with tears. "Oh, no, Sammy," I say, a thought striking me between the eyes. "Did I cause you not to be chief?" I eke out the words in a whisper.

He stares at me, unsure for a moment what I mean, then reaches up to touch the slight crook in his nose. He throws back his head, laughing. "No. Paul was better suited, more tolerant, and patient. I love being a cop and didn't want to give it up. I let my younger brother take the spotlight," Sammy winks.

An awkward pause takes hold, the kind where two people who once knew each other run out of things to say. Carolyn gracefully breaks the tension, "Well, it was nice to meet you, Sheriff, but I need to get this young lady to her mother's. Don't want to be late for that." She smiles, and he returns an understanding nod.

"Tell Brenda hello for me, and Running Bear, too." I drift in my memories of people and days past.

"Will do. You take care, Sera." Sammy turns to walk away.

"Hey, Sammy," I call after him.

He pauses at the door. "Yeah?"

"What kind of feather is that?" I point toward his head. "It's different from when we were kids."

Sammy reaches up, stroking the feather, "It's an eagle."

I smile, "That makes me happy for you, Red Feather."

———————

We arrive at Heatherwood Care Center thirty minutes after our gas station stop. Mom is sitting in a chair in front of a window, staring out at the lawn. Nothing moves outside to hold her gaze, but she's content, focused on nothing, and becomes agitated when I try to get her attention.

"I'm watching," she yells, batting my hand away when I touch her shoulder.

An attendant comes over to calm her and tries to help her understand. "Helen, your daughter, Sera, is here to see you. Can you turn around and say hello?" She speaks to mom as if she's a child.

Mom's eyes focus, and she turns to look at Carolyn, then at me. A glimmer of recognition flutters across her face, and her lips turn up at the corners. She reaches out a hand, "Sera, you've come home."

———————

Carolyn and I drive back to Boise in the morning, bypassing the canyon's hieroglyphs. We stick to the main thoroughfare. I keep the music off and my eyes shut, not wanting to interact or explain my life. Carolyn has questions; I can see them in her eyes. She's bursting to know what my mother had meant when she said, "You've come home," and she's doing everything she can to contain herself while I feign sleep.

"I only visited at Christmas," I blurt out two hundred miles into our drive home.

"What?" Carolyn jumps, startled by the broken silence.

"After Dad died. I only visited at Christmas. I guess I blamed Mom. Not like she killed him, but for his misery. He wasn't happy." I stare out the window. "Dad wanted to travel and experience life. Mom didn't. Simple as that. And they grew apart. Dad called me the summer before he died, saying he wanted a divorce, that he had given her fifty-two years, and he couldn't give her any more. He asked me to draw up papers." I take a breath and roll my head until my eyes are looking straight at Carolyn. "I refused. I told him to suck it up, buttercup."

Carolyn giggles but keeps her attention forward.

"I encouraged him to stay, telling him he would lose more than half of everything he had worked so hard for if he left. He told me he didn't care. But he also wasn't willing to hire any other attorney. I refused him, Carolyn. I forbade my father to divorce my mother, and I refused to represent him; I refused him his happiness. And within a few months, he died a lonely, miserable death."

"Sera. He had a heart attack."

"He lay on the bathroom floor the entire evening, vomiting

278

and in pain. She didn't even call an ambulance until six the next morning." In the pause that follows, I reflect before saying, "I cleaned the bathroom; he suffered."

"I'm so sorry."

We ride in silence for the rest of the drive to Boise.

CHAPTER

36

"Sera, are you awake?" Dr. Z squeezes my hand, and I do my best to open my eyes and push the brain fog away.

His appearance during Carolyn's rare absence is not happenstance. I know he's enlisted the nurses to alert him when she's out of the room. During our alone times, Dr. Z and I have frank conversations about my health without the two cents of my well-meaning, though often pain-in-the-ass, caregiver. Waking to his presence, therefore, is neither surprising nor bothersome. His behavior, however, is alarming. He shifts his weight and wrings his hands, avoiding my gaze completely.

"What is it?" I ask.

He sits on the metal stool next to my bed. "As you know," Dr. Z glances at the fresh bags of blood and platelets hanging from my chemo tree, "your numbers are dropping as expected." He sighs. "But they are not rallying. Your white blood cell count is high, indicative of infection, metastases, or secondary leukemia." He pauses, his eyes moist. "It doesn't look good, Sera."

Through an exchange of private emails at the onset of my diagnosis, I made Dr. Z promise to pull no punches, explaining that I'm a realist and can't live in a false world of rainbows and unicorns. He gave me his word, and he has kept it.

I reach for his hands resting in his lap, his fingers laced together. This posture was the clinician's way, and I'd seen it many times. They stop themselves from reaching out to their patients, remain detached, forgo the natural urge for the human touch to stay objective. Loss is prevalent on this floor. To continue being effective in their jobs, nurses, and doctors must separate themselves from the patients, wall themselves off, remain safely distant.

I weave my fingers through Dr. Z's and squeeze, "Thank you for everything." I unabashedly let all my emotions show and feel a tear streak down my steroid-round moon face, "How much time?"

He stammers, doing his best to maintain his composure. "We need to run tests. These are preliminary findings, unfounded. I may have spoken too soon; it's just that you and I . . ." His words trail off, and he glances down at our hands folded together then back to my eyes. "Less than a year, six months, I would guess."

"Thank you," I say again, grateful he's keeping his promise of full disclosure. "I appreciate you." I pause and then ask, "What's your name mean, Dr. Z, your actual name, not your doctor-patient persona?"

"Rafa," he says.

"How does that translate?"

Rafa blushes. His flustered appearance gives him the look of a much younger man. "In Polish, it means 'God heals,' 'well-being,' 'the giant.'"

"It's perfect," I whisper, my eyes heavy from medication. I feel myself drift into sleep.

I enlist Matt, Stefan, Vance, and Marta on a video call to assist me in a plan I've concocted during my last days of round three in the hospital. I joke with them, calling it Operation Don't Tell Carolyn.

"Marta, I need you to keep Carolyn occupied at work, shuffle something around, call a partners' meeting, whatever it takes. I don't want her at my next scan."

"I gotcha covered," she grins and gives a brisk salute into the camera.

"Stefan, I need you to work on the logistics of transportation and doing whatever necessary to keep Carolyn out of my condo. If she notices I'm gone, she'll call in the National Guard." That earns more chuckles.

"Matt, you know your part?" He nods, giving a wink.

"What about me?" Vance asks, jumping in his seat next to Stefan.

"You, my friend, will accompany me."

Vance smiles, dabs an imaginary tear, and blows a kiss at the screen, "It will be my pleasure."

"Okay, you all know your jobs. Meet me back here tomorrow, same time. Marta, will you please send everyone the video invitation?" she nods. "And don't tell Carolyn," I remind everyone as we say our goodbyes and exit the chat.

It isn't a comprehensive plan, nothing stellar or earth-shattering. I merely want to attend my scan alone and hear the news of my fate without the well-meaning meddling of my now-constant companion. I want to give Carolyn a break as much as myself. She looks exhausted and haggard; her Yves Saint Laurent suits hanging like unfashionable sacks on her too-thin frame. A break will do us both good.

I make my way to the couch, slide under my afghan blanket, pulling it under my chin, and close my eyes. The buzzing phone rouses me. It's Marta in our group chat. Her text reads: "The package will be detained," and a wink-face emoji.

Seeing Marta's thrill in my mind's eye, I smile, knowing she's enjoying herself.

The next message is from Stefan. "Transportation arranged. You will be picked up at 2:00 p.m. tomorrow, alone." A second message follows; it's a thumbs-up meme. A third message, this one from Vance, reads, "Alone with me, of course, LOL."

"Of course," I tell the screen, texting back a smiley face. *I love you two goofballs.*

My anxiety and impatience rise as I wait for the third and final piece of the plan, Matt. I know his job will take more time than the others', and I force myself to calm down by snuggling back into the blanket. I've washed it a dozen times since bringing it home from Doris' house but can still conjure the aroma of homemade bread whenever I inhale into it deeply.

Two hours pass before my phone lights up with Matt's message. "I have your information. I'm coming by within the hour."

My hands are shaking as I text, "OK."

I work my way up to a sitting position and then stand, reaching out to steady myself, then pace, doing the chemo shuffle; feet sliding, arms out in case I fall, constantly scanning for the next closest place to rest my weary bones. A couple minutes in and I'm spent and curl back up on the couch.

A soft rap at the door and a click of the master key in the lock announce Stefan; he's let Matt into the condo. Tired, I pull myself up to a sitting position but don't stand.

"Hey, friend," Matt greets me where I'm at, bending down to give me a peck on the cheek and a light squeeze of my shoulders, "How are you today?"

"It's a good day, Matt." Good days now qualify as little-to-no nausea, controlled pain, and finding myself in the company of those I love. I offer him a sincere smile and pat the cushion beside me.

He sits, trying not to brush against my frail body or cause it to topple from the depression in the cushion made by his weight; it's all I can do to keep myself upright. "It's not great, Sera," he says, staring down at the folded papers clutched in his hands. "We don't have to do this," another warning.

"Whatever it is, Matt, I blame you for nothing." During my long days of treatment, I'd taken to heart the messages in the books Carolyn had snuck into my life; all people are hurting and broken, and it's up to everyone to make this world better. My days of reading boil down to a few simple absolutes I now live by: be kind, forgive before being asked, appreciate even the smallest of gestures, and tell everyone you love them.

Matt looks at the folded papers, hesitant to hand them to me. The first page is familiar, disclosing current address and other occupants in the house. Then come the details about military service, credit, and any bankruptcies. And then I reach the line that reads *public records*. Here, my heart stops. In letters that seem to jump off the page and mock me are two words, *marriage license*.

I sit dazed, staring down at the paper and the words that shouldn't feel so earth-shattering. I knew this, knew it down deep in the place where I shove everything uncomfortable, which includes the truths I don't want to acknowledge. This hidey-hole of sorts is where I tuck away any trace of things sad or worrisome since childhood, where all my defeats and regrets get stuffed, and where I keep all the insults ever slung at me. My heartbreaks, failings, shame, guilt, all of it buried layer upon layer, in what my counselor calls my shit bag. She warns me against continuing to cram more into the bag, telling me it will reach maximum capacity one day and burst. I laughed at that, at her, when she said this. I am masterful at compartmentalizing, putting on a pleasant face, and pulling myself up by my bootstraps. Why then do I feel a tremble of warning coming over me?

"Thank you, Matt," I say, doing everything I can to hold my composure. "I'm grateful for your honesty." Matt's gaze meets mine. His eyes are shiny, filled with a look of regret, pain, sorrow, and worry. "We've been through a lot," I say, leaning in to rest my head on his shoulder. "I love you, my friend."

Matt sits with me, quiet, both of us lost in our thoughts. "Would you mind leaving now?" I break the silence, "I would like to be alone." I do my best to speak the words in a non-offensive, gentle tone.

Looking both concerned and relieved, Matt gets to his feet, gives me a last soft hug, longer than usual, and leaves. I curl back into my safe-place afghan, and weep and weep and weep. The dam breaks, and a tsunami of grief, pain, and loss flood my heart, sweeps away my dreams, and empties my shit bag.

CHAPTER
37

Time has lost all meaning and no longer dictates my routine or bodily functions. When I'm tired, I sleep; when I'm hungry, I eat, regardless of the hour. It seems a lifetime ago that I would wake to an alarm, rush to attend meetings and court hearings, and eat at the prescribed hours of six AM, noon, and six PM. Since my diagnosis, and especially during treatment, I'm more awake during the evening and less hungry in daylight.

I cried myself into a deep sleep after learning of the marriage license and wake the next day with new clarity. I've had a change in perspective. There's a gnawing inside my belly. Hunger maybe, or perhaps reflux; I can't distinguish the difference anymore. *No,* my inner voice corrects me, *that is an ache, and you know what you need to do.*

I reach for my phone, my hands shaking. My voice will be too, but these words need to be said aloud. This is the end of my life, and I will tell my truths, no matter their ugliness, no matter their cost.

I scroll through the contacts until the familiar number shows up, and then I touch the call button, going straight to voicemail.

Try as I might, my words come out jittery and husky, "Hi, it's Sera, please call me." I end the call and pray.

A minute later, my phone vibrates with a voicemail.

Strange, it didn't ring. I listen to the familiar voice that's left a message, "Hey, it's me, call me back."

I push redial. The call is answered on the first ring. "Hello?"

"Hi," I stammer, "it's Sera."

"I know who it is," the voice on the other end says.

"I need to talk to you. Can we meet? Usual place? Tomorrow at four?" My scan will be complete by then.

"Sure," the response is quick, and then, "I'm glad to hear your voice."

My heart chokes in my throat, making it impossible for me to speak. Instead, I nod. It had been months since I'd heard from him, since just before I got sick, but his voice still stops my heart. I disconnect the call and don't sleep again until morning.

An hour before the scan, I shuffle into the closet, change into a dress that hangs oversized on my wasting body, and layer on a bulky sweater that will provide warmth and hide my deterioration.

I accessorize with big earrings and bright lipstick (the trick Carolyn mentioned on the day of my diagnosis) and tie a beautiful gray and red silk scarf around my baldness. I grab my purse, sling it crosswise over my body, pause, swallow hard, and then grab my cane. My shoulders sag.

"Ms. Kincaid," Stefan's gentle voice calls out through the intercom, "your car has arrived."

"Thank you. I'll be right down."

"Do you need help?" Stefan, ever the gentleman, asks when I exit the elevator.

"No, I can manage." I make my way into the lobby, and Vance rushes to my side, cupping my elbow with his palm. It is nice to have the steadiness of him on one side and the cane on the other. Vance sits beside me in the car as it makes its way to the imagery center and waits outside while I have my scan.

———

When I climb back into the car, I'm weary and trembling. I can feel the color drain from my face.

"Sera?" Vance asks.

I shake my head, the news is not good.

We ride back to the building in silence. Vance helps settle me back into my condo just before Carolyn pops in for her afternoon check.

"How's everything?" she asks, suspicious at seeing Vance.

"Oh, hiya," he says, leaning to kiss Carolyn on each cheek. "I'm just leaving, gotta go to work. Toodles," he says, rushing out the door.

"I'm exhausted, Carolyn; come back tonight?"

———

After I wake, I apply more color to my lips and call for my ride; it's only eight blocks to the café, but there's no way I can walk it. I arrive early and sit for a moment in the back seat of the stranger's car, wringing my hands.

"Let me help you," the driver says, jumping out of her seat and opening my door, extending her hand to me. Since Seattle, I've never accepted a ride share from a man.

I lay mine in hers, apologizing as my cane clunks into the back of the seat as I exit. I make my way to the front of the Flying M and check my reflection in the glass. Startled by what I see staring back and me, I avert my eyes and pull open the door. Sitting at the corner table, leaning against the window, sits Zac, his anticipation and nervousness filling the room.

Our eyes meet, and he leaps from his chair, reaching me in a few steps. He gathers me in his arms, holding me, forcing the air from my chest.

"My God, it's so good to see you," he says, loosening his grip just enough to take in my face.

I see Vance out of the corner of my eye, standing behind the counter, his mouth agape. He covers it with one hand, giving me a thumbs-up approval with the other.

Zac steps back to assess me and asks, "Can I help you?"

I shake my head, steadying myself with my cane, feeling the familiar rush of heat flood my face as I stand close to him. I close my eyes, breathe in his woodsy musk. I want to imprint his smell on my brain. We move toward our table, Zac slows his pace to match the speed of my shuffle.

"Sera, what . . . ?" His words fall off as we sit.

"I have terminal cancer, Zac." There's no need to wade in the pool of niceties.

He deflates in front of me, his eyes welling up with tears. "What? When?"

"Lymphoma, in a nutshell. Diagnosed a while ago, and . . ." I pause, take a breath, and say the tough words, "I knew you'd gotten married. Well, I just found out you got married, but I knew it long ago when I stopped hearing from you. I didn't want to burden you with my illness or step between you and Anne. It is Anne, isn't it? I've no place there."

His gaze drops to the floor. "Why didn't you tell me?" he asks. I'm not sure he heard what I said, that I knew he was married.

He sits shaking his head, lost in what can only be disbelief. And when he looks up again, I can see he's holding something back. I see it in his eyes, the way they dart back and forth to mine, the flare of his nostrils, and the way he nervously licks his lips. I wait, and he finally says, "I would have been there for you. Why didn't you call me?"

"It wasn't right."

"Then why did you call me now?"

"It still isn't right, I know that, and I'm sorry, but I just needed to tell you something."

He leans across the table and grasps my hands, waiting. I take a breath and open the floodgates.

"You are the most important person in my life," I say. "You have made me feel whole and complete, fixed a brokenness I didn't think possible." Snot and tears converge into a single river flowing down my chin. "I love you."

"I never stopped reaching out to you."

"What?"

"I never stopped texting you." His voice is low. "You never texted back," he says. The hurt and anguish in his words pierce my soul.

"I-I got no texts." I wipe the wetness from my face with the back of my hand, questioning Zac's words; *is he lying to me?*

"I swear. I've texted you so many times." He picks up his phone and scrolls through the messages. "I've deleted everything," mumbling, he scolds himself. "Give me your phone," he demands. "What's your password?"

I give him a knowing grin, "I don't have one."

"Of course, you don't." He smiles and begins scrolling through the list of names in my contacts, looking for his.

"You're just a number," I bite my bottom lip, embarrassed, "at the bottom of my phone."

Zac scrolls to the bottom and taps a few buttons on the screen. "My number is blocked." He thrusts the phone in my direction, showing me the screen with its slide bar highlighted in green next to the word "block."

"I-I don't even know how to block someone."

"I believe you. You are not the least bit techy. But it's blocked. Is it okay if I unblock it?" He waits for me to nod and swipes the screen, laying the phone face down on the table. It vibrates, notifying me of an incoming text. I ignore it; sure, it is Carolyn. Another vibration rattles the table, followed by another, and another, and yet another until the notifications come in a steady barrage.

Flustered, I grab the phone. "I'm sorry, I don't know what's going on," I say more to myself. "I'm sure it's Carolyn."

I feel my jaw go slack. "Oh my," I whisper. "There are seventy-four missed texts." The phone continues to vibrate in brief spurts, *buzz, buzz, buzz*. Messages populate the previously stored texts that, until moments ago, sat unseen, waiting in the wings. I lift my gaze to meet Zac's, "They're all from you."

"What?!" Zac jumps, recoiling in disbelief and unease. "No way."

"This is the first I've seen of these."

"I thought that's why you called." He's looks mortified, "Because you finally decided to respond to one of my texts."

I offer him the phone.

Scrolling through the texts, he goes red, "Oh, my God—this is embarrassing."

The first message in the thread has a date corresponding to my diagnosis. It only reads, "Hello."

The subsequent text, a day later, says, "How are you?"

Still, a few days later, another message. "I hope you are well."

In the following days, texts say, "I'm going to coffee, meet me at eight? Usual spot."

The next text, time-stamped an hour later reads, "Sigh" and a sad-face emoji.

I continue scrolling through the dozens of texts as Zac squirms in his seat. I read through some texts aloud:

"I miss you."

"Thinking of you."

"Would like to see you. Lunch?"

"Maybe next time."

There's a pattern. Zac reaches out every few days, asks how I am, gives a meeting spot and time, and then texts his disappointment when I don't join him. There is the occasional random sexting, where perhaps he was missing me more than usual, or maybe he thought they might elicit a response.

"I want you."

"I can taste you."

"Meet me in the stairwell?"

Dozens and dozens of unanswered texts span the days, weeks, and months. All since I've been diagnosed and all since, he had gotten married. Zac has indeed never stopped reaching out and never given up, even when I didn't respond.

Stunned, I scroll to the very end, hearing his voice in each message. "I didn't know." My words so soft I can barely hear them. "Yet, you never stopped." I look at him through my sobs. "And you're married," I whisper, sad and confused.

"It's not like you think. I love *you*, Serenade," tears brim in his eyes. He opens his mouth as if to say something more he but holds back.

There are so many things I want to say. I had planned out this meeting with precision. See him, thank him, tell him how much he meant to me, say goodbye. *But now what? He never stopped trying to see me? What about his wife and the baby?*

What about Vance? I realize that if Zac came to the Flying M over and over, Vance saw him and said nothing to me. I twist in my chair and glare at Vance, who is occupied with a customer.

"I asked him not to say anything," Zac's voice answers my unspoken question, "begged him, more like it." I turn back to face Zac, unsure how I feel now.

"I didn't know you weren't getting my messages," Zac continues, still holding my hands across the table. "But I kept showing up. I think the poor guy felt sorry for me." An embarrassed chuckle escapes Zac's throat. "He started bringing me two cups of soy chai lattes, both with a splash of vanilla and sitting them on the table without me asking. I would sip one and wait, leaving the other untouched, just in case."

"But why didn't he tell me, anyway? He's my friend and knows . . ." My tongue hitches, and the words *I love you* stay in my mouth.

"Sometimes, Sera, the kindest thing is not to tell. I think Vance thought this would hurt you more than help you, and given your—your condition, which I assume he knew, he probably thought he was making the right call."

CHAPTER

38

When my marriage dissolved from infidelity, I promised myself I would never spend time with a married man. I am admittedly breaking that promise. Zac and I spend every moment we can together. He stops in at my blood draws, a place that Carolyn avoids because of her propensity to faint at the sight of blood. He sits in my hospital room with me when Carolyn departs for work. We share food and laughter and tears during sappy movies in the middle of the day. We hold hands as we walk through the park when I feel up to it, frequenting Catherine Albertson's downtown so I can watch the wildlife. But we don't have sex. I won't, can't most days because I'm too ill, but wouldn't even if I could; I know the hurt of being the other woman. Regardless, I'm ashamed of myself but I don't want to die without this experience of love. I also know sooner than later I'll no longer be any woman's threat.

My phone vibrates. I lie snuggled on the couch with Doris's afghan blanket, watching reruns of *Friends*, eating fried hamburger and macaroni and cheese. I look at the screen and read the text.

"Hey love, meet me at the Riverside Hotel. I have a surprise for you."

I message back. "I'm not sleeping with you."

He has again agreed to my terms, and our intimacy and pleasure come in a unique form now: conversation, holding hands, kissing, and laughter.

"Just meet me. I promise I won't seduce you."

I can hear Zac's smile through the message. *You always try to seduce me.*

"Room 228."

He gives me no choice, not that I want one. I force myself off the couch, do the chemo-shuffle to the closet and throw on something other than fuzzy pajamas. Over text I ask Stefan to hail a car.

The driver drops me off at the Riverside, and the lock clicks as soon as I tap on the door; he's been waiting for me. He pulls me in and holds me close, whispering in my neck, "I've missed you." He leads me to the bedside, sits me down, and kneels in front of me, holding my hands. "How are you, Sera?"

Putting my best face forward, I smile and lie, "I'm alright."

Zac pauses a moment, staring into my eyes, then reaches up with the back of his fingers and strokes my cheek.

"I'm so sorry, Sera. I'm sorry I can't be there for you more of the time." His eyes fill with emotion.

"I appreciate the time you give me. It means more than you could ever know." I kiss his fingers as they brush across my lips.

Taking my hand, he helps me up and leads me into the bathroom. "Here's your surprise," he says, stripping off his jeans and t-shirt. My heart races as he kneels in the bathtub.

"Since when do you wear underwear?" I giggle.

"Shut it," he smiles. "Reach into the bag." He points to a dark gray gym bag lying on the floor.

"Is something going to bite me?"

"Just reach into the bag," he scolds. Childlike, I inch my hand into the folds of canvas and pull out a pair of hair clippers.

"Go ahead," he says, waiting.

"I-I can't."

"Why not? It's just hair. It will grow back."

"But your . . ." I can't say "wife," can't give Anne the label she owns, the one I so desperately want. "It's not like you can hide this." I drop my gaze, shame rushing through me. "You don't have to do this."

"I don't have to do anything." Zac grabs the clippers. "And no one will notice or care," he says. There is a bite to his words. He buzzes a swath down the middle of his head, handing the shears to me. "Now finish it," his grin melts my heart.

When I finish, Zac reaches up and rubs his hand back and forth along the stubble. I catch sight of a subtle indentation on his left ring finger where his wedding band has worn a grove. Nausea takes hold, and I slump onto the toilet lid.

"Are you okay?" Zac asks, frantic.

"I'm a little queasy."

———

Carolyn helps settle me into the hospital for my next round of chemo. It's only been a few short weeks since the last time I was here, when Rafa and I had our frank conversation about how the cancer was outpacing the chemo. My private scan results, the one I had without Carolyn, had not been good, and Dr. Z and I had agreed this treatment would be my last, and it was, in his words, a Hail Mary.

As I change into my comfy pajamas, ready for my port to be accessed, Carolyn busies herself setting up her makeshift office. While fearing her wrath, the nurses also seem to respect her tenacity and her care of me as upon arrival, they supply her with an extra bedside table, a straight-back chair, and a fan; the drugs cause me to shiver, which results in my request to turn up the room's temperature.

"Are you settled, Sera?" asks Brea. She was my first nurse, the one with the bouncy ponytail. We've become friendly, and she's assigned to my care with each of my admissions.

"I am." I climb into the bed and pull my afghan blanket around my chest.

"Time for doxorubicin," Brea says, then leans in. "The red devil."

"Ugh."

Dressed in her full hazmat suit, complete with hood and plastic face shield, Brea sits beside me, injecting tiny milligrams of the brilliant, ruby-red serum into my IV until the combination of drug and saline becomes a pale salmon color. She then pushes the fluid into my port, where it will course through my body. This drug is serious business and takes time, experience, and a steady hand to administer.

"What's on your mind," Carolyn asks, sliding her chair close to the bed.

"My party," I answer, staring at the concoction as it travels up the tube and into my body, "I'd like to plan it."

Carolyn stiffens at my request, but she honors her promise

made when we started this journey and says in a choked, low tone, "Okay, let's do it."

"What's the occasion?" Brea asks, concentrating on the push of the red devil and the pull of the saline.

"A live celebration of Sera's life, one that she will attend."

"Oh," Brea says and then smiles, thoughtfully, "I like that idea."

"Right?" I jump in. "I should be present at my celebration of life. Otherwise, it should be called a celebration of death." There's an awkward pause followed by uncomfortable laughter.

"I'd like little gift bags filled with stupid fun mementos, Tic Tacs, and yo-yos," I say.

Carolyn jots down notes. "And Doritos and Milk Duds, all your favorites," she adds.

"And 'fuck cancer' bracelets," Brea offers, not looking away from the nasty red poison.

"And 'fuck cancer' bracelets," Carolyn and I say in unison, grinning at each other, sharing another Thelma and Louise moment.

"I'd like turkey dinner with all the fixins," I say, remembering my date with William and his father at Paul Baptiste's restaurant. I wonder for a second if William and his wife ever worked out their issues.

"Turkey, stuffing, rolls," Carolyn dictates aloud as she types, having switched from a writing pad to her laptop.

"Sweet potatoes with the little marshmallows," I add.

"Green bean casserole," Brea says. "My mouth is watering."

"Mom's recipe," Carolyn and I again chime in together.

"My mom makes the best," I brag to Brea.

"And the gelatinous cranberry sauce in the can." I rub my palms together.

"Eew," Carolyn stops typing and wrinkles her nose.

"Oh my gosh, I love that kind." Brea shoots a quick look in my direction and then looks back to her task. "The kind that makes the slow slurping sound when it slides out of the can, and you cut it with a knife?"

"That's the one." I lean toward Carolyn, "Be sure there is that kind of cranberry sauce, okay? I don't want your fancy-pants kind with the real little berries."

She rolls her eyes. Her phone pings, and she turns it over. "Stefan and Vance are already on it. They've reserved the Grove for Friday night three weeks from now; they have the DJ booked too."

"Impressive," Brea says.

"We've had this planned for a while," I confide. "I was just waiting for the, well," I pause, this new reality sinking in, "the right time."

The three of us sit, lost in our thoughts. Brea finishes up with the treatment and slips out of the room as Dr. Z steps in.

"Hello, Sera," he says, smiling at me and placing a hand on my shoulder. To Carolyn, he nods and says, "Good to see you."

"Doctor," Carolyn has a suspicious look in her eyes. "What can we do for you?"

"I'm here as the bearer of not good news," he says, looking at me for reassurance; I give him a quick go-ahead blink. I made him promise to do this when Carolyn was here, since she'll never stop looking for miracles unless these words come directly from him. Dr. Z draws in a deep breath and says to Carolyn, "This will be Sera's last round of treatment. I'm sorry, I can do nothing more. I suggest you contact hospice."

"What?" Carolyn jumps to her feet, wobbling, reaching for something to hold.

Then to me, he says, "Sera, it has been my pleasure." He bows at the waist and turns on his heel.

"Wait! You can't leave," Carolyn yells to his back as he's partway down the hall. "You can't drop that bomb and then walk out. You owe her more than that." And then she screams, "You fucking coward!"

She stands outside the door for a long minute, her fists balled at her side, her body shaking. When she turns to face me, she has streaks of black mascara running down her cheeks. Through clenched teeth, she says, "You knew, didn't you?"

I nod.

Carolyn's lip quivers, and I watch a gamut of emotions wash over her face. She slides onto the bed beside me, nuzzling into my neck. I feel her defeat and impending loss as she sobs, coming to grips with the finality that she will soon lose her friend forever. She lies in my bed for hours.

"Carolyn," I whisper in the night.

"I'm here," she says, her voice soft, buried between us as she lies curled next to me.

"Please start the legal processes we talked about."

I feel the nod of her head and hear a faint sniff.

CHAPTER

39

Each day beyond chemo finds me with more energy and less fatigue. I've cut down on all my medications and am using marijuana during the day for pain control; still illegal in Idaho, but accessible forty miles away over the state line in Oregon.

Carolyn enlists Matt's help in finding people from my past who positively affected my life and whom I want to honor. While labeled a celebration of my life, my party will be my way of honoring and thanking others; they just don't know that, yet.

Matt reaches out to people from my hometown in northern Idaho and as far away as New York, where I bolted right after high school. It was short-lived, my time in the Big Apple as a nanny, but I made a few lasting friends in SoHo and want to see them. He helps me find random people I had connected with in airports and at seminars that made a lasting impact or an effective change in the way I thought of the world. And he helps get addresses for those as close as city hall and the prosecutor's office. My goal is to let these people know they have mattered in my life, that their presence and their existence has been profound. The list of people has grown to hundreds. This makes me proud.

I have four outfits for the party, wanting to arrive at the celebration in one ensemble, change twice during the dancing and festivities, and then leave in the fourth outfit. I opt for a chic A-line dress in a raspberry hue with matching kitten-heel pumps for my entrance ensemble. I will change into a floor-length ball gown that will twirl as I dance around the floor. My third outfit is a stunning, backless, black jumpsuit with wide legs and a plunge to my navel. I will wear a long necklace to show off my decolletage and long earrings for accent. My fourth and final change is the plushest velour pajama set I could find; I will leave in comfort.

"Are you sure you don't want me to escort you?" Carolyn says on the evening of the event, fussing over invisible lint on my dress.

"Positive. Now go, I'll meet you there soon." I hug her and shoo her out the door. I look around at the bare walls of the condo, patched where pictures and photos once hung. The beautiful wooden floors are now covered with boxes filled with my things, each labeled and addressed to where they will be shipped or delivered or donated.

There's a small box of throwaway items. I glance in it, mostly filled with paper and personal items, significant only to me. I smile at the bundle of keys in the box. I found them in the back of a drawer. They were ghoster Cary's, belonging to his horse trailer.

Next to the discard items, a donation pile overflows with my clothes and shoes, handbags, and accessories, as well as kitchen and bathroom items. Nothing from either of these piles will make the next leg of my journey.

The lock clicks, and Stefan calls out, his voice echoing, "Ms. Kincaid, I'm here to escort you."

I said goodbye to Zac a few days earlier. I won't allow him to attend my party; it would be too much for me. I would never mingle, wanting to spend every second with him. I was also afraid he might never leave. But he's not coming with me, where I'm going, and I need him to go back to his life, the real one with his wife and the child they're raising together.

"Please, move on with your life," I had begged him.

We had cried in each other's arms, doing our best to ease the other's grief with promises of meeting again, at another time, in another life.

"Thank you, Stefan." I come back to the present and walk out of my room, my progress slow.

"You look beautiful, Ms. Kincaid," Stefan gushes. I don't deflect his compliment, although I know I am gaunt, bald, and not near as glamorous as I envisioned I would be for this event.

"Please, call me Sera," I smile. "I am no longer a tenant here." The place sold in a day, fetching an outrageous price; real estate in Boise has skyrocketed for years, and I reaped its reward.

Stefan stumbles with his words, "Ms. . . . er, S-Sera. You are doing a wonderful thing."

I hold up my hand to stop his effusing and hold back my tears. "Let's go," I whisper and turn off the light.

———

The buzz of the crowd drifts out to the lobby where Stefan and I stand, preparing to enter. Stefan reaches for the handle, always the doorman and waits for my approval. I nod, and he pulls open the enormous door. We are met by a crowd of hundreds, chatting and drinking, mingling, and nibbling.

"They are all here for you." He is clearly astonished, as am I.

"Yes, I suppose you're right."

The DJ stops the music mid-song and announces, "And here she is! Everyone welcome our friend, Sera."

The room erupts in clapping, and people rush to greet me, swarming around me, speaking all at once.

"Let her through, folks. Sera, would you like to say something?" the DJ asks above the din.

I make my way to the front of the room and grab the microphone. "Thank you, thank you all for coming. I'm overwhelmed to see so many of you made such long journeys to be here." I cup my hand over my eyes, shading them from the lights and staring into the sea of people.

"Oh my gosh, Trevor? Is that you?" I laugh. "Everyone, I met Trevor on my trip to Australia after college. He was kind enough to save me from a hoodlum pickpocketing eight-year-old on the Metro. Trevor got my wallet back, empty, of course, and lent me two hundred American until my mom could express me some money. The check's in the mail, Trevor." I give an exaggerated wink, and the room laughs.

"Mrs. Elvin?" I cover my mouth with my hand. "She, folks, was my high school English teacher and gave me a D in her class. The best lesson I ever learned in school: stay awake in class." More laughter.

"Doris?" my voice squeaks, and I choke. Carolyn rushes to my side, ever the caregiver. She had been waiting in the wings, just in case. She holds me until I regained my composure.

"Thank you," I whisper, directing my comment to Doris. I won't elaborate.

I gather myself, drawing in a breath. "As you all know by the invitation, this is my celebration of life. I decided, during treat-ment, that I wanted to be with you for the party, with those I love, before riding off into the sunset."

An uncomfortable wave of nervous laughter ripples through the crowd.

My throat tightens, emotions getting to me. "You are each here because you have made a positive, lasting difference in my life. This celebration is about you and us. I'm not sure I can address each of you this evening. Still, please know, however, whatever our interaction, be it little or great, the time we spent together was meaningful for me, enough so that I want you here now. You are my people, my tribe." I pause to more murmurs. "I appreciate you, and I have never forgotten you." I choke, my voice cracking, hot tears flowing down my cheeks. "I love all of you."

A collective "Aww" rolls through the room.

"We love you too," a man's voice calls.

"I love you, Sera," another unknown voice shouts, and another, until the room is at a deafening volume of clapping, whistles, and shouts.

CHAPTER
40

"¿A donde?" the cab driver looks in his rear view for my response.

"Steve's Bar, por favor."

"Si."

"¿Cual es tu nombre?" I ask the friendly driver.

"Javier." He flashes me a smile through the mirror. Javier turns on the radio. "It's okay?" he asks, using his best English.

"Si."

He turns the volume low, and I catch his curious look through the two-way. Everyone stares at me these days, but today I'm too tired to explain my situation to this stranger. Closing my eyes instead, I choose to ride in silence.

"Señora, aqui; Steve's Bar." Javier says loudly.

"Gracias." I rouse, dig in my purse, and ask how much, "¿Cuanto es?"

"Diez dólares." Javier holds up all his fingers.

"Gracias." I give him an American twenty. "¿Espéra por favor?" I'm hoping he will wait outside for me.

Nodding, Javier jumps out of the car and, taking my elbow,

assists me up the stairs and through the bar door. A wan smile crosses my lips, and he gives a knowing nod.

After acclimating to the pub's dim light, I shuffle over to the bar, where the blaring television drowns out my thoughts. Steve stands behind the bar, washing glasses, watching a soccer match on the screen. I totter over and stood in front of him.

"Hello. How can I . . . ?"

Staring at me, taking in my gaunt face and hollow eyes, the scarf covering my head and my clothes hanging off me, a glimmer of recognition sparks in his eyes.

"Sera," I answer his silent question.

"Oh, my God," Steve runs around the bar and hugs me, holding me in a gentle squeeze. "Let me help you." He scoots a stool behind me and guides me onto the seat. "Sera, love, what happened? I mean, I can see what happened," he stammers, his cheeks turning red.

My fatigue shows through the tiny upturn of my lips and shallow breathing. Steve wastes no time. "Let me get Marin." He starts toward the back of the bar, stops, and turns back toward me. "Are you okay?"

I nod, shooing him with my hand, and he continues his way to the back.

Marin rushes out from the backroom, drying her hands as she walks, "Sera, sweetheart," she says in her gruff Chicago accent. "What the hell happened to you?" Pulling me close, she gives me a long, soft hug.

"I fought like hell, but cancer's winning. I've stopped treatment, and I've come here to spend my last days." Marin and Steve pass a glance between them, and tears well in their eyes, Marin's spilling onto her cheeks.

"Oh, Sera," she whispers, clasping her hand over her mouth. "I'm so sorry."

I've heard those words so many times in recent weeks, everyone saying they're sorry.

"I'll be staying at New Amber resort. Carolyn will come down in a few days. If you'd like to join us, we'll be there until, well . . . until the end." I punctuate the statement with a coughing fit.

"Could I have some water? I need to take some meds." Steve appears thankful for something to do and rushes around the counter to fetch my drink.

"Thank you," I say, taking the cold bottle.

Marin wrings her hands. "How long?"

"I don't know. A month or two, probably less." The air becomes thick and Marin fans her face with her hand. Steve clears his throat.

"I have a cab waiting," I say and stand.

I hug them and lumber to the door, where I stop and turn to them. "Thank you, my friends. Cliché, but true, you were always a port in the storm." Marin hugs herself, and Steve wraps an arm around her shoulder. I hear a sniffle as I pull open the door to find Javier leaning against the cab, smoking a cigarette; *he waited.*

"¿Adonde?" Javier asks, as he helps settle me back into the car.

"New Amber." I lean against the door, having no option but to trust my driver, as I close my eyes and drift fast, the oxy hitting my bloodstream quick through my near-empty stomach. I am surviving on not much more than dry toast and crackers, which keep the pills down and nausea at bay. I still have times when I'm up and walking and feeling well, but those days are less and less frequent.

"¿Señora?" Javier whispers, "¿Señora?"

I look up to find Javier peering over the top of the seat. During the drive, I had slid down the door, curled up, and slept the twenty-five minutes to the hotel. I try to lift myself to a seated position, leaning on my elbow to catch my breath. Javier throws open his door and then mine. "Espere a que te ayudaré." Javier's telling me to wait for him to help.

He lifts me upright and waits for me to regain my strength before assisting me out of the cab. Javier then yells in rapid-fire Spanish to the doorman, a younger man in his early twenties. He commands the younger man to bring a wheelchair.

Javier and the doorman settle me into the wheelchair amidst my useless protests. He grabs my bags out of the trunk and hands them to the other man. "La ayudaré." Javier insists on helping me.

The bellman argues with Javier in Spanish, "This is my job," the young man says, waving his hands.

Javier wins the fight and pushes my chair through the lobby, to the front desk to check-in, and then onto the elevator. The bellman follows behind, fuming and lugging my bags. Javier waits when the doors open on the fourth floor for the bellman to exit the elevator with my luggage. He then pushes me after him, the wheelchair bumping over the metal doorjamb. "Lo siento," Javier apologizes.

"Estoy bien," I respond.

The bellman opens the door and steps aside. Javier pushes me through, and the junior man follows with my bags. The rush of air-conditioning reinvigorates me.

"Will you need further help with your bags?" says the younger of the two in perfect English.

"No, thank you. I can manage. Are you from Vallarta?"

"I am. I went to university at San Diego State—Go Warriors!" He pumps his fist.

"That's fantastic. What did you study?"

"Architecture. I'm waiting for my paperwork before I can apply for jobs. I'm hoping to open a firm one day," he says, proudly.

"What's your name?"

"It is Daniel, senorita."

"Daniel, you speak excellent English without a hint of an accent. I'm surprised four years in the States accomplished that for you."

He shrugs. "Both my parents also went to university in the States. When they married, they raised us kids in an English-speaking household, giving us a 'leg up,' as they say. When we were outside the house or with our grandparents or other relatives, we spoke Spanish. I've known how to speak both languages all my life."

"Your parents were forward thinkers."

He smiles a full-faced grin and nods with pride. "What may I call you?"

"I'm Sera."

"Miss Sera, anything else?" Javier struggles to say in what is likely his best English.

"No, gracias, Javier. Has sido de gran ayuda."

"I'm happy to help. Call if you need," Javier says slowly, exaggerated, and hands me a business card with worn edges and smudge marks. It has his number and name, Javier Ortega-Villa. I make a mental note to take him up on the offer for a ride in the future.

"Gracias, Javier, gracias."

"De nada," he says, settling me into a chair, looking out over the ocean before he pushes the wheelchair into the hallway. Daniel follows Javier, holding the door so it shuts with only a slight *click*.

I survey the suite, a luxurious room with marble tile, Jacuzzi tub, and private dining. A mirrored version of my room is next door for Carolyn when she joins me. Separate spaces will afford each of us privacy, yet proximity for my healthcare needs. These rooms will be where she and I live until I live no more. I shuffle to the bed, pull the afghan blanket brought from home up to my chin, and close my eyes.

CHAPTER
41

Every morning is a surprise. I no longer take for granted waking up after I close my eyes. One of these days, I know I won't.

On this morning, like every other, I assess my pain before rolling out of bed. I move my neck, *not much pain*, arch my back, *stiff but manageable*, flex my muscles, *nothing excruciating yet*. I grade my days on a scale of "I've lived through worse," to "best day of my life." Today receives a mark of excellence.

It's nice to have a day alone before Carolyn arrives; she stayed in Boise, wrapping up my legal affairs before joining me for the last phase of my life. My condo sold for a staggering amount of money, my meager retirement (after Clint took his portion), and a few other assets have enabled me to gift decent sums to deserving persons, keeping most of my charity local.

I make my way to the patio overlooking the ocean, pull my floppy hat low, and cover myself with a towel. I open the novel I've tried frequently to read, but I wind up drifting again, pondering my life—an act I seem to do every day now, wondering if my life matters, whether I made a good and lasting mark. As with every evaluation, I pause at the memory of individual people and certain times; my failed marriage, my stepdaughters, Elise and Hailey, my lost child, who would be orphaned if he or she had survived.

I push the negative from my mind and focus on my beautiful life, filled with great intellectual stimulation, adventure, and romance. My career, taxing and challenging as it often was, neither consumed nor defined me. My family had always been supportive and loving, something too few can say. And I acquired a passel of friends who filled most of my voids. In all honesty, I am quite fortunate.

My memories jump from my dearest friend and most significant pain in the ass, Carolyn, to Meg, Vance and Stefan, Matt, and Zac, always Zac. I close my eyes, drawing on my memories of his smell, kiss, touch, and how he was never mine, but I was always his.

"Hello, Miss Sera." I open my eyes to find the young bellman, Daniel, standing beside me. "I hope you don't mind. You didn't answer when I knocked or rang. I used my key." He stammers, apologetic, "Miss Carolyn gave permission, saying to keep an eye—"

"Daniel, under these circumstances, you may always come in. I appreciate you checking on me. I was just resting, thinking."

"I brought you some complimentary bottles of water and a snack. We have standing orders from Miss Carolyn to bring you a bite and something to drink every three hours until she arrives." His face turns red.

The door of the room next to mine opens, and I hear the familiar voice calling out instructions.

"Daniel, please put my bags in the closet. And don't forget bottled water every day. Oh, and snacks, healthy ones. I sent a list, dear." Her commands drip with honey. "You are a love. Sera is right." I want to hide.

"Hello again, Miss Sera."

Looking up from where I sit on the couch, I smile at Daniel.

"Is there anything I can get for you?" he asks.

"No, thank you, Daniel," I'm embarrassed he knows I spoke to Carolyn about him.

"Please let me know if I can help." Daniel steps out of the room.

"How are you feeling?" Carolyn asks, flopping down in the chair next to me.

"I'm not too bad. I think today is a good day."

She leans on her elbow and smiles. "It's good to see you, Sera."

"Did you get everything done?"

"I did, just as you requested."

CHAPTER

42

Carolyn and I lounge around the rooms for the first several days of my hospice, unsure what to expect, fearful my end will come quick, then surprised when it doesn't. We take to sitting outside in the mornings, playing cards in the afternoon, me sometimes dozing between hands. There are times I wake from a stupor to find Carolyn reading next to me on the bed. When I stir, she glances at me and smiles from over her book, checking in to see if I need anything.

On healthy days, we call Javier, and he takes us into town. Our outings almost always include a stop to see Steve and Marin. They greet us with resounding joy, bottomless drinks, mine of the juice and water variety, Carolyn's generally tequila, and all the wings and soda crackers we want. It's easier on them each time we stop by; the tears are fewer, and the conversation more relaxed. They, like Carolyn and I, are wrapping their minds around my impending death.

Within a few weeks of arriving in Vallarta, my hair looks like peach fuzz on a teenage boy's lip, soft and baby-fine. Although, unlike a youthful person, mine has a generous sprinkling of gray.

Javier is now on standby. Carolyn pays him full-time to run errands, escort us on outings, and wait for us as we shop or check in with the doctor. He's become a trusted and dear friend, as has Daniel.

"Javi, please take us to the church," Carolyn says. She gave up trying to speak Spanish weeks ago.

"Catedral de nuestra señora de Guadalupe," I translate.

"Si, señora." He smiles and nods approval of my Spanish.

Javier parks in front of the cathedral in the center of the old downtown tourist hub, just a few blocks from Steve's. He runs around the car, opens my door and helps me out, pops the trunk lid and retrieves the walker Carolyn purchased from the *farmacia* where she also purchased Benadryl straws, a forehead thermometer, a shower seat, and a baby monitor.

Carolyn and I were close to blows over the baby monitor. "I'm not an infant," I yelled in the pharmacy's aisle, leaning onto the walker for support.

"But you are ill, and I need to hear you," she'd said, leaving no room for further discussion.

As time passes, I will need adult diapers, wipes, and underpads for the bed. But for now, I'm still upright and continent. However, a baby monitor is a necessity, or so I am told.

Upon entering the church, I dip a finger into the holy water at the front entrance. I then touched my wet finger to my forehead, middle of my chest, and then my left and right shoulders. It had been years since I had performed this Catholic ritual but thought it couldn't hurt.

Carolyn eyes me, and then she, too, dips her finger.

The church is exquisite with its high marble white columns,

decorative cornices, and gold embellished filigree and scrollwork. Behind the altar there's an enormous portrait of the Virgin Mary, her hands clasped together in prayer, holding a rosary. Her son, the well-known carpenter's boy, is painted high above her. A golden glow encircling his head angelic-like—an image I would guess is every mother's vision of her child.

I shuffle to a pew in the middle of the church. Unable to genuflect, I bow my head, cross myself again, and then slip in between two pews, leaving my walker in the aisle. Carolyn follows my lead, also lowering her head and crossing herself as she sits next to me. I pull down the hassock from under the bench in front of us, scoot forward, and rest on the hard wooden plank. With my hands folded, I bow my head and pray. Carolyn copies my motions.

Lord? It's me, Serenade. Sorry it's been so long. I pause, feeling childish, but wanting to make sure God knows it's me. I shift in my seat, my kneecaps aching on the hardwood kneeler. *Please let Carolyn be happy. She's been with me for so long; I'm not sure she will know what to do when I'm gone. I pray for Marta, Lord, that she has a good retirement. She was terrific to me.*

I peek through the slits of my eyelids at Carolyn, kneeling beside me, hands clasped in prayer, eyes closed. I smile. Faith looks good on her.

I turn my focus back to my prayers.

Please bless Doris. She's already an angel, but maybe you can elevate her status to "saint." I almost giggle but refrain, reminding myself this is serious.

You know this, I think, but I feel I need to say the words, "I've forgiven Rodney." I would ask that you help him fight his demons. I can't dwell on this subject.

God, please take care of Zac. Keep him safe and help him find some peace with his wife. I pray he finds joy and fulfillment with her child . . . their *child. And God*—I pause and take a deep breath—*please don't let him forget me.*

My breathing is difficult, and my face wet. It's been a long time since I sat in a space of sincere prayer, and I'd forgotten how relieving and uplifting it feels. My shoulders straighten, and my chin comes up, my world nearly righted. But there's one more thing I need to address. I settle back into my thoughts.

God, you broke my heart by not answering my lifelong prayer. You know I wanted a family since I was a little girl. "Ask, and ye shall receive," you said. Well, I begged, but you never gave. I hated you for a long time for not giving me children. I wipe my nose before continuing. *But I guess you always knew my children would end up without a mother.*

I stay motionless, waiting for God to smite me. I open my eyes and survey the room. No locusts. No earthquakes. No trumpets. Closing my eyes one last time, I tell God, *I forgive you.*

A shiver runs through me. Carolyn's hand rests in the middle of my back, rubbing small circles, consoling me. I'm weeping, sobbing for my losses, the unborn children, my broken marriage, my unrequited love. She hands me a tissue, a staple she carries for me in her bag. We sit for a few more minutes. The tacit knowledge that we will never return passes between us.

When we exit the church, we find Javier standing outside his cab, leaning against its side, smoking a cigarette. His back is to us, and he is startled when I touch his shoulder.

"¿Me podría ofrecer un cigarrillo?" I ask.

Surprised by my request, he reaches into his shirt pocket and pulls out the box, fumbles with the lid, and hands me a cigarette. I put it between my lips. Javier holds the flame of a worn but well-polished silver lighter to the cigarette's tip. I take a drag, careful not to invoke a coughing fit, close my eyes, and let the rush of nicotine find its way through me. I blow the smoke into the air and watch it rise and disperse as I rest on my walker.

"Gracias," I whisper, as I draw another small lungful.

"You are welcome." He's been practicing his English.

Carolyn stands by for a moment, watching Javier and I smoke, and then throws her hands up, "Oh hell—give me one of those, Javi." She holds open two fingers, a child imitating a smoker. Javier wastes no time, reaches into his shirt to retrieve another cigarette, and places it between Carolyn's fingers. She sputters and chokes on the lit cigarette, her eyes watering. She doubles over, coughing, and swearing.

"Who the hell would ever want to smoke these nasty things!" She throws the offensive cigarette to the ground and crushes it out of existence with a twist of her foot.

Javier and I chuckle.

The sun is setting when I open my eyes from a much-needed nap. Carolyn is out on the patio, a half-filled glass of wine next to her with a book lying open across her chest; her head is tilted back, her mouth wide.

My caregiver's work and stress are not lost on me. I smile, and my heart fills with love. Trying not to wake her, I fiddle with the lid on my pills. The rattling bottle startles her, and I see her head pop up, alert, a sentinel, a meerkat. Eyes wide, she jumps to her feet.

Damned baby monitor.

"Sweetie, why didn't you call me?" Standing next to me, she picks up the bottle and pours a glass of water.

"You looked so peaceful."

"Don't be silly. I'm here for you."

I swallow the pills and smile at her. "And for the tequila."

CHAPTER
43

"Thanks, Steve. I appreciate your help." Carolyn shuts the door to her room as I trudge out from the bathroom with my rollator. I've advanced to a walker with a cushioned seat, so I can sit when I get winded. It has brakes on the handles to help me stop and a wire basket to carry my daily supplies of tissues, Oxy, a water bottle, and wipes. "A real honey," my dad would have called it.

"Was that Steve?"

"Yeah. He just stopped by for a minute. You were in the bathroom. He and Marin will come by later for a visit if you're up to it."

"I'm sorry I missed him."

"How are you feeling?"

"Meh, you know, this hurts and that aches." I try to downplay the severity of the pain, which has become near debilitating, coming in waves that suck the breath out of me and cause me to double over or need to sit. Hence the recent purchase of my cherry-red Cadillac-style walker.

"Steve brought you a little something." Carolyn's grin says it all.

"Oh?"

"A little ganja."

"What?"

"A spliff, a J, a doobie—you know, some four-twenty."

"Oh my God, Carolyn, when did you get so gangsta?" I wipe my eyes and cough. "You're killing me."

"Ha-ha," she mocks. "Come on, let's sit out on the patio and have some Indica."

"In da couch." I flash my best gangster sign, causing Carolyn to belly laugh.

I push the walker onto the deck and sit under the shade of the table umbrella. The ocean's waves hold my gaze. Carolyn lights the joint and passes it to me.

"Remember the first time Meg brought you back some weed from Oregon?"

"Holy crap, yes." I choke on the words, holding in the smoke as best I can. "Here's a little something-something for you," I say, doing my best impression of Meg.

Carolyn chuckles and takes another hit, holding the smoke in as she speaks. "It's ridiculous Idaho doesn't allow medical marijuana," she says, letting out her breath.

The cannabis soars through my body and eases my ridged muscles and joint pain. I relax and drift, listening to the waves lap against the rocks below.

"What is it about Zac?" Carolyn's voice crashes into my thoughts.

"Huh?"

"Zac, what's the draw? I mean, this tattooed bad-boy, Harley-riding persona, what is it?" Her words are muffled by cottonmouth, and she giggles, trying hard to remain sincere.

"He's the ice cream to my cone."

"Oh, for fuck's sake." Carolyn bursts out laughing, losing all the smoke from her lungs in a single *puh*. I crumple into myself and laugh until the coughing takes my breath.

"No, seriously, he's . . . well, I don't know." I stammer, trying to describe the "Zac effect."

"He's the bee's knees?" she says, laughing.

We pause for a few minutes, catching our breath and regaining composure. Carolyn passes me the end of the joint; I shake my head and wave it away. "No thanks. I'm stoned."

"Me too," Carolyn giggles, her voice a peep as she holds in her last hit.

"He's not a bad boy," I whisper.

"Then what is he?"

"He's likely the most caring man I've ever known."

"How so?"

"He gets me. He lets me be who I am and doesn't control any part of me. I can come and go, cry and rage, fuck him with abandon, and never worry that he will use my fantasies or fears against me. He's my yang."

"But are you his yin?"

I pause, close my eyes, and think for a moment. "Yin is the water, the contraction, inside, downward, cold, obvious. Is that me? Maybe. But for him? Maybe not."

"That's heavy, man," Carolyn says in her best stoner voice. "Real philosophical."

"You are such a shit." I slap at the air. "Zac is contrary to me in every aspect. He is complementary to my personality and brings me a sense of duality. He would be my fire, my hot, my enigma, my opposite." I nod with the veracity of a sudden thought: "He completes me."

There's a split-second hesitation before what I say catches up to us, and both Carolyn and I burst out laughing until we cry ourselves to sleep, still sitting on the patio.

––––––––––

We sleep for a solid hour in an Indica-induced coma. The sun is beating down when I open my eyes, and my skin is pink.

"Hey, Sleeping Beauty." Carolyn's voice is in my ear. "Let's get you inside."

"I'm starving," I blurt.

"That's great. I'll call Daniel."

Over chips, salsa, and Dos Equis beer (my thimble-sized serving compared to Carolyn's bottle); we revisit our patio conversation.

"So, you were telling me about how Zac was the moon to your sun or some weird crap. But what about your crazy relationship? Why didn't you two ever get together?"

"Because I was the lover, not the beloved."

"Huh?"

"In every relationship, there is a set of scales. One side is weighted by the lover—the person who does the loving—and the other side weighted by the beloved, the person who receives the love. Depending on how the scales tip will depend on how things turn out; I wasn't his beloved."

"Who are you? You did do a lot of reading."

I nod. "I did."

"So, who is his beloved, the Lamaze chick?" Carolyn asks.

"The little boy, Connor." I sigh, shaking my head. "Zac felt Connor needed a father, so he committed himself to being that."

"Well, that's all great, but what about you? You were with him before el prego and the kid."

"Nice Spanish," I say with sarcasm, rolling my eyes.

She waves her hand. "Whatever happened there?"

"I wasn't ready."

"Bullshit. You were always ready."

I dip a chip into the picante sauce and open myself up raw to her. "I chameleoned."

She takes a second to remember the word I coined. Eventually, Carolyn nods; she understands. "You became what you thought Zac wanted from you instead of being yourself?"

"Exactly."

"And what did that look like?"

"I became the listener, the independent chick that didn't want or need a man and just wanted to play." I bite my lip. "And as time went on, there was no way I would even try to take him away from that child."

"Jesus, Sera. Did he ever know this?"

"It's not like I told him, but I'm sure he knew. Didn't everyone know how I felt?"

"Yes, the entire world—except maybe Zac."

CHAPTER
44

I wake around nine o'clock, surprised as always to see another day. I run through my physical checklist of pain and rate today as reasonably good.

The baby monitor announces I've woken by broadcasting the rustle of my bed covers. Carolyn floats into my room clad in a bright yellow and white dress with a wide-brimmed floppy hat and stylish sandals.

"You look great." A jealous pang runs through me.

"And you look like shit," she says, smiling. "Let's get you up and showered. I want to try a new routine with you."

"Ugh." I pull the sheet up to my nose.

Carolyn grabs the linen and pulls it back down. "Perhaps if you get up earlier, you can enjoy more of the day."

Carolyn assists me into the bathroom, where I let the silk night-gown fall to the floor. I see her stare at the sight of my bony figure. I push the walker into the shower, and she helps me settle onto the bathing stool. We have a good shower routine, one where Carolyn only gets a few wayward drops of water on her. I often spray her with the nozzle just for fun, but this morning she looks so lovely, I don't have the heart.

Finished washing, I soak long enough to soothe my aching bones. Everything hurts these days, including my hair follicles. Carolyn helps me out of the shower and stands by, waiting patiently as I towel dry. My hair, what there is of it, requires little more than a back and forth with a towel to dry it. I've grown fond of and accustomed to its simplicity.

"Why don't you also put on a nice sundress? You always love wearing dresses," Carolyn suggests.

"Is there a reason I can't lounge around in my jammies?"

"Come on, Sera, you must keep trying. I went shopping, and I think it will do you good to get out of your pajamas for a day," Carolyn says. "Lift."

I put my arms straight over my head, feeling like a small child. She shimmies a soft blue and white gingham checked sundress over my head and past my hips. She zips up the back and cinches the tie around my midsection, but then thinks better of accentuating my thinness and loosens the tie.

"I look like I stepped out of an episode of Little House on the Prairie."

"It was the only thing in your size. And you look great." Carolyn smooths the dress down around me. "Let's put on some earrings and lipstick; that always makes you happy." She reaches into her bag for a tube of pink gloss.

"What the hell, Carolyn? What's going on here?" I swat at her hand.

Swatting back, she warns, "Hold still, or I'll make you into a clown." She doesn't bat an eye.

I stand motionless as she applies the pink color.

"There. Nice." She approves. "I think Javi should take us for a drive later. Would you like that?"

It's apparent she's trying to make me happy; I nod.

———————

There is a soft knock, followed by the click of the lock, and Daniel enters, pushing a cart filled with delicious cuisine from the kitchen and a protein shake for me; I don't eat much actual food these days. He sits with us for a few minutes, catching us up on his fun-filled, twenty-something-year-old life while Carolyn nibbles and I slurp. Daniel's become quite a fixture in our lives since we arrived in Vallarta, and he pops in, checking on us once or twice during every shift. Sometimes he even stays for a cocktail in the evening. He and Javier are now integral parts of our lives.

My new routine entails a lot of sleep, including naps after most events: shower, nap, eat, nap, shuffle outside, and nap. After brunch, I doze.

"Sera, Sera, sweetie, time to wake up." Carolyn shakes my shoulder.

"Why? What's going on?" I peel my lips apart. My tongue is dry and thick from narcotics.

"Javi's here. Remember, we're going for a drive." She looks anxious.

"I'm too tired, Carolyn," I moan, "You go." I close my eyes, willing her to disappear.

"No, Sera, you need to wake up. I told Javier we would be down in ten minutes." Carolyn lifts my body to a sitting position, my arms, and legs lifeless, flopping from side to side. "Sera," she says, her words are loud and irritated, "if you don't get up, I will put you in a wheelchair and push you." She stands with her hands on her hips, peering down at me.

"No wheelchair." My words slur as I push the drug-induced cobwebs aside and will my legs to stabilize beneath me. Carolyn pushes the walker to within an arm's length and steadies me so I don't topple backward.

Javier is waiting, poised in his usual spot, resting against the cab, smoking a cigarette. Gesturing to me, I decline his offer to join him. He puts out his cigarette and assists me into the car. He then throws open the trunk and chucks the walker, it lands with a thud. Javier then runs to the other side to open Carolyn's door.

"¿Cual es la prisa?" I ask, trying to catch Javier's eye in the mirror.

"What's the rush?" I turned toward Carolyn.

"No rush," she says, clearly lying. "Javi told me he has somewhere special to take us, and we can't be late."

"Late for what? What are you two in cahoots about?" Javier smiles in the mirror, and one corner of Carolyn's lip rises.

"Your lip twitches when you lie," I say. Carolyn touches a finger to her mouth.

Too exhausted to fight them, I rest my head on the back of the seat.

———

"Sera, Sera, we're here. Time to wake up." Carolyn is shaking my shoulder. My eyelids raise and I recognize we are at the airport.

"What are we doing here? Are we going somewhere?" I ask, rubbing the sleep from my eyes.

"We aren't going anywhere, sweetie."

We sit in silence, the three of us staring in front of the car. For what, I'm not sure.

"There!" Carolyn leans into Javier, pointing. "See?"

336

Javier throws open his door and holds up his arm. I can't make out the person walking toward us. The figure draws near with a confident saunter. A tall man, muscular and in shirtsleeves wearing black glasses. And then I see him grin.

"Oh, Carolyn." I gush. "Oh, my God." My eyes brim with tears. I would know that smile anywhere.

She wraps her arms around me and whispers, "You're welcome." Carolyn hops out of the backseat and climbs into the front of the cab.

"Hello, Serenade. Got room for one more?" Zac slides in beside me and pulls me to him. I rest my head on his chest and breathe him in with deep gulps. My cheeks are wet when I look up and into his eyes. I touch his face with my fingers.

"You're here."

"I'm here."

CHAPTER

45

At hotel New Amber, Javier retrieves my walker. I look up at Zac, sheepish and embarrassed. He kisses the top of my head and whispers, "It's okay, babe."

He called me "babe."

I shuffle into the lobby, feeling alive and almost spry. Daniel catches sight of the addition to our entourage and rushes over. "Ah, you must be Zac? I'm Daniel, so nice to meet you." He thrusts his hand toward Zac, who shakes it with enthusiasm.

"Did everyone know?" I shoot a glance at Carolyn, who refuses to engage me but smiles as she turns away.

Javier helps get me settled in my room and leans down to give me his now standard, friendly, quick hug. "Enjoy, Miss Sera."

"Thank you, Javier." I understand his effort and appreciate it. He's a great friend.

"Is there anything else you need?" Daniel asks, looking around. I shake my head.

"Okay, well, I'm here to help. Shall I come up after my shift?"

"Of course," Carolyn says.

"You're always welcome, Daniel," I say.

When he leaves, I turn my attention back to Zac.

"I can't believe you're here . . ." My words trail off, and I notice Carolyn slip into her room, quiet as a church mouse.

"Carolyn reached out. She said you were, well, that you were, sleeping a lot. She said I might want to visit."

"Ah. You mean Carolyn said I was near death, and you better hurry if you wanted to see me before I kick the bucket?"

Zac chuckles. "Yeah, that's more accurate. How are you doing?"

"Well, I guess she's not too far off the mark. The oxy isn't working anymore, and Carolyn has the doctor coming over tomorrow to start me on morphine. The pain . . ." There is no way of ending that sentence that can convey my suffering.

"I would take your place if I could," Zac says, sitting next to me on the bed. He grabs my hand with both of his. They appear extra-large now compared to my bony, thin-skinned, wrinkled, old-lady hands.

He's still married. I trace the indent of the missing ring with my finger.

He looks at my hand in his, and then back at my face. "I didn't expect to see you again."

I lean into his chest, and we lie down together on the bed. I curl into him and drift.

When I wake, Zac and Carolyn are sitting outside on the patio, deep in conversation. I turn off the baby monitor, not wanting to interrupt them. With the assistance of the walker, I shuffle to the bathroom to relieve myself, wash, and on instinct check my reflection in the mirror.

Nope, still no hair.

I run my hands down my dress, trying to smooth out the wrinkles before deciding it is somewhat flattering. And with whatever spring I have left in my step, I use it to scoot with my walker out onto the patio.

"There she is," Carolyn says as she stands to help me into a chair.

"Hi, babe, how did you sleep?" Zac helps me settle.

"I slept well." My voice catches in an unexpected choke, and tears roll down my face.

"What's wrong?" Zac and Carolyn ask in unison.

"My two favorite people are with me." Unashamed, I allow my feelings to fall out of my eyes and slide down my cheeks.

"I invited Steve and Marin to come over tonight, along with Javi and his wife, and Daniel and his new boyfriend."

"Daniel has a new boyfriend?"

"He does. And he sounds fabulous."

"Oh, that sounds lovely and exhausting," I said.

"Don't worry, I've told everyone to be here at seven sharp and that we would kick them all out by eight. It will be nothing more than a couple of drinks and a few laughs. I know you hate the word, but will that be, okay?"

"I do hate *that* word. But it makes me wonder how Meg's doing, and that's nice."

Carolyn explains who Meg is and how she inappropriately (at least to me) used the word "okay" a lot. When she's finished her story, I brighten.

"A party sounds splendid. Thank you, Carolyn, Zac, both of you. Thank you for everything." More tears fall.

"Baby don't cry. It's all good." Zac kneels in front of me. "Can I get you anything? Water?"

"Yes, and a Xanax. I'm a mess," I say. "Half, though, please. No, wait, half of a half; I guess that's a quarter." I rub my forehead. "Damned chemo brain . . . I don't want to be a zombie at my party." I smile, trying to lift the mood. "People might mistake me for already being dead."

Zac and Carolyn chuckle at my attempted humor, and Zac walks back into the room to cut an anti-anxiety pill.

"Thank you, Carolyn," I whisper as I watch Zac through the glass door.

"You are so welcome, sweetie. I love you. I'd do anything for you," she says. "Jesus! Now you're making me cry." She wipes under her eyes, careful not to smudge her mascara.

———————

There was a knock on the door at seven o'clock. All six of our guests stood together, waiting in the hall.

"Wow!" Carolyn exclaims. "Did you all take the same cab?" She looks at Javier. "Come on in." She beckons and makes introductions. Daniel takes an extra minute to introduce me and Carolyn to Felix, his new partner.

Felix, unlike Daniel, speaks only broken English. His family could not afford to school him in the States, and he's a current student at the local school of higher education. He's studying to become a primary school teacher. Felix's story warms every heart in the room.

"So nice to meet you." Steve gives Zac a firm handshake and

slaps his back. "Marin and I have been hearing about you for quite some time." He introduces Marin, who reaches up on tiptoes and kisses Zac on the cheek, giving him a hearty hug.

"Thank you for making our girl so happy."

Zac turns to me and smiles, his eyes warm.

"¿Como estas?" Javier asks Zac, shaking his hand.

"Bien," Zac says. "Gracias por cuidar a Sera."

I'm surprised to hear him speak Spanish.

The party lasts well past nine, breaking up after my first stifled yawn. When the last guest leaves, I change into a silk nightgown and climb into bed, exhausted but overjoyed.

Zac says good night to Carolyn, who gives him detailed instructions on what to expect from my evening. "Sometimes she struggles, you know, coughing, gurgling, almost choking. Be sure to roll her on her side."

"Okay, thanks. Goodnight, Carolyn."

"And sometimes she whimpers a little, sort of a moan and cry sound. This usually means she's in pain. The meds are on the nightstand."

"Gotcha. Goodnight."

"Oh, and . . ."

"Carolyn, I've got it. Really. You can take a break, get some rest. I'll let you know if I need you." Zac pauses, then reaches to her with open arms, Carolyn falls into his chest, looking overwhelmed and frail.

"Thank you for being here."

"No place I'd rather be," Zac assures her and quietly shuts the door.

He walks over to my side of the bed and reaches for the baby monitor, turning it off; I see him grin. He then undresses and climbs into bed next to me, wrapping his arms around me and enveloping me with his warmth. I'm drifting off to sleep when he kisses the back of my neck, then my shoulder, caressing my back with feather-light touches. I feel his arousal and roll over onto my back.

"Is this okay?" he asks, his voice soft.

"Mm-hmm."

"Are you sure?"

"Yes," I whisper. The moment I saw Zac at the airport, I knew he held me far above any casual sex-mate and that he was willing to jeopardize life as he knew it to be with me. He loves me.

He is careful and gentle with a soft, slow touch. My pain gives way to pleasure, and I do my best to meet him stroke for stroke, arching my back to join his lead. I pull my legs, atrophied and weak, up to his waist and wrap them around him, and we become one as I claw at his back and pull him to me, as close as possible, begging him not to stop.

"I'm close," he says.

"Please, please don't stop," I plead as the surge from deep within me mounts. I move my hips, knowing, remembering. Zac moans and I scream out with pleasure. I collapse, spent.

———

Our morning is lazy, and we spend it lounging in bed. We take turns giving and receiving soft kisses, caressing each other's nakedness, and talking about things gone unspoken. We spend hours laughing, crying, remembering, dreaming. I close my eyes and trace every inch of Zac's face, memorizing its topography and storing it in a place I hope to take with me. I breathe him in as deeply as I can, searing his scent into my mind to recall later. My fingertips land again on the divot on his ring finger. I rub over the smooth dimple a few times. "Why her?" I finally ask.

"I had to."

I flinch at his words.

"Even though the boy's not mine." Zac pulls himself to his elbow. "Sera, I need to tell you something." He takes in a long breath. "It's a complicated story; let me get us some breakfast, and I'll tell you everything."

CHAPTER
46

As requested, the funeral is small with no pomp and circumstance, no doves released, no lengthy eulogy or open mic with stories of Sera. She didn't want that. In keeping with Sera's wishes, there is only a graveside service with few attendees: Meg, Vance, Stefan, Matt, Mel and her husband Martin, Doris, Zac, and me.

Steve and Marin said their goodbyes in Puerto Vallarta, as did Javier and Daniel. Sera's mother transitioned to full-time memory care, and not only was she unable to attend the funeral, she had forgotten altogether she even had a daughter. The few in attendance were the closest to Sera and were the only ones to whom she asked me to deliver her handwritten invitations.

Dear loved one, if you are receiving this invitation, you have remained in my inner circle until the end, and the end has arrived. I would appreciate you being present at my interment this Sunday afternoon at four p.m., at Hillcrest Cemetery. I love you ~ Sera.

Upon arriving at the cemetery, I give each person a bouquet of Sera's favorite flowers to place at her headstone: sterling rose, lilac, gardenia, lily of the valley, lavender. A single Stargazer lily, a funeral flower, as Sera called it, is tucked into each nosegay. Their heady fragrance and beautiful colors contrast the gray, overcast sky and damp chill. Today looks like a funeral day.

No one speaks as each person takes their turn to place their bouquet on the fresh-turned dirt, stand for a somber, reflective moment, and then step away, allowing the next person to say their goodbye. Meg steps up to where Sera rests and begins humming. A few bars into Amazing Grace, and Mel and Doris sing along. My legs tremble, like my voice when I join in. The song ends and the group slowly disperses, leaving only me and Zac. He is standing back from the crowd, dressed in a long, black wool overcoat and dark glasses.

"She was in complete and utter love with you," I say, walking up to him.

"I know."

"It crushed her when you got married."

"I know that too."

There is an interminable pause as we stare at the headstone, *Beloved Serenade Kincaid.*

The sky is dark, and thunderclouds rumble overhead. Zac wraps his coat tighter and takes in a deep, shaky breath.

"Did Sera have time to tell you about my marriage?"

"She tried to, but after you left, she didn't have many lucid moments; something about it wasn't what she thought. She mentioned you and the Marines and some other gibberish."

"When Sera and I first met, she asked me about my days in the service. Given that we were just going to be, well, you know . . ." He doesn't finish his statement.

"Fuck buddies?" My words are blunt, much harsher than I actually wish.

"Yeah." A hurt-looking, crooked smile sits on Zac's ashen face. He takes a moment, reflecting, looking lost in his memories. "I told her about being shot in Somalia and how Smitty saved my life and lost his face in doing so."

"She mentioned that a long time ago."

"Smitty came to see me after Sera and I started seeing each other." He drops his gaze, shifts his weight, and continues, "He just showed up one day, out of the blue, banging at my door. He was all kinds of messed up. Life had taken a toll on him after the Marines. I didn't tell Sera he had come around. I didn't see any reason for it."

Zac pauses, reaching into his shirt pocket, and pulls out a pack of cigarettes. He puts one in his mouth and offers one to me. I shake my head. He flicks open the familiar, worn but well-polished silver lighter, a gift to him from Javier, and takes a big draw. His voice is low and rumbling like the clouds that have overtaken the sky when he says, "We went out, Smitty and I, down to the One Twenty Seven Club, the shitty little dive bar downtown, and threw back about a dozen whiskeys. The two of us were shit-faced when Anne and her girlfriends walked in, so young and innocent, all dressed in their going-out clothes. You know, a little risqué, all sexy looking." He flicks the ash from his cigarette and takes another long drag. "I introduced the two of them, Smitty and Anne, and she introduced me to her friends. I mean, what the hell, right? Just a couple of guys enjoying the company of some giddy girls out on the town. No harm, no foul."

"What happened?" A shiver runs up my spine. "This will not end well, will it?"

Zac stubs his cigarette out on the ground, pocketing the butt.

"Sera used to do that," I whisper.

"'Doing my part to keep the world clean,' she would say." Zac smiles, repeating Sera's phrase from rote.

My knees knock together. The wind has picked up, and my linen pants are no match for its biting cold. I snuggle deeper into my coat.

"Come on. We can sit in my truck."

"But—"

Zac's look relays he has no intention of leaving the rest of his story untold.

Tucked in the warmth of his truck, he continues. "I'm not sure of the details between the time the taxi dropped me back at my condo and the time Smitty woke me up the next morning."

"Oh, my God . . . did he . . . ?"

"No. Definitely not."

"Well then, what happened?"

"All I know is everyone was lit up drunk. I checked the video from my doorbell cam. And sure enough, it shows Smitty and Anne stumbling up the walk to the front door. In the morning, he begged me for help, told me I *owed* him. There apparently was no used condom to be found when they woke up."

"Christ."

Zac bends over the steering wheel, his hands clasped in his lap, reliving the day.

"So, what, you took the blame? How does this work?" I ask.

"No, nothing like that. You should know, Anne was no saint." Zac holds up his hand to stop any ensuing attack. "I'm not saying she did anything wrong, I'm saying, she got pregnant, but wasn't sure by whom. And, I'm saying, she admits she and Smitty were consensual."

I glare at him, looking for any hint of a lie, daring him to point blame toward Anne. There is none. Relief floods through me.

"Anne was my friend, is my friend. She was young, alone, in trouble."

"Buy why you? What about Sera?"

"When Anne first asked me to be her Lamaze coach it seemed flattering, I guess. And when I found out Smitty had refused her attempts to reach him, I actually *did* feel some responsibility, an indebtedness, even if the kid wasn't his."

"And Sera?" I was losing patience.

"I broached the subject of being a Lamaze coach with her, she told me it was quite the honor for a woman to ask someone this, and that I should do it. She seemed, I don't know, aloof."

"Jesus, Mary, and Joseph."

"I always wanted a kid, a family. So, I did it, became Anne's birthing coach. Of course, our friendship grew into love. I think that's only natural, given the circumstances, but it wasn't her I wanted to be with, it wasn't her I was in love with, it was Sera. But by then, Sera had ghosted me. And the little man was born."

Zac smiles. I can see his memories of the baby wash over his face, a proud father. "I did that," I whisper, nauseous, gulping for air. "I ghosted you on her phone, not Sera."

"I know. She knows or knew." He corrects himself, and his words fade.

"She knew all this?" My face is wet, and I wipe mascara streaks with a tissue.

"She knew before she . . . I told her everything, that Anne and I married for the baby and that Sera was the one I loved, always had loved."

I'm numb. More numb than I was during the minutes prior staring at Sera's headstone.

"We're separated."

"What?" I lift my hand to my mouth. Zac's story is too much on this day. I'm not sure I can take any more.

"Anne and I, before going to Puerto Vallarta. Sera had told me she would never be with a married man. I had to be with her, one more time."

"Did Sera know this too? About the separation?"

Zac nods. "If even for a few days, I needed her to know she was the most important person to me."

The weight of Zac's story strikes me like a hammer. I choke down a sob. "That's why she wanted 'Beloved' written on her epitaph," I say. "One of the last things she said."

"She forgave you." Zac's voice is timid. "She forgave us."

He looks at me and sits silently, allowing his tears to roll. Quiet minutes pass.

"Are you coming down to the bar?" I ask Zac when we both gather our composure, "There's something Sera would like you to see."

Stefan opens the door for Zac and me. "Welcome to Serenade. Our specialty drink is, of course, the Serenade, comprising vodka and cranberry juice with a splash of soda and a twist of lime, in memory of our benefactor." Stefan tucks his chin and gives a slight bow, and Zac and I enter the renovated pub in the city's rehab district.

"Benefactor?" Zac's eyes, red-rimmed, light up, and a grin crosses his lips.

"Oh, there's more," I say, patting him on the back. "Sera had me put her money into a trust. We used part of it as a down payment on this place for Vance and Stefan to start this business; a hand up, not a handout. It requires they pay back a portion of the down over time so that the Serenade Foundation may continue to help other young people with dreams and ability but no funds."

"How did I not know this?" Zac asks, awestruck.

"She didn't tell you everything."

"Touché."

Vance stands behind the counter, an apron wrapped around his waist, pouring shots, and pulling handles. "Hey, Carolyn, Zac. What can I get you?"

"Two Serenades, of course," I say.

I grab a spoon from the bar and clink it several times to my glass. "Now that I have your attention, I would like to thank you all for coming. Thank you for loving Sera and thank you for your support through her illness. To Sera." I raise my glass to my lips.

"To Sera," the room answers.

"Now, Stefan gave each of you a sealed envelope when you entered." I turn to Stefan, who nods his confirmation. "Please open your envelopes."

A thrum of murmuring and tearing paper fills the air, followed by, "Are you kidding me?" "What the hell?" "Oh my gosh."

I tap the spoon again to my glass, yelling, "Attention, attention."

Zac lets out a whistle between his teeth, and the room silences.

"Yes," I address the crowd. "This is all true. What you see written on your paper is what Sera has gifted you."

"What is on those pieces of paper?" Zac leans in and asks, looking as if he is enjoying himself.

"Sera hated Matt's beater pick up, so she gave him her Cuda."

"Are you shitting me? She gave Matt her Barracuda?" Zac throws his head back in a laugh.

"Vance and Stefan got a down payment and a grant from her foundation to start this place. That they named the bar Serenade was on them, not a requirement from Sera or the Foundation." I take a drink and add, "She gave Marta a hefty early retirement bonus."

"Aww, the assistant who insisted on calling her Ms. Kincaid. Sera held much respect for her," Zac says.

"And who's that? I didn't see him at the service," Zac asks, pointing to Sheriff Roberts.

"That is Sammy Red Feather Roberts, Sera's nemesis from her childhood on the reservation, the Chief's son, well, brother now, his father has passed."

"She gave him something as well?" Zac's eyes are open wide.

"Red Feather is merely acting as an ambassador for the Tribe. Sera gave back her family's land to the tribe. Her great-grandfather legally staked it in the eighteen hundreds, but the land had been stripped from its indigenous people. Sera is giving it back."

"Wow." Zac lets out a massive breath and finds the closest barstool on which to sit.

"She had no one to pass the land down to, and she always felt a nagging sense that the land should go back to its rightful owners. She wanted to do what she thought was right."

"Mel and Martin got letters too; what could she have given them?"

"They were the reason you two met, of course, so they get an annual bottle of celebratory champagne and a cruise." I shrug.

"Sera felt they needed a get away from their kids."

"And then there's Doris." I point to the older woman sitting alone, dabbing her eyes with a tissue. "Doris received a grant to help fund Night Guardians, a nonprofit that helps women in the Seattle area get home safely after dark."

Zac sits quiet for a moment, taking in all this recent information. I throw a look to Stefan, who reaches into his breast pocket, pulls out an envelope, and walks it over to me. "There's one more envelope, and it's for you, Zac."

He takes the envelope, drains his glass, and opens it to find a check and a brief handwritten note.

Zac, you are the most important person in my life and the most respectable man I know. Please use this money to help take care of your little boy. Your Beloved Serenade.

Zac shakes his head, sniffs, and wipes his brow. "There's an envelope for you as well, Carolyn."

He summons Stefan, who again reaches into his jacket, removes an envelope, and hands it to me.

The color drains from my face. Seeing my name written in Sera's loopy handwriting on the outside, I choke back tears. Inside the envelope are two pictures and a note. The first picture is a landscape shot—a highway running over a creek with a rock wall in the background covered in graffiti. In the foreground are the long shadows of the photographer and a vehicle; the picture has a date stamp on the corner from several months ago. The place is familiar. The second picture, with a more recent date stamp, is much closer than the first and shows a freshly painted circle in silver-white around the words, *Wax Sisters, Jen, Kate, Jill, Sera,* and *Carolyn.* A sob catches in my throat.

I unfold the note and read the words Sera had written in her shaky, end-of-life scrawl.

Carolyn,

As an only child, you understand the longing for a sibling. As a female, you know the desire for a sister. As one of the most important females in my life, I would like you to be an honorary Wax Sister, a chosen member of the sisterhood. You, too, are Beloved. Sera.

I collapse onto a stool.

"Are you okay?" Zac leans down and asks. I nod and look up at him, speechless, my eyes filled with questions.

"She took the picture when she drove up to see her mother months before the two of you took your girls' trip," he explains.

I blink hard.

Zac chuckles, laying a hand on my arm. "Sera had this planned for a long time. She wanted to make sure you knew you were one of the most important people in her life."

"But—" I cannot speak, my throat aches.

"How did your name get up there?" Zac asks the question I couldn't. I nod, still mute.

Zac grins. Stefan and Vance have gathered behind him. "We took a guys' trip," says Vance, who hops up and down clapping his hands.

My tough exterior cracks, and I fling myself into the three men, sobbing, kissing their cheeks. "I love you guys."

Zac lifts his glass and yells over the crowd, "To Serenade."

The room echoes back, "To Serenade!"

ABOUT THE AUTHOR

Lynda Wolters is the author of two non-fiction books, *Voices of Cancer* and *Voices of LGBTQ+*. She resides in Idaho with her husband and their Pekapoo, Max.

For more information about Lynda and her books,
visit lyndawolters.com.